LOST IN THE ARCHIVES

Published by Lethe Press | lethepressbooks.com

ISBN: 978-1-59021-723-8

Cover design: Ryan Vance
Typesetting: Ryan Vance

Lost in the Archives

Speculative Stories

E.Saxey

Contents

Reading Guide

Near-future pessimism:
Not Smart, Not Clever; Sunslick; A Day Without Sunshine; There is a Willow Grows Aslant a Brook; The Librarian's Dilemma; Missing Episodes; Lucidity; Raising the Sea-Drowned

Fantastical optimism:
No Children; My Rightwise Home; Since You Ask Me for a Tale; Red Kite Kindred

Historical oddities:
Windows into Men's Hearts; A Marvellous Neutrality; Anxiety; Uranus

Unhelpful universities:
Not Smart, Not Clever; The Librarian's Dilemma

Troubled dreams:
Anxiety; Lucidity; Raising the Sea-Drowned

Coastal waters:
No Children; Sunslick; Raising the Sea-Drowned

Adventures with animals:
No Children; Red Kite Kindred; Anxiety

A Day Without Sunshine

I don't waste time. I study, I work, and when I go out, I can squeeze a month of fun into one night. Tonight I'm squeezing it into a tiny club in Peckham, south London: no air, and the walls are sweating. I can't drink tonight, so I'm dancing hard instead, moving my head so that my braids skip around my face.

But across the delirious dance-floor, in the far corner, there's a pool of stillness. Nobody dancing, everyone chilling, and you, leaning on a wall. You're a little guy with luscious eyes, gazing all around you.

I fight my way through the dancers to get to you. I dodge feet, get tangled in arms, but I finally reach you.

"I'm Michelle."

"Could I buy you a drink?"

"Nah, I've got a lecture tomorrow. Are you a student?"

You're Hesham, twenty-eight, from Cairo. Not studying anything.

As I look at you, my skin tingles. Then I flinch, hearing a police siren wailing past, too loud—of course, we're next to an open fire exit. That's why there's a pool of coolness all round you.

"This is all excellent," you say, waving an overpriced beer bottle at the club. I laugh.

"You must be on some good stuff."

"I'm not! I like places where people are making the most of every moment." You sound shy, formal. My mum would call you ***well-brought-up***.

Later, you sneak into my sweaty arms. You're shorter than me and kind of delicate, but you don't make me feel clumsy. Just strong, as though I could scoop you up.

Like I said, I don't waste time. "Are you going to invite me back to yours?"

I reckon you'll be conned by the unlicensed minicabs hovering outside. But somehow you summon us a proper black cab. We sit on opposite sides of the big back seat. Up the mangy Old Kent Road we go, across the dark river with both banks twinkling. Past the City, castles of light.

The taxi meter ticks up and up. How can I pay half, how can I get home in the morning? "Hesham, I can't afford this."

"Oh! I should have said. It's on me."

Your place is surrounded by high hedges, a big dark old block. "Lights all out," I say.

"Oh, yes. My neighbours will be in their pods by now."

"Why, are they ill?"

"They pod most nights. Why get eight hours older while you're asleep?"

"Seriously?"

"And if they get fed up with the Winter, they pod all the way through to Spring."

Inside your flat, the thick carpet eats our footsteps. I can't relax, imagining your neighbours above us and around us, frozen under glass. "What a waste. Missing whole months."

"But when they're awake, it's always Summer." Your lilting voice doesn't calm me.

Everything's spotless in your flat, everything's beige. It looks like the waiting room to a private clinic.

"Don't you ever use a pod?" you ask.

Of course I don't. I stack shelves on the night shift to help my mum pay our rent, I couldn't afford to use a pod. I've never met anyone who has. There was a guy at my college who podded for a month before a Batman film premier. But that was a publicity stunt, and the film distributors paid for his pod.

"My mother pods while my father goes skiing," you tell me.

I snort. It's such a ludicrous sentence. Like 'I've dropped my Rolex in the champagne *again*'.

I don't want you to know I'm out of my depth. "Hasn't she got anything better to do?" I jab back.

"Sometimes she visits her friends in Maadi. Then if my father gets home before she does, he pods until she gets back. They're very devoted." You take my hand, link our fingers, and lead me down a corridor.

We pass photos on the wall: a man with a moustache on a mountaintop, a woman wearing tweed and laughing and holding a shotgun. How would it look if my mum had a photo of herself, on the wall of our flat, holding a gun and laughing?

We reach your bedroom.

I stall at the threshold. Do you do this every week? Go south of the river, pick up someone like me—someone big and confident, maybe a bit cocky—then mess with her head? With the taxi fare, and your show-home flat, and your podding relatives?

"Your family's weird, mate." That feels good to say. Easier than *your family's so rich it makes my ears bleed.*

"I suppose so. Yes." You smile.

"Come here, then."

•

One month together. You take me to gigs and shows and you buy me some pretty fantastic meals. But I don't feel I owe you, because I know I'm good for you. "I used to float through life," you say. "But you make me connect."

One Sunday morning, I get lost on the way back from your bathroom and I open the wrong door.

It looms at me from the centre of the room. I can't even identify it: a techno-coffin? A giant wine fridge?

It's a pod. Open, empty, hungry for an occupant.

You own your own pod, and you never mentioned it. That's a significant omission.

"Hesham!"

"What is it, sweet?" Your voice laps at me, all loving and sleepy. You're in bed and you want me to come back.

"I found your pod, Hesh."

You stumble up behind me. You say: "It's not dangerous."

"That's not the point." What *is* the point? Why is my heart thumping? Because we agree—we laugh together—about how messed up your family are, with their rich-people hobbies, their floating from Ascot to the Emirates and podding in between. They're nothing like me. Head-in-the-clouds versus feet-on-the-ground. And you may be one of them, but you've sided with me. Haven't you?

"I only do it when I need to," you say. "Do you want to see how it works? Press the buttons?"

"No."

"Why not?"

Because the thought of it shrivels me up. "What if I do it wrong?"

"I trust you."

So then I can't refuse because I'd be mistrusting your trust, or some nonsense like that. You show me what to press.

"Wake me up in five minutes," you say as you clamber in, wriggling down in the headrest just the same way you snuggle into my shoulder when we hug. "Shut the lid, then."

"Shut it yourself."

I don't like needles. I kept my eyes on your serene face as your eyelids lower. The mist from your breath whitens the whole visor once, twice, then dwindles to a tiny spot, like the moon in fog.

I can't keep still. I ought to watch you, keep a vigil, but I pace the flat instead. I could open every door, snoop and discover what else you've got hidden. It's the perfect opportunity: when you're asleep, you could wake up. When you're out, you could walk back in. But right now, you can't surprise me.

I march myself back to the pod room and press where you told me. The pod whirs.

You open your eyes and unlatch the lid from inside. You're dopey from the double shot of drugs: the ones to knock you out, and the ones to wake you up.

"Give me a kiss," you say.

I won't bend my head down into the mechanism. "Come up here and get it."

•

Three months together. I like the pace of us. We see each other every week. You don't pester me with messages between dates. You respect that I've got too much work to do, no spare time. You're not clingy.

But something's not right with you. You're slipping.

When I phone, why do you never answer, but always phone back a couple of hours later? Why did you let me think you'd been to a gig last week, when you didn't go at all? You just read the reviews and repeated phrases to me. Are you cheating on me? Losing hours and days to drugs?

You hold me close. "Michelle, love. You know Anthony and Cleopatra, in Shakespeare? Cleopatra says: *give me mandragora to drink, so I can sleep out this great gap of time that Anthony's away*."

I say: "Who's Cleopatra, in this scenario?"

"When you're not here, 'Chelle, it's just a gap."

"So what have you been drinking, to get through it?"

"You know, there are a thousand other poems about how amazing it would be to be with your beloved, all the time. And now it's possible!"

"What? No. It isn't. I've got to work, I've got to study..."

"It is for me. I can kiss you and fall asleep and wake up and kiss you again."

A light-bulb comes on in my head; a bare bulb, it's bright and it hurts me. "You're telling me—you only get out of the pod if we're going to meet?"

"Why would I want a day without you in it?"

The light-bulb in my head swings, throwing shadows that swerve around and won't settle. "Are you ill? I mean, do you only have a few years to live, or something?"

"Everyone's only got a few years to live."

"Oh, very clever, very philosophical. You're only twenty-eight, Hesham."

"Some people would think it was romantic."

"Don't wind me up! You knew I wouldn't like it, or you wouldn't have lied about it."

"I didn't lie."

"You implied."

"You assumed."

You keep podding.

•

Four months together, for me; twenty days or so for you, I reckon.

I have to cancel a date, to babysit for my cousin. You're sweet about it, but I can tell what you're thinking: that I've wasted a whole day of your precious life.

I think that's when you decide to wake up just an hour before our dates. There are clues. Sometimes, by the time you see me, you haven't scrubbed the pod-breath out of your mouth.

I'm tired one night, so I let you send your car for me. It glides into my road like a pike in a pond and swallows me up, then races through the City up to your neighbourhood, all manicured lawns and security cameras. The high dark hedges round your home seem to part, to let me in.

At your door, I understand: you want someone to fight their way in to your weird closed-off life, past your fossilised family, and save you. To give you a reason to stay awake, just for a day, just for an hour.

And when I'm longing to see you, when I'm ringing your doorbell, I think I could be that fighter.

When you buzz me in, you're wearing your bathrobe. You've just stepped out of your wet room. Your machine has woken you up, timed it to perfection. After we kiss, you ask, "Would you want to wake me, some time? Like you did before?"

I freeze. "Why?"

"I just have this picture of you waking me up with a kiss. But it doesn't matter."

I can't do it. I'm not your fighter.

•

Five months together, for me. Twenty days, and what—sixteen hours for you?

I see us as wheels on gears. I'm the tiny wheel, spinning round seven times, while you're the sluggish wheel moving less than one rotation.

Of course, you never have any news. So I ask you about your childhood, then your dreams. Even if we see all the same things, we can't dream the same dreams.

"I don't really remember them," you say.

Little fights spring up between us like seedlings. One late night we turn into your dark driveway and an urban fox is loping away from us, a big auburn leggy one. I hold your hand tighter.

"We'll never know where he goes," I whisper. "Isn't it brilliant?"

"We can have a pretty good guess, though, can't we?" There's a scratch in your voice. "He goes through bins and he pisses on doorsteps. Just because he's mysterious, doesn't mean he's glamorous."

"I just like him. I wasn't liking him *at* you." You're being an arsehole but I let it go, because I don't want us to argue. I just want us to differ.

One time we're in the Tate Modern gallery, looking at a great battle of blue brush-strokes. You look at the painting, to me, and back again. As though you're reading my face and adjusting your focus, tweaking your reactions to whatever I'm feeling. Trying to fuse our gazes into a single gaze.

I still think of you as laid-back, not clingy. But you don't need to be clingy. Because you don't exist when you're not with me.

I wish that was why I was breaking up with you. "Hesham, I can't live without the give and take of different experiences." That would be so high-minded. But it's more shabby than that.

We've been meeting once a fortnight, because of my end-of-year exams. That's a good thing about our arrangement: you don't mind how often we see each other. You aren't twiddling your thumbs, waiting for me to visit. Two days in the pod is the same as a month, to you. Same as a hundred years, probably.

As soon as I get you alone in your flat I kiss you. You taste like hot fresh bread and I melt like butter.

You give me a hug you could give your Grandma and say, "Shall I make us coffee?"

We're gears. I spin. You only turn a tiny bit.

In my world, we've been having sex once a fortnight. In your world, we've been doing it *every four hours*. While I've been spinning fantasies, you've been in your pod. You're not ravenous for me, you're still basking in the afterglow from last time.

I should wait until I'm calm to bring it up, but I blurt it out.

"It's not a problem," you say. "I can fix it. Viagra would work, wouldn't it? I'll get a prescription..."

"I don't want you taking pills!"

"What do you want?"

I don't know. Not this.

"Do you want a pod? One of your own. I could get you one."

Both of us stare, like the other one's pulled a knife.

•

Breaking up with you is another thing I've done on my own while you've been in your pod, another bit of news that I'll tell you later. I sent you an email to end things. Sorry about that. But I wouldn't want to waste your time on the conversation.

Six months later, you've been sending begging messages and I give in. Strict limits: we meet in a café, you have one hour to talk.

You look just the same.

"How are you?" I ask. "Using your pod much?"

"I know you don't approve." In your voice I can hear the strain which your unchanged body can't show. "But wouldn't it be weird if I'd given it up to please you?"

"Maybe. Whatever."

"Anyway. I'm going to start feeling better soon."

"Yeah? Good. How?" You could afford therapy, a round-the-world holiday. You could buy a puppy, a puppy who's trained as a therapist. I resent you so much. It hurt me too, you know? But I didn't take shortcuts, I did the work and I got over you.

You rub your temples. "My subconscious is working on it while I'm asleep. I just need more time."

"Time in the pod? That's not a plan, that's hiding."

"It'll be like podding through the Winter."

"Hesham, you can't mope like a teenager, you're nearly thirty. And it's been six months since we broke up."

"I'm nowhere near thirty," you say. "It hasn't been six months."

No Children

My unmarked tatty white van carries the two of us along the coast road: not sea-side, but scrub grass and wind-chill in no-man's land.

It's best to be cautious so I let the van stutter to a stop in a layby some distance from our client's house. We skulk there between heaps of bramble bushes until my phone pings, and a moment later a red car shoots past us in the other direction.

"Was that Mr Jones?" asks Bronwyn.

"Better hope so."

Our clients' house is a modern white bungalow, flimsy as a holiday cottage, not sturdy enough for the weather we get round here. I notice the lead flashing pulling away from the roof-tiles. I'm a builder, but we're not here to fix the house. That would be simpler.

The sea is at an extreme low tide, a twisting white ruffle, right on the horizon, twenty minutes' walk across the sand.

Bronwyn, my cousin and my painter, sighs as she clambers from the van. "It's so much easier at high tide." She pushes her curls into a hat, and buttons her overalls across her wide chest, hiding knitted roses. I hop into my own overalls, turning us both into nondescript grey tubes.

"The tide'll be back in by midday," I tell her, grabbing my toolkit.

"Will we not be done, by then? What about that wet-room job in Llanelli, we could get started this afternoon."

"I don't think this will be quick. The husband built this house." The shoddy bungalow could hold a lot of secrets, which will make for a long day's work. "That's why we need your Marie."

A chugging roar tells us our final crew-member has arrived. Marie, Bronwyn's kid, halts her much heftier vehicle and leaps down onto the grass. She's got purple hair, which makes her overalls look pretty punk. "Where's the husband off at, then? And where the fuck has the sea gone?"

Bronwyn tuts at the swear-word. I don't mind the swearing, but I could do without the tutting.

"Husband's just left for a family funeral," I tell Marie. "Other side of the Brecon Beacons."

Marie whistles. "That's stone cold, that is."

"Got to make sure they're out of the way," says Bronwyn. "Learned that on the Porthcawl job."

Bronwyn has a habit of mournful reminiscence. I don't join in.

"So he just comes home, and *bam*?!" Marie asks.

"He's had his chance," says Bronwyn.

Marie's been working with us for a year—mostly tiles and plastering—but this is her first side-job. I'd wanted someone young on the team. Bronwyn and I are nearing fifty, now. Our clients are younger. That is to say, our clients look younger.

"No children, though?" Bronwyn asks.

"Aw, so are you the heart of the operation, Mam?" mocks Marie.

"She's also the common sense," I say. "And I'm the muscle. So I don't know why we brought you along. And no, there's no children."

"What's the legal position, then," asks Marie, "If there's children? What about the Dad?"

Bronwyn fetches her tools to avoid the conversation. I lower my voice. "The legal position is he can fuck right off out of it."

Our position is only legal in as far as our side-jobs are so wildly improbable.

We don't go mob-handed to the house, in case there's still company. We wait until the door opens, and the wind snatches it and slams it back against the wall. Is this Mrs Jones, her ankle-length dress flapping in the wind? I've not yet met her. When she comes closer to the van, I'll see her face, and I'll know.

"Don't you stare," says Bronwyn, elbowing Marie in the ribs. Then she sighs. "Oh, Sal. It's so soon after the last one."

"You know I didn't pick the date." Our clients come in an uneven trickle. Through the women's refuge in Swansea, through a network of barmaids, my phone number ends up in the hands that need it. "And the last one was hardly any trouble."

"It's not the attention I'm worried about, Sal." She nudges me with her big shoulder. "It's *you.* You're not as tough as you think you are."

Family always want to take you down a peg.

Mrs Jones pushes against the wind as she walks. I move to meet her. Bronwyn is half-right, in that this job has come sooner than I expected. Most clients call me three or four times before they set a date. Sometimes, when I call back, the client pretends not to know me: "We don't need any work done, goodbye." Or she'll turn us away at the doorstep, and tell her man we were charity collectors. I have to have the patience of Job.

By contrast, Mrs Jones has been frighteningly decisive. One phone conversation to set the date, and here—close enough to touch—is Mrs Jones. She looks no older than Marie, maybe twenty. Her eyes are inky and wide, almost circular, her hair slate grey and glossy.

"You're Sal?" she asks.

"That's me." I smile. Behind me, Bronwyn will be smiling too, and she's better at it.

Mrs Jones holds out one arm in invitation.

As we cross the patchy lawn, young Marie is silent, perhaps for the first time since she was born. Last week, when I explained these side-jobs to Marie, she asked, "How do you know they're not ordinary housewives? Pissed off at their blokes?" Now Marie has seen Mrs Jones, and the sheen of her skin, and her bottomless eyes, she won't ask again.

We tramp across Mrs Jones' threshold in dusty work-clothes. Ordinary clients tolerate our invasion because they want a loft extension, or a nice new open-plan lounge, and they still get teasy, fretting at us to wipe our feet. I never saw a homeowner less bothered than Mrs Jones. I suppose we may be the last people she ever welcomes into her tasteful modern kitchen.

I catch Bronwyn surreptitiously checking the fridge for kid's drawings. Soft-hearted, and she never takes my word for it. I also spot Marie placing thumb and finger on the metal knob of a cupboard door, starting to unscrew it. I kick her and she stops. Does her Mam know she's bloody light-fingered?

"What happens first?" asks Mrs Jones.

"We look through all your storage. Sometimes that's enough."

"I've searched..."

"Always in the last place you think of looking," pipes up Marie.

Sometimes our clients back out at this point, particularly the ones who've been married for longer. They flinch at our mucky hands rifling through their belongings, with no promise of success. Even half a life is worth keeping.

"We'll be careful," I tell her. "You don't have to be here, while we work. You can wait in the garden." That scruffy garden, clinging to a saline incline.

Mrs Jones stays.

The drawers are the most distasteful part: shoving aside bras, mementos, bills marked FINAL NOTICE. I prefer to search the impersonal spaces, like the gap under a chest of drawers, the inches behind a wardrobe. The places that kids find when they play hide and seek, or hunt treasure.

Marie is small and bendy enough to wriggle right in under the bed. Her questions, slightly muffled, keep coming. "Couldn't she leave him, anyway, even if we don't find it?"

"That's not how it works," I say. "You want to go up in the attic, look there?"

Marie holds up a bedside photo on the way out. "He looks like a weaselly little scrote. She's a good looking woman, hey, Aunty Sal?" She tries to wink at me like a woman of the world.

"Don't start," I say. "And don't pocket the kitchen fittings."

"I was just seeing if they were proper pewter."

"We can't risk you gleaning." We get away with this line of work because our crimes are too strange to report. Stealing is ordinary, stealing will bring us down. "Bugger off and check the attic."

Left alone, I fish with a long slim stick in the cavities of the built-in bedroom set. There's a snag, a tug of resistance, and I work my hand in deep. My fingers tingle, brushing something warm, firm, supple.

A figure moves between me and the window. Jesus, is it Mr Jones? I jump back, yank my arm free.

Mrs Jones stands silently behind me.

"Might be something back there," I say, keeping my voice level. On the third job, I found something this way, and now I always let the client pull it out. It felt indecent to touch it. And it was hard on my heart, to pass it over.

Her arm is longer than mine. When she brings her hand back out, between her fingertips is an ordinary heather-coloured jumper. She flicks it away like a dead thing.

Marie bellows down through the attic hatch. "There's nothing here! Can I rip up the insulation?"

I look to Mrs Jones. Mrs Jones nods.

I pace around the outside of the house, to see if we've missed a garage or a boat-shed.

I stop in the sloping garden and look out to check the tide, but the wind makes my eyes water. I grew up in a seaside house, with salt ghosts on the windows and everything corroding. There's another white bungalow further along the road, and a figure in the doorway. They turn as I watch and the door slams behind them. My van, and Marie's truck and trailer, disturbed the neighbour, and the sight of me has put the seal on it. I know with sinking certainty that Mr Jones, on his way to his uncle's funeral, will be getting a phone call. I hope reception is bad over the Beacons. I very much prefer not to be interrupted.

I hurry back to the kitchen for the next stage. With Mrs Jones' permission, we set crowbars to the kitchen tops and lever them off, prise the sides from the fridge-freezer cabinet. "He's done it shoddy," scolds Bronwyn. "Look at that, it's all spit and glue."

Not much dust, I notice. House-proud, Mrs Jones must be, but she stands coolly by and lets us peel her house like a satsuma. While I work, I watch her. I see a family resemblance in her snub nose and short upper lip. Then I look away before I get caught staring.

We work well together, a real family business; Uncle Justin, Bronwyn's dad, taught all three of us. We yank plasterboard free, show the spaces inside the walls. There's one tricky corner, and Bronwyn raises a sledgehammer to knock a hole.

"It's not there," Mrs Jones says. "I'd have felt it." She holds out her hands, like she's warming them on a fire.

Is that true? None of our other clients have mentioned it. The sledgehammer wobbles in Bronwyn's hands, and she looks to me, uneasy. Is this just an excuse to stop, the first sign of Mrs Jones getting cold feet? In a panic, I calculate if we can replace everything we've torn away, before Mr Jones returns, summoned by the Neighbourhood Watch. Whether we go forwards or back, the clock's surely ticking.

"Go ahead," says Mrs Jones, and Bronwyn swings, and then I step up next to her to rip the hole wider. Our hands are clumsy with eagerness and relief, but the thing we need isn't there. Mrs Jones was correct.

I have to maintain a professional demeanour, not sweep our client along with my plans, so they can always back out if they need to. It's very hard to hide my satisfaction as Bronwyn and I go wild on the floorboards: putting your whole back into it, rewarded by the first creak, then a gratifying shriek as the nails pull free. All the better for knowing that Mr Jones probably hammered them down himself.

But every space we reveal is empty.

"What's that?" There's something fluffy at the tip of Bronwyn's boot. Only a mouse's nest, and the husk of a mouse. "Oh. Poor thing."

Marie marches in, soot in her purple hair. "Awright, Mary Poppins! There's fuck all up the chimney, I gave it a good rodding."

"Is there a chance Mr Jones buried it in the garden?" I ask Mrs Jones.

"It's in the house."

"Can you feel it? Can you…" I wave around my hand like a metal detector.

"No."

I blush. She looks less than half my age, but I feel her disdain like I'm a child clinging to her knee. "Then the next steps, we discussed…"

"Do it," says Mrs Jones.

"I'll turn off the water and gas," says Bronwyn.

•

When I broached the subject of this job with Marie, last week, I asked: "Do you know about the other jobs, what your Mam and I do?"

"Is it smuggling?"

"What?"

"I reckon it's illegal, and you go down the coast road to do it. Never up the valleys."

She's smart as a whip, is Marie. Now I have to stand back and trust her as she trundles a mini-excavator away from its trailer and right up to the house. I've previously only seen Marie handle a wallpaper steamer.

"She's got a good light touch," says Bronwyn, soothingly, as Marie bops around like a muppet at the levers of the JCB. I hope that isn't a motherly over-estimate.

"Still, maybe I should have done it."

"On the Rhossili job," asks Bronwyn mildly, "Didn't you drive that digger into the quick-sand, then whinge about it?"

"Where first?" I ask Mrs Jones. She raises her hand and points, the seaward side of the house. Her dress in the wind ripples like kelp in a current. Marie rocks the machine back and forth, an ugly eight-point turn, graunching great scars into the pitiful garden.

Marie flays the side of the house with precision. The sharp teeth break the skin of brickwork, deafeningly loud. Water sprays briefly from a sheared-off pipe. Electrical cables snag and then snap. The bricks don't fall apart smoothly but stick, like a box of Lego holding shapes from the last game.

"Break it up, Marie," I shout out.

The JCB rakes its scoop back and forth, Marie swaying to match it and cackling. Bronwyn has a tattoo on her ankle with Marie's name and a rose. I wonder how she expected her kid to turn out.

Marie asked me, last week: "Do you ever just punch them?" Meaning the husbands.

"No."

"I would."

"Not if you work with me, you won't."

"How do they think they'll get away with it?"

"I don't know. You know, the factories closed. The women went to the cities where they can get work. The men turn to the sea." It's a fairy tale my aunties told me, Bronwyn's Mam, Marie's Gran. I'm surprised to hear it come out of my own mouth.

"They can turn to a sock full of liver," suggests Marie. "And stick their nob in that."

What can you tell a teenage girl about companionship, or wanting a family?

But why would I argue that you can build a family on an act of kidnap?

The digger lifts its triumphant head and freezes in that pose. Mrs Jones walks in under it, the maiden poking about the dragon's hoard, and Bronwyn follows behind.

Something moves in the corner of my watering eye: a car? No, it's the vigilant neighbour, striding over to us, a pillar-of-the-community type, pristine in her pastel sweater. "What's all this, then?"

"We're under Mrs Jones' instruction."

When we started in this line of work, I used to say: we're helping Mrs So-and-so move out. That always set off an avalanche of moaning.

"He's not a bad husband," objects the neighbour. Even when I say nothing, some people hear condemnation. "I know there were a few unfriendly comments. Because she isn't from round here."

"She is from round here," I say. There is nobody who is more from round here, *right* here, than Mrs Jones. The neighbour scowls, perhaps noticing that I don't look quite local, myself.

Mrs Jones is picking through the rubble of her own house like a beachcomber. Marie runs over and mucks in with her Mam, the two of them heaving aside the bigger blocks.

"You can't do this, you know!" the neighbour yells. "It's illegal!"

"Am I his wife?" calls back Mrs Jones.

I'm surprised. The clients don't usually like to talk, once they've made up their mind.

Her question flusters the neighbour. "It's none of my business, whether you're married."

"If I'm his wife, this is my house," calls Mrs Jones, and goes back to the search.

"She's gone mad," offers the neighbour. "Because of her kid."

My breath catches. It's as though the tide has finally come in, and filled up my lungs. Mrs Jones said there were no children.

"Losing the kid, it's sent her mad," the neighbour confides. "But it couldn't live. Deformed, it was."

I find my breath again, and use it. "Piss off and drizzle your bile into someone else's ear."

"He'll be back here, soon," she gloats, before she stalks away.

"*Hi ho*," I hear, "*Hi ho...*" Marie is singing, while she and Bronwyn haul up a lump of brick-work, letting Mrs Jones dart in to search beneath it.

The red car swings around the corner and skids to a halt on the grass. Mr Jones jumps from his car, jerky with shock and anger, a wiry man past forty failing to fill out his funeral suit. His mouth hangs as open as his home.

"What? What the hell is this?" shouts Mr Jones.

Mr Jones has come back to catch his wife cheating, or leaving, and he's found his place turned into a doll's house, its insides displayed to the world.

Bronwyn runs up to form a wall beside me, between Mr Jones and his bride.

"What is this? What?"

"We're acting on behalf of Mrs Jones," I say.

"Well, I'm *Mr* Jones," he replies, like he's playing his trump card. He has a smoker's mouth, lips like a cat's arse. He moves to the left, we lean to the left. He sees he shouldn't try to dodge to the right. Marie was right: he's a weaselly scrote. "You're telling me I can't talk to my wife?"

I shrug. I look big when I shrug. "Talk yourself hoarse."

He calls to his wife. The wind plucks his voice away. She could plausibly ignore him. But she raises her head, fixes her great dark eyes on him. He starts bellowing, vile things, foul things, touching on everything from her face to her sexual propensities.

I can't show it, but I'm scared. With Mr Jones hopping mad at ground level, Marie can't use the JCB. He could run forward and have his head knocked off, tidy. Could we restrain him? I could punch him, and Bronwyn could hold him down, but a small crime like assault is a tool in the hands of a petty man.

Then Mr Jones' insults are drowned out as loose roof tiles drop in a deafening shower.

Marie screams, and my heart jumps, because she could have been hit. But I see her at once, jumping up and down and pointing upwards: "Look! Look there!"

There's mineral wool insulation, in clumps and strands, flapping around. But there's something else, dark and supple like a sheet of suede. It whips back and forth, lithe in the sea wind.

"I'll get it!" calls Marie, and before I can stop her she's shinning up the neck of the bloody JCB. Foot on a piston, hand on a hinge, like she's spotted a fiver growing in a tree.

She tugs and yanks and the sheet-thing comes free. It billows into every wild shape as it falls down into the arms of Mrs Jones.

I shout cautions as I run towards her: "Mrs Jones, wait!"

She is elated. I saw Bronwyn hold Marie, when she was new-born, and her face looked this way. "Not until you're near the water!" I swear the tide has come in early, to rescue her. It's streaming and foaming only two hundred yards away.

(And Bronwyn is hanging back to protect Mr Jones, just in case. We learned to do that on our messy third job, down in Porthcawl.)

Mrs Jones nods. She holds the thing we have found, and we walk together towards the water.

The foam rushes over my boots and her feet, which are bare now. She wrings her hands, like someone miming regret, but then holds out the ring she has removed, offering it to me. I shake my head; who'd want a souvenir of this marriage? She drops it and it winks out of sight in the foam.

I tighten my fists, feel the slight webs between my fingers strain. I no longer need to be professional, or carefully neutral. There is no chance, now, that Mrs Jones will back down. Now I might bring out one of the hundred questions I carry in my chest. I draw in a lungful of briny air.

Simultaneously, the yelling starts up again.

"Gwen, don't do it!" Mr Jones has decided he can bellow her back to him. "We were happy! We were going to try again, for a family!"

Mrs Jones changes.

She sheds her dress like a wet dog shaking, stands stark and fearless. She swings the skin up over her head, high like dark wings. The fierce wind can't take it from her, it strokes her shoulders and won't let go. It clads her arms, which are shorter than arms, now, and covers her head. The dark hood becomes a powerful thick neck. The skin clings to her torso, cloaks her legs. She falls to her knees, and that sharp drop turns into a sinuous roll.

I want to hold her. I'm ten years old again, and I want to cling to her and drag her back up the beach. Of course I don't, but of course I cry.

She lollops towards the water. It only takes a couple of undulations before a wave comes in to scoop her up. God it's freezing, but she quivers joyfully all along her dark body, from her muzzle to the tip of her tail. A twitch of her fins sends her scooting off into the blue-black water. We watch her round head bob, and then dive, and her flank curves after it, curling in a perfect arc. She doesn't resurface.

I walk back to my crew. Bronwyn squeezes my shoulder.

Mr Jones is sitting in a crumple on the ground. Bronwyn and I climb into the van and belt up.

"It'd be a nice house, in the summer," says Bronwyn, of the building we have just demolished.

Maria sticks her head through the open van window. "Can we get chips for lunch in Llanelli?"

"I want those nobs, Marie," says Bronwyn. "You get paid by the hour, same as when you're plastering."

"Aw..." Marie, shamefaced, starts to decant handfuls of pewter doorknobs from her overall pockets.

"Leave that, now." I want to move off before Mr Jones notices my van has no number-plates. "I'll buy you a drink, later, down the Red Lion."

Marie stomps away, to drive the JCB back to the plant hire company.

"She's got a good heart," says Bronwyn. "Just needs a firm hand."

I pull the van back onto the road, thinking: we need a better plan. What if there had been a kid?

I do hope anyone would want their mother to be free. Even if it meant never seeing her again, and being raised by heavy-handed aunties. Even if it meant going off the rails for a while, until Uncle Justin stepped up and taught you bricklaying. Eventually, you'd want the best for your Mam.

But it's too much to ask of a kid. If they held their mother's freedom in their hands, warm and firm and supple—what kid would willingly pass it over?

Bronwyn turns on the radio, finds Abba, and gives me a nudge which nearly knocks me over. "Come on, you know it! *Nothing more to say, dah-dah dah-dah play...*" She warbles the chorus as our van trundles through Pwll.

Today, at least, there were no children.

There is a Willow Grows Aslant a Brook

"Jenny, come to the Rush Street bridge quickly. But don't look into the river."

How could Jenny not look, after that phone message? Really. Especially when there's a little crowd, leaning over the parapet.

And when the body stands out so starkly in the dark water. White torso and forked legs rolling to and fro, in the long tassels of green river weed. Hair given life and moved by the current, too; she looks like a creature native to the river. The police screens are perfunctory, so everyone can see the officers trying to catch her with a boat hook. Hauled up by an arm, dangling and dripping, dropped again.

Jenny has always liked the way that people know each other by sight, in this town. But today, that means that when the body is dragged up one last time, and flops onto the ground, everyone in the small crowd recognises her face.

It is Jenny's face.

"Poor you! Poor you!" cries her friend Sarah, the one who left her the phone message, running over. "I told you not to look."

•

It had been Sarah's suggestion to try online dating. The town was small and friendly, but there weren't many newcomers. Old people do it, too, Sarah had told Jenny.

The men on the dating site were friendly. It was her own profile that Jenny came to resent.

Some versions of yourself expand you. Playing the teacher, Jenny is more fair and patient. Playing the widow, saying the traditional responses had helped her to hold back waves of pain. So Jenny was content to be someone slightly different, online—only a reasonably accurate reflection.

But her dating profile hollowed her out. Lively and engaging, it somehow sapped those qualities away from her. Men sent polite messages, but Jenny fumbled all her replies.

Her profile picture was (said Sarah) quite pretty, but nonetheless looked (to Jenny) like a malicious impersonator. So last month, Jenny tried uploading a scan, as well. Just her face; her nephew hinted that body-scans were for young people with specific concerns.

"You want to know if they've really got what they say they've got," he'd explained. Then he'd blushed.

Jenny sat in a booth at the copy shop on the market square. Then she added the scan to her profile. She liked the way you could spin it and tilt it. She flew round her own face like a tiny plane round the Sphinx of Giza. It absolutely looked like her, she couldn't argue with that. But she didn't like it.

She'd taken her profile down, nearly a week ago. And this afternoon, Sarah had called her because a body that looked like Jenny was bobbing under the bridge on Rush Street.

•

It's easy to revive her account, and discover which three men downloaded her face-scan. One had never contacted her at all. One had moved to Scotland (or had he?). The third was Paul—nice, but no chemistry—who Jenny now considers a friend (or is he?).

Jenny should call Paul. For comfort, or interrogation? In the end, she simply invites him for dinner and explains the situation.

He is a wonderful audience. He hasn't seen it, that's the important thing. She can tell him as much or as little as she wants. After the awful exposure of the bridge crowd, gawping at her, it's wonderful to regain some control.

"So it looked like you? Good Lord..."

"Just my face." She remembers the line round the neck, where the skin changed tone and peeled back slightly. "It had been printed out and stuck onto the head of a kind of artificial woman."

"How macabre!" He hasn't twigged what she meant. He's thinking of dress-shop mannequins. But it had been clear enough to the bridge crowd why that body had been chosen: the globular breasts, the splayed legs. "Was it some kind of horrible practical joke?"

"No, it was some kind of sex pest."

"You mean it was an *inflatable* woman?"

He's so incredulous that Jenny smiles. "Not actually inflatable. A shame it wasn't, it might have deflated..."

"Yes! Popped!"

"And been swept away, and I'd never have seen it!"

They've made it into a funny story, together. It's almost bearable.

But after Paul leaves Jenny at her cottage door, she is seized by visions of what happened to her watery twin before it was abandoned. The police have taken the doll away to check her for prints, and euphemistic 'other evidence'.

Enabled by ginger wine, Jenny becomes screamingly angry.

A man stole her face to use.

A man who'd never even sent her a message! Who'd viewed her profile a few times, but who had decided in the end that he'd rather steal her face and glue it over the gormless features of a sex doll and do—what? Obvious things.

This man had decided that he'd rather do that than suggest, for example, a trip to the Festival Theatre together. Or an Autumn walk in the nearby woods.

It was an insult. It was as though he'd said to her *you'd be nicer if you didn't talk.*

And then he'd been overcome with remorse, perhaps? Thrown the whole botched mess over the bridge. Thought it would carry downstream. Not enough remorse, though. Not nearly enough. *Cry me a river,* thinks Jenny.

•

"How do you want it?"

"What ways can you do it?"

The copy shop assistant lays out samples. 'We can do it in vinyl—nice colours. Or for something a bit special, we can do metals. Pure silver, even, but you'd have to have it small. Is it a present? Retirement? Anniversary?"

"No, just a—an office birthday. A joke." Jenny had scanned her face in this shop. Now she wonders if the man printed off her face, here. Will the shop tell her, if she asks? No, she mustn't get involved. The police will do all that. "I'd like it about four inches high and as cheap as possible."

"Sintered gypsum would be the cheapest."

She takes her new acquisition to the Rush Street bridge. She stands him on the parapet in the bright sunshine.

Absolutely accurate, of course, but in the end it doesn't tell you much. It doesn't give you a sense of the person, not really. His hands rest on his thighs, with his fingers close together. It's an odd posture, but she remembers from the booth instructions that you have to stand that way, because printers have trouble with the delicacy of free-hanging hands and open fingers.

If this thing can't even show you a proper hand, then can it really show you a face? His nose looks a little blocky. The cheeks have swirling contour lines on them. Other than that, he looks boring.

The man who stole her face looks boring.

Really. Why have yourself scanned, when there's nothing interesting about you? When if you wrote "I am a white man in my sixties", you would have said all there is to say?

Jenny has purchased two items in the ironmongers. Now she holds the small man with the kitchen tongs, and applies the cigarette lighter.

The gypsum blackens from smoke licking across the rough surface. Smudges, nothing substantial. Jenny holds the figure out over the edge of the bridge, and keeps the lighter trained on his feet. She hears the first sputter as a portion collapses in on itself, leaving a crater like a burst blister. He's properly charred, now.

His feet writhe, then drop off and she wishes she'd started with his head, with his stupid face, but you keep a degree of respect, don't you? Even when it's only a model of a man, you hold it the right way up, you don't hold it head-down and melt it face-first.

She rotates the tongs to push his features into the flame.

Her thumb on the lighter is starting to scorch. She'll have to drop it soon but she will watch his face melt, before she lets him go.

His nose slides off all at once, and she drops him in the same instant. He sticks to the tongs, so she has to drop them too, clattering down into the water. She sucks her thumb and sees them sink, covered up by the green shifting curtains of weed.

•

Afterwards, Jenny doesn't waste much thought on the event. Except sometimes while crossing the Rush Street bridge, she feels a flicker of anxiety, and wonders if she's being watched.

On these occasions, she squeezes her handbag to check the can of pepper spray is nestled in its depths. "Best-case scenario," Paul had said when he gave it to her, "You never need to use it."

Best-case scenario, Jenny isn't being followed at all.

But second-best case: it's the man who stole her face. And he's decided that an imitation isn't enough, and he's come looking for the real thing.

And Jenny's hand grips the can because in those brief moments, she feels the same way.

Lucidity

Ah, what it is to be young and in love! Utterly wretched. I loved you for four years. That's not many, perhaps, but they were the formative ones. From scrubby eleven years old to furtive fifteen.

I remember clambering out of an upper window onto the roof of our Victorian-Gothic boys' boarding school, and setting my back to a redbrick chimney stack to watch you below me on the cricket pitch. Two-and-a-half years older than me (I knew your birthday), your fringe fell like a raven's wing over your eyes. You fielded with such grace that you looked like an elf from Tolkien (which I was reading that week). I was a late developer. I had a slice of fruitcake in my pocket, I still fantasised about flying, and you were my first more adult enthusiasm.

I hid myself on the roof and spied because I was too young to be your friend. Even speaking to me would have brought mockery on both of us. You were untouchable. (Which was convenient, because *love unobtainable has* a great legacy behind it, while *love basically incompatible* would just be a terrible let-down.)

My first year of love was ennobling. The next two were pathetic. By the time I was fourteen, I'd heard jokes and rumours about sex and drugs: what they were and where to get them. I knew about Lucidity and I had to try it.

•

I asked Thom, drugs kingpin of the lower sixth.

"Lucidity? Bloody boring drug," he said. "You want to expand your horizons, kid, not doze off."

I shrugged. I was content to be thought of as a boring boy, in the service of love.

Thom knew a dealer who dropped off a mid-week delivery. I sneaked into the sixth-form common room the following Wednesday, and skulked behind the older boys when Thom brought in the package. He brazenly distributed rations: tiny squares of resin, pills in ones and twos. Thom flicked a twist of paper over to me. "Here you go, you boring bugger. Eat cheese."

"What?"

"This is how you use it!" The internet not having been invented, I listened intently to his guidance. "Sleep the wrong way round in your bed." That was no hardship. "And wear an acrylic jumper," he said. I wondered if he was winding me up. "It'll mess up your sleep, so you dream more. Look at your hands." I did. "Do that all through the day. Think: *Am I dreaming*? And then you'll do it in your dream. You'll realise: I'm dreaming! Do it to get lucid, OK?" He had the sincerity of the stoned.

Ridiculous advice. Whoever wanted to see their own hands as much as I wanted to kiss the boy I loved?

•

I took my first dose in my little dormitory cubicle. I pulled on a crackling nylon jumper, moved my pillow, gobbled a big lump of cheddar I'd stolen from the kitchen. Poured the powder into a glass of water and drank it, bitter as hell, just before bed.

Falling asleep was a series of muffled bumps into the dark, like sliding down a long staircase. Then warm light surrounded me. I could see my hands. I was dreaming. Beyond my hands, I could see the floor tiles of the school entrance hall.

I went off to find my love.

I paced along the school's longest corridor, past photographs of triumphant rugby teams. I thought, I will turn into that classroom and you will be there. With your dark hair, with your back turned to me.

I saw you before I entered, through the little window in the door. Wearing cricket whites. I had conjured you up.

I felt the weight of the wooden door pressing against my palms. You turned and were surprised to see me there. Your hands were very warm. I could even smell laundry detergent on your cricket jumper.

It was more real than any dream I'd ever had before. But I didn't worry that I was awake. Nothing told me I was dreaming more clearly than the fact that you returned my kiss.

•

I took Lucidity most nights, spending all my pocket money. I meant you no harm, it was only an extended fantasy. Someone I explained it to, much later, asked why didn't I just masturbate? I told him that Lucidity was better. Actually, I did both.

So every night, my unobtainable love was obtained. I wasn't too young at all. But then I had to see you over my cornflakes, blissfully unaware of me, while I fought off a comedown like my brain's rusted cogs slipping and grinding.

Even our dream liaisons were limited. I didn't know how sex worked. After a few frustrating attempts at complex manoeuvres, I restricted myself to kissing. I didn't know what kissing felt like either, and sometimes it was like eating cake and sometimes too much like dentistry, but at least I was close to you.

I experimented in other directions. In the school woods I placed stone cliffs, a tumultuous river. I scoured encyclopaedia to stock up my bank of dream imagery, and was able to dot the riverside paths with temples and castles.

We sat beside the river. I summoned a hummingbird for your delight. It was only fair; I'd summoned you for mine.

•

I thought that true love simply was obsession. I'd read Nabokov and Thomas Mann as instructions, not cautions. I didn't know that love can be part of depression, dragging the brain's chemistry down in a whirlpool of adoration. Lucidity allowed me to graunch my brain along the same rut, night as well as day. It didn't satisfy, and didn't nourish.

Then came the term when you left the school. I assumed (the internet not having been invented) we would never meet again. It would only be as bad as before, I told myself. It might even be less painful.

It was worse. I took the Lucidity on the last day of term, a Friday evening. A week's worth in one mug, cloudy and acrid. I combined it with some sleeping tablets, also supplied by Thom.

I stood, in my dream, on the school lawns at night-time. The school was on fire. I ran down to the river, where the temples I'd built reflected, burning, in black waters. I willed you to appear, but you were on the far side of the water. In the real world, you'd left me. The anger made my arm muscles clench, the skin of my palms was full of roaring heat. I held up my hands to ward you away, and fire pulsed out of me. I watched you burst into flame.

I looked at my hands. They were on fire.

My housemaster was shaking me awake. It was lunchtime on Saturday. My drugged sleep had terrified my dorm-mates.

The rest of Saturday was hectic and dull: rushing to hospital for checks, then (when I was definitely safe) a parental grilling. They knew I'd taken pills but I lied about which ones, and I never mentioned Thom. I never mentioned you, either. Instead I blamed stress and anxiety, lacrimae rerum, the common or garden bone-deep sadness of things.

My GP believed me, and gave me a different drug: Prozac.

One drug made you larger, the other made you smaller. I still loved you, but I found (over the Summer holidays) that it was not so very great or terrible a thing, after all. I talked my way out of expulsion, and went back to school.

When you appeared in my dreams—less vivid, a mere echo—you stayed on the other side of the river.

•

Until my first breakup.

I was at Uni. I'd kissed boys (and compared those kisses with Lucid kisses—I'd misjudged the pressure, the sliding, the hotness). I'd woken up in bed with a thirty-year-old man, and remembered you with a jolt of nostalgia, seeing that the two-and-a-half years that divided us were meaningless now. But otherwise I'd barely thought of you.

Then I'd been dumped.

I had a few miserable nights of nightmares (rehashed arguments, reconciliations that evaporated with the dawn). Then at the Union one night, I overheard a muslin-wearing hippy woman talking about Lucidity and its revelatory powers. "You can find out so *much*."

"About yourself?"

"About everything. The horse spirits tell you mysteries!"

I nodded along to her theories about the equine gods of the dreamspace.

"Have you used it before?" she asked, as she slipped a sachet into my hot paw.

"No." I feared she'd ask what I'd learned about myself, or about the horse gods, during two years' nightly use.

"Be strong," she advised. "Be honest with yourself. Oh, and most important—you *must* look at your hands."

In my grimy digs, I wrapped a pinch of the powder in a Rizla paper and swallowed it. I put my ex-lover's T-shirt under my head, hoping the smell would make him manifest.

Instead, I found myself back on the lawns at school. Yew trees in the distance, larger than I remembered, with darker shadows under them. My ex will be there, I thought. In that patch of shade. I looked for his pale, shaved head.

But when I arrived, there was dark hair instead. You turned, and were surprised to see me.

You were eighteen, caught in amber, exactly as I'd last met you. My head only came up to your chest. I was fourteen again. But now I knew how kissing felt.

•

I popped back between relationships. Sometimes we didn't even kiss, just explored together the dream-landscape of my childhood. I supplemented the school grounds with sights from my travels, placed Angkor Wat beside the roaring river.

Friends told me they had anxiety dreams about school, but I had only these weird, crystallised moments of delight. The whole experience reminded me of glacé fruits: a season preserved but transformed, made golden and slightly sickly.

Then love—proper love—arrived, and it was savoury and nourishing and nothing like those glacéd memories. Love had grey stubble and a sly wit. I was with my husband for ten years. I never took Lucidity.

Sometimes you popped up accidentally, with your bird's wing fringe. But I'd learned that love was something that happened between two people. Give and take, back and forth. Unrequited love began to sound like a category error. What was loving about banging one's head against another person's indifference?

•

Bereavement I cannot describe at all.

For nights I didn't sleep, so I was grateful when I finally felt myself falling under. I slithered over a lumpy track in the darkness. Why was that sensation so familiar?

I smelled cut grass, felt the sun, knew I was back at school. My body was whittled down to eleven years old. I stood stock still.

Then from the shadows of the chapel, you appeared and walked towards me, coming to comfort me.

I could have been grateful for some guilt-free, no-strings kissing. But you were too young. In my dream I looked short and spotty but I knew I was really forty, while you were perpetually eighteen. I didn't need—on top of everything else—to feel seedy. Plenty of men have younger boyfriends, my devilish side observed. My better angel raised an eyebrow: younger *imaginary* boyfriends?

I wanted rid of you. By then, the internet had been invented, so I found Thom, my juvenile Mr Nice.

Synthetic oneirogens, he wrote. *How stupid were we?*

Very stupid, I agreed. *How can I get shot of it?*

Put the drug back into its original religious context, he told me. *Mental preparation, and a full day of chanting. Helps you to control it.*

I asked: *Have you tried that?*

Course I have, mate. Did it in a church hall in Dalston.

I wasn't sure the problems caused by my youthful idiocy could be remedied by middle-aged cultural appropriation.

Keep me updated. It's funny, said the man who supplied me with a daily dose of an illegal drug for two solid years, *I almost feel responsible.*

I despaired. Part of me was permanently glacéd. I would never escape childhood.

It was ridiculous, because look how much I'd changed since school. How much Thom had changed, as well; even a thumbnail photo of his adult face made it hard for me now to remember how he'd looked as a teenager. The way I'd always known him had become—in an instant—just a precursor.

Of course! If I could see you again, then I wouldn't dream of you as a teenager. What would you be, now? Forty-two. (I could still remember your birth date.) I'd find a picture of you online. A video, even. Bearded would be best, or greying—some definitive break. If I couldn't drive you away, I'd make you respectable.

I looked you up.

A picture appeared immediately—you had a beard. Excellent! But the same magnetic eyes, and your hair still dark (despite the hairline creeping back). You were beakier, creased across the brow—but still you, still the cricket captain. I feasted on your features, telling myself that I needed to concentrate while my dream-memory overwrote your younger face.

But while I looked, an old fault-line reopened. What if I could step into the same river twice—a different river, a deeper river? What if the mistake I'd made wasn't loving you, but stopping? I wasn't too young, now, to be your companion.

Then I looked at the words that accompanied your photograph: *jailed for four years for possession of a 'hoard' of images.*

I wasn't too young for you at all. I was, appallingly, not young enough.

Someone should write to you in prison, I thought. Human contact reduced re-offending.

Someone should write, but not me. I was salivating at the chance to have you as a captive audience. I'd grabbed at your ghost for years. I couldn't teach you a thing about human contact.

•

That night I was back at the old school again. Down the same long corridor, tapering into darkness. I passed the first door, looked in through the small window. In a pool of sunlight, you looked up from the book you were reading. I hurried on. In the next room I passed, you were playing the viola, and set it down on the floor when you saw me. Every room held a version of you, trapped in treacle. In each one, you were coming to life, smiling and wanting to speak to me.

I picked up my pace. I passed a room where you were standing close to the door, already scrabbling at the handle. Bearded and changed, a middle-aged man in cricket whites. I pushed past you, and you staggered after me.

I ran across the lawns. I heaved on old instincts and willed a rope bridge across a rock chasm. After I crossed it, I made the ropes fray and flutter down.

In the dark of the forest, you re-spawned in front of me.

In desperation, I held out my hands and pushed heat from my palms. Heard spitting, cracking. I set the forest on fire, and you, and myself.

I burned for a long while before I managed to wake myself up.

•

Mostly, these days, I eat cake and fly.

I'm spending a lot of time on an exercise bike, to sweat the drug out (a tip from an online forum). The exercise gives me a useful craving for sugar, which carries over into my dreams. If I find myself in that endless school corridor, my first thought is: *I will walk into this classroom and there will be chocolate sponge, with thick rich icing.* Childish, perhaps, but it works. I don't think of you.

While I cycle at the gym, I watch television. I'm stocking up my mental library with images. Documentaries about the Blitz, to absorb the aesthetics of ruins, the buddleia and barbed wire. The images need to be imbued with emotion, I've found, to pass into my dreambank, so I need the pity of war—zombie films won't do.

Why ruins? Because when I burn the school, it comes back. I need, when I've finished my cake, to smash it to pieces, brick by brick.

Later, I relax with a superhero film. I watch in slow motion as the camera swoops around the city skyline, and I try to immerse myself and feel childish awe, so that later I'll be able to recall the feeling of acceleration.

On nights when the cake fails me, and the walls won't crumble, when you hurry towards me—still in your cricket whites, bearded, silent—I spring into the sky, and fly away.

My Rightwise Home

I am Prince Elwin of Norland. I have been Prince for fifteen years. *My land from sea to mountain owes obeisance to its rightful Lord.*

So I'm furious to be deposed by a back-stabbing bastard in the stable-yard of an inn. I've been travelling with my retinue, making our slow Autumn loop round the North of my Kingdom. Now my treacherous Uncle Harlow sips his beer, and hems and haws.

"Fact is, we've got a new Prince."

What now, what now? No kin of mine, false greybeard... "Why?"

"We need the money, Elwin. We can't go any further North this year, the mist's come South too soon." He's right. Despite the stink of horses, I can smell the grey mist settling around us in the yard. "If we company turn back now, we cut six towns off our tour. We could halve our profits. So we need a real crowd-pleaser."

"I'm a crowd-pleaser. I'm the best Prince there is, you know it." My voice is resonant, my movements elegant. I've studied my rivals, stolen whatever worked, ditched whatever jarred.

Harlow shrugs. "That youngster we saw last night, from Kenn's company—he wants to travel."

Oh venomous and venal snake. The youngster is a dew-faced curly-haired moppet who doesn't know the speeches. Fine for the small towns on a county circuit. But we're better than that.

"I wouldn't pay to piss on him."

"But he's young." The unanswerable accusation: *you're old*. "Come back South with us," says Harlow. "You could be a good King Nicholas."

I'll stop your mouth! My sickle knife will make your throat sing out... "King Nick's an old man!"

His eyes slide sideways to my temples. There's grey hair showing there because I've run out of walnut powder. I'm Prince Elwin, I'm nineteen at most. I've made the Prince as subtle as I can, but the essence of Elwin is youth: promise, vitality, headstrong arrogance.

My Uncle concedes an inch. "Well, a youngish King Nick? Perhaps?"

"With you?" Our company doesn't perform that cycle."

"You could come South with us, find another company at the Winter meet at Elmsbury." So I must depose some lesser ruler to regain a crown.

Like a newt's tail sloughed when the foul perch grips, your Gods-sent Lord you cast aside. But I can't speak those lines. I'm not Prince Elwin any more.

•

The next morning, I don't leave with them to go South. How could I watch the wonder-boy fumble his lines every night?

"Where will you sleep?" asks Harlow.

"I have friends."

Harlow's travelled with me for years. He knows I have no friends. But I speak with authority (*my land from sea to mountain*) and he doesn't press me, because it lessens his guilt. The company push off down the coast road, disappearing into the mist, scarves over their faces and wrapped round the horses' noses.

It's a bleak region. The thin grass anchors some poor soil to the black rocks, while the sea wind tries to sweep it all away.

On the horizon, closer to the cliffs, is a castle. We pass it twice a year. When I play the attack on Castle Wistan (*my rightwise home I'll claim or cleave*) I picture its squat towers.

I don't have any other home, so I set off walking towards it.

There is no view out to sea, only a pearly wall, the waves invisible. If I stay outdoors much longer, clammy grey rime will grow on my clothes. Which would be a waste—I've stolen some of my costume tunics and I'm wearing them all for warmth, prince-in-waiting blue over coronation crimson.

I tire quickly. I drank a lake last night, and I'm not a young man.

The smell of the sea steals me back to my early life. I was a fisherman's daughter and a net-mender, but neither of those stuck. I could learn a speech by hearing it twice, and I was tall and handsome, so I was taken on by a local company at fourteen. The best Princes aren't boys. Why train up a new lad then watch him grow bearded, croaky, spotty in three years? When folk like me could play the Prince for twenty years, improving every season.

I won't go back to mending nets.

The castle is dark rock but less fortified than I thought. I walk the wall until I reach an orchard, where a woman saws a dead branch from an apple tree. Her grey dress tells me this is a Sister-house. Not a Castle, but a cold place full of old women, singing.

I call: "Peace to you, Sister." She lays down her saw and approaches. She isn't old. She isn't young. Her hair is covered, letting her face jut out from the scarf, as sharp-angled as a gardening tool.

"I know you," she says. "I saw you yesterday, on the common. You're the Prince."

•

"You can't walk South," says Sister Annys.

We're in the guest hall, eating stew at a long table. We have a half-dozen morose companions, with blanket bundles on their knees. Sister Annys tells me they're refugees from further North; the mist's taken their farms and they can't bring in their harvest.

"Some of these folk will be going South, surely?"

"Probably. But I've told them what I'm telling you: you need a horse, and a house to sleep in each night. Do you have friends between here and the South?"

"But my company never has trouble. We walk, with a wagon."

"It's worse this year. Go and look at the carts outside—their covers are all corroded."

"It can't kill you."

"It *has* killed."

"In other lands."

"On the North coast of this land, this year."

The Sisters have good messengers. Players like me carry the news from town to town, but we're like beetles, proud to know more than the worms, while the crow sees everything. So I ask: "Why is this year so bad?"

"Maybe some cold thing in the far North growing colder, or moving closer." Or some great heat in the South that has protected us is damping down, and mist is the natural state of the whole world. I can guess, as good as she can.

"Can I stay here, if I can't leave?"

"All Winter? Could you pay for it?"

"You shock me! What of mercy?"

"The merciful must eat, too. And you're not an invalid. You could help to bring the vegetables in before they rot." She eyes my shoulders. I have muscles—I grew them for show, but I could turn them to digging. "You don't have any books?"

"Books?"

"This Sister-house collects them. That's why the scholars are here." At the far end of the long table, three men in good heavy robes hold a muttered argument.

I tap my forehead. "Do you want plays? I have the Elwin cycle, entire..."

"...and we would have only to provide the vellum and the ink and the hours of writing. Or do you write?"

I write badly.

"Besides, we own Elwin. Several versions."

Other versions? That draws my curiosity. Then I remember my forced abdication.

"The Duke's Downfall? Sweet May?"

"Yes, we have those too." She not unfriendly, but she's impatient. She reminds me of someone, and that reminds me of something I might trade.

"I've been to Laeverland. Four years ago." I boast it casually, though I heaved on the sea trip and they hooted at our shows.

"You have books from there?"

"I know the Princess Rovena cycle by heart."

She takes a berry from the bowl and chews it. She wants it but she doesn't want me to know it.

"Could you dig the vegetables, as well?"

•

The House forms a C around a cloister; one side for the visitors, one side for the library, one side for the Sisters with a heavy oak door. No men beyond that door. So Annys and I meet in the library the following night.

My body aches; digging asks more of me than sword-fighting. I've worked from the moment the mist was burnt off in the morning to its insidious return at nightfall. More farmers, haunted and hungry, have stumbled up to the House;

most of the vegetables I unearthed were cooked for dinner (if they weren't rotten with mould from the mist).

I wear my gold and red tunic, looking very fetching by lamplight. The Sisters have leant me a grey one to wear while I'm digging, but I've changed back into my finery so I don't muddy the library.

We sit with a table between us.

I start to recite.

I'm not used to speaking aloud into silence, and getting no reaction. I'm not used to switching character every other line. I don't know whether to throw myself into every mood, or drone through it quickly.

Sometimes I'm interrupted by shouts—profanities—from the visitor's wing of the house. The scholars are in disagreement.

Annys doesn't take my words down in pen. Perhaps she doesn't trust me, or perhaps she needs to hear it all to judge how to set it out on the page. She writes with black-lead, whispering across scraps of vellum.

When we stop the first night, Sister Annys says, "Your memory's excellent. Do you eat sennage?"

"Grief, no. Only poor players need it."

"I eat it. We grow it in the gardens." She's prickly. "It helps my work in the library."

Over the next few nights, I recite the early parts of the cycle: the Princess abducted, the sorrow of the queen. ***Would that my breath had been robbed from me, too.*** The princess raised by wolves, ***found in the fur of the forest beasts.*** The Princess discovered by a hunter: ***see, how the bald beast pipes back to me!***

The words take me back to Laeverland. The sunlight was sharper. Few of the audience knew our plays. We over-exaggerated, mimed, bellowed in the thin bright air to try to move them. But when we saw the local companies, we understood: the whole style of show was different, over there. More elaborate in some ways, very lax in others. Trying to understand, I'd watched the Princess cycle three times through.

The Princess vows revenge on her enemies. An alliance, a betrayal, a parade of suitors...

"What are you doing?" asks Sister Annys.

I was making the hand gestures. I translate them to Annys: the turning fist for *anger controlled*, the flutter that shows *confusion*, and the behind-the-back flicking that showed ***a lie believed to be believed***. "The players' hands were painted white."

"I see. Now, should I note the gestures down with the speeches? Or are they more like the backcloth, or the clothes—oh, I shall have to read other books to see how it's done. You're smiling."

"You're very open. You don't need hand gestures."

"Am I?"

"For a Sister. You're supposed to be calm."

"You don't know many Sisters."

She's right. I see them dragging around, but I don't talk to them. Why would I?

"We're not all born to the life. Some take the vows that suit them," she says. "Some the vows they need. It's difficult for me to be calm, to be obedient, to stay in one place. But it's a useful struggle."

It doesn't seem useful to me, always to be flapping against your nature like a fish in a net. But I envy her in one regard, and tell her so: "You're lucky to have found your place."

She frowns. "We may have to leave this House, if the mist keeps moving. We own land here, but if nobody can grow food, it's little use."

The shelves of books run as low as the floor and as high as my head. "How would you move all this?"

"Oh, we would lose the library. Perhaps we could rescue some of it, next Summer, but..." She waves her calloused hand: *despair that does not want comfort.*

"Things can be moved," I say, to cheer her. "Today at noon, I saw white fluff bobbing along the horizon—a whole herd of sheep, passing down the coast road."

"The mist is killing animals, further North."

I will need to leave soon, myself. I can't stay the whole Winter. While I dig, in borrowed clothes, I'm nobody; each night, in the library, I'm half a dozen people all at once. It's been a week since my arrival. Were I still Prince, I'd have been ten times crowned in that week, and ten times to bed with a woman.

•

I tell Annys the speeches of the suitors. *Woman your worth far out-paces me.* One each night. Show me what labours would honour you. Two who fail, one victorious. *Can there be unfallen fruit so ripe? Let your arms prison me...*

Annys' black-lead stick never stops moving. By the triumph of the third suitor, I am raging with lust.

I'm not locked into my room above the guest hall. I could creep across the fields to town. I see myself in an inn, smiling, wooing...

Am I wearing my gold tunic? Or the grey?

When I walk into an inn after a performance, my clothes announce me. I'm the Prince, and there will be women who've watched me who want to know me. They'll want to hear me speak the words.

I imagine myself in a grey tunic, wordless, and my lust is numb.

•

"What is the Princess like?" Annys asks.

"Glorious. She had clouds of dark hair and she was taller than I—she made herself seem small in the early plays, I don't know how. They have the opposite tradition to us, there; the Princesses are rarely drawn from girl-players. She was forthright, not patient. Long fingers, good for the gestures. Her voice was so rich—I envied it..."

The room is silent, still, but Annys is laughing at me, biting her lips.

"I meant the *character*," she says. Sometimes while I recite Annys has asked for pieces of context: where is this city, what is this food. I should have understood. "I meant her *clothes*, and so forth. Goodness." She is mocking my misunderstanding and my affection.

"Is love very amusing, for Sisters?"

She stares me down. "Are Princes usually so spoiled?"

But I haven't been a Prince for weeks, now. "Forgive me. I probably chose the life that suited me, not the life I needed."

"Well. You might choose again—your life's hardly over."

I've not told her why I'm here, and I wonder if she's guessed, or if she gives that advice to every stray.

"So did the Princess player impress you, then?" she asks.

She is trying too hard to sound light-hearted. I know what she wants to know; it roughens her voice.

"She helped me to learn the speeches." My memory hadn't been as good as when I'd learned Elwin. "She was very clever—knew a lot of history."

"You were close to her."

Why does she care, being a Sister? "When you leave here, will you go to another House?"

"I may."

Now I understand. She wants to know what it would be like, if she left the House to be a common woman. She wants to know about common love. But she's asking the wrong person. I've been a Prince.

But her openness moves me. I owe her honesty.

"Yes, we were close." My throat closes, and I tilt my head back to open it, a players' trick. "But what could we do? With a woman from the crowd, I know what to say—Elwin's words. That's what women want. They want to entertain a Prince. And the same for her, she told me: with a man from the crowd, she was the Princess."

"So?"

"Prince Elwin and Princess Rovena—they had never met. They played no scenes together."

It seemed foolish now. It had seemed impassable, then.

"But a Prince would have things to say to a Princess."

"We were from different places. No—different tales. I fight my uncles with my sword. She battles the sea gods with incantations, to stop Laeverland sinking into the waves."

"That's quite a lot to talk about." Annys is laughing again.

I manage a smile. "Let me alone! It was hopeless. Our metre was different."

"Your metre?"

"This is me." I beat it out on the table with my fingertips. "My *un*cles *damned* the *throne* have *coz*ened, *court*ing the *aw*ful *wrath* of *Hea*ven… You see? Double beats. Heartbeats."

"I see."

"This was the Princess: *Suit*or, your *speak*ing is *ser*pent-like; *Where*fore these *ef*forts to *wor*ry me?" I pull my hands back into my lap. "Triplets, you see. It runs off your tongue."

Annys doesn't reply. A grey silence thickens between us.

Then shouting erupts from the scholars' rooms. "Such a disturbance, those men," Annys says. "At least most of my Sisters have left, and don't have to hear it."

"I thought there weren't many of you, for such a large House."

"They've gone South." She looks out of the library window. "I'm on my own, on the first floor."

She points across the dark cloister.

•

It's too cold to sleep that night.

The Princess changed her costume in front of me, a few times. Such an expanse of warm skin.

If I went through the great oak door to Sister Annys' cell, would she welcome me? Would she be wearing her grey robe, still?

I walk into the cloister, a grey algal bloom making the flagstones slippery.

I turn to the garden, first. I can smell the sennage, sweet and musky, like a fox in a flower patch. I pick a handful of it, chew it (it tastes rank, like cat's piss), and wonder how soon it takes effect.

I want to remember every detail of this night.

And I will, indeed, always remember it: how the mist in the garden got into my mouth and eyes and numbed them. How the oak door of the Sister's hall faced me down.

What could she and I say to one another? Some people don't need words. I do.

So I will always remember how my own door creaked with scorn when I returned to my room. And, as I lay cowardly and alone, each increment of dawn's arrival. *This is a dismal tricksy light, a candle hid behind a hand—I cannot tell my friends from foes...*

•

I ask the scholars if I can go South with them, when they leave. They're wealthy, and can rent rooms in each of the towns. I will memorise certain texts for them before we leave, which they'll transcribe while we travel. I may have to ride a donkey.

"But the Princess cycle's not finished," Annys says.

"They're my last chance."

"But where will you go?" I'm following her advice, but she's angry.

"I'll find another company at the Elmsbury fair. Can I use the library to learn King Nicholas before I go?"

As I read, I find that Uncle Harlow complimented me, when he said I could play King Nick. Nick's a deep man, with a lot to say, not an advisor or a courtier. A grown man, not an old man.

Nick doesn't do too much wooing, though. I wonder if the women in the inns wait for the King, wanting him to say certain words to them.

The last night, Annys makes me recite until midnight, and the cycle is still unfinished.

"If it doesn't suit you, you could come back here." She stares at her black-lead stick. "At least until the House closes. Your memory would be useful, for the library."

"I'll think on it."

"It could be a home for you."

"A home where I could never enter the door?"

She raises her eyes. "You could live either side. It is the vows that count: obedience and stability. Nothing else. Many of us have not had straight paths to our Houses."

She is giving me honest words and I try to return them.

"Annys, I wanted to be a Prince, and I did it. I want to be a King, and must attempt it."

I had meant to conclude by saying: if I find I would rather be a Sister, I will return here. But I can't say it, I can't see it, I would rather live as a fisherman. Whatever happens, I am going South to the sun. I want to get away from this grey place, this grey-robed raw-hearted woman.

I'm wondering if a King would have something to say to a Princess. I am dazzled by a crown, and cannot see beyond it.

Not Smart, Not Clever

The lecture theatre I'm trying to enter holds three hundred, but the security doors only admit two people at a time. Smart. I wait with the gang—Isha, Barb and Zach—in the underground atrium.

"Lin," Isha asks me, "you totally don't have to tell me, but are you on brain-rec?"

"No. I mean, not yet, anyway."

"I am," Isha admits.

The gang gasp. Isha is normally squeaky-clean.

"I didn't cheat! I was on face-rec," Isha explains, "but then I was writing my Decadence essay and the face-rec didn't know who I was, because I was wearing a hat. So the department put me on brain-rec, too." She frowns. "It's not fair. It was my thinking hat."

The gang coos. Isha is adorable.

The gang were thrown together in a hall of residence in their first year of University. Isha is sweet, Barb is melodramatic and Zach is nerdy. Not well-suited, they nevertheless became fiercely loyal and emotionally pot-bound. Now, in their second year, they're renting a house together. I'm shy. I'm not one of the gang, yet. I'm Zach's girlfriend.

"What do they do if you fail the brain-rec?" Isha asks.

"They've got truth drugs," says Barb.

This is a peril of studying literature: scientific illiteracy. I don't tell them that truth drugs don't work. I don't want a reputation for being a know-it-all.

We don't discuss the subject we're studying. Maybe it's too personal, or too easy to say something clueless. So we keep talking about plagiarism, probation, punishment. A vision of a grubby grail hovers before us: undetectable plagiarism.

"My mate said his friend's, like, cracked the code," Zach tells us. "He's not doing any work, just twiddling his thumbs, and he's going to stroll out with a First."

Isha reminds everyone that plagiarism is foul and most unnatural. I say something bland about fear and failure.

Barb bellows at me: "You don't have to worry about failing, you swot!" Then backpedals: "You're totally not a swot, sorry." My family's Chinese, and perhaps Barb doesn't want to stereotype me. But it's fair enough, I'm pretty swotty. I don't talk about it, but the girls have guessed that I still live with my parents, and they're academically pushy.

Complaints about how much everyone is paying in fees, how much everyone is working, how much everyone is expected to write, are passed up and down the queue like a bag of crisps.

"What did you get for the Decadence essay, Lin?" asks Isha.

I drop my head. Zach hugs me. We've reached the card-slots and cameras of the security doors.

"Don't worry about it, Lin." Barb says. "Decadence is the least of our fucking problems."

She swipes her card to and fro, fast as a hummingbird. We all shove through the doors together.

Barb issues a significant invitation: "You should come to Club Sandwich at the Union with us. It's horrible."

Whenever I pass the Union it smells of bleach, beer and vomit.

"I totally would," I say, "But I've always got a lecture the next day, first thing."

"Swot!"

I scan the rows of the lecture theatre. I can see twenty women who look a little like me. Six of us have the same hairstyle. A few of them are wearing gold eye-shadow. I might try that. I tend to copy people. I wish I could be more original, but it feels risky.

Zach and I sit next to one another, and our knees touch as Zach gets out his department-issue device, logs on and shares his thumb-print, to type his notes. I crack open my paper notebook, and he smiles because I'm old fashioned.

•

My ex-boyfriend, Linton, became entranced by plagiarism.

He was writing a doctorate on a handful of black American writers and their inter-textual influences. Doctorates are very specific. But they need momentum to get going. So you generalise a little, add a slug of confirmation bias, so you can believe you've got something huge.

Linton began to see inter-textuality everywhere. Anything 'new' grew out of revision, transformation and theft. We weren't just standing on the shoulders of giants; the giants threw us in the air, and we hauled them up with us. He told me when we met: we dance with giants in the air, man.

I probably encouraged his exaggeration. Relationships need momentum to get going, too.

Around the same time, Linton's University made him sign a four-page document stating that he wouldn't plagiarise.

It took him a week to reason himself into it. He got philosophical and then incredulous and then paranoid and then did them all again, drunk. He argued it out with his tutor, and his tutor said "Yes, but Linton. Seriously." He found that the text of the anti-plagiarism document had been copied directly from another institution's anti-plagiarism agreement and he rolled on his bedroom floor with hysteria.

But he signed it. Then the bad faith ate at him.

He started to talk a lot about undetectable plagiarism.

First, he was going to write software that would generate essays.

"It's a problem crying out for a smart solution. You know what smart is?"

"I'm smart."

"No, you're clever. Smart is when you have huge datasets, and a bit of processing power. You ask a question, the smart-thing pulls in data and filters it and personalises the output. Like, you ask where can I buy..."

"Dinner for my girlfriend, who helped me work on my thesis today?"

"Yeah, dinner! The smart-thing checks restaurant locations, menus, reviews. Now, there are databases full of essays, articles... If I create something smart, it can pull them in, and answer an essay question."

"'Is Hamlet mad' isn't the same as 'Can I have extra mozzarella."

"In some ways, it's identical."

Linton programmed a simple Markov bot. He fed it essays and the bot learned their rules. Then he asked it to churn out new essays, unoriginal but unique.

The new essays were like a child babbling down a crackly phone line. Linton swore and started again.

•

Later that day I hear Isha crying in her room. She can't find any relevant material for her essay, and the deadline's at midnight. I offer to help her.

"Would you really?"

"It'll take an hour. I can teach you how to use the databases."

"Oh, I couldn't. That wouldn't be fair, you've got your own work—"

"Buy me a pint at Club Sandwich, some time."

Isha plugs in her dedicated device. An oval light shines up at her: the face-rec. She isn't wearing her thinking hat, this time. I stay away from the camera so as not to confuse it and risk her reputation. She sticks two cheap sensor suckers to her temples, embarrassed, and tucks the wires into her cardigan. Brain-rec. I've not seen it in action, before.

I talk her through the big databases in our subject area, the differences between them. I set her some test exercises and make her a cup of tea while she completes them. Then on to the fun part—refining search terms, pinning down page numbers, whittling irrelevancies.

At the end of it, it's taken two hours, and we have six good articles, and she knows how to do it for herself next time.

"You're sooo clever," she says, correctly.

"Well, I'm smart. Just, you know, ask if you need anything else."

"You're so kind." She sounds uncertain, as though I'm trespassing on her territory. I want to reassure her: I'm shy and swotty but I'm not really sweet. She can keep sweet. And she doesn't know how kind I'm being.

•

Linton studied the leading text-matching service. It besmirched the white innocent page of the essay by highlighting unauthorised quotes, each separate source in a different colour. A plagiarised essay would light up like a Christmas tree.

Linton made a programme which turned all the Es in an essay into something that looked like an E but wasn't, so that the text-matching service couldn't recognise it. The service became a blustering idiot: Fourscor3 y3ars and t3n? Never heard of it! I hav3 a dr3am?!

Essays treated with Linton's programme had a 0% match, were white as snow.

"But that's just as suspicious as a 100% match," Linton admitted.

Linton made a synonym swapper. He told it that the plot of the Sensation novel, in essence, owes much to the Gothic novel. It told him that the scam of the funky tingle, in pith, is in hock to the Barbaric quirky.

"It sounds good, yeah?"

"It sounds like an encyclopaedia with a head injury."

"It's getting there."

Linton tried to teach code to write like people. Like hung-over, distracted, overworked amateurs. Like students.

Linton realised that he was trying to simultaneously solve all the major problems of language and computing and creativity, to invent a product that he could never sell.

•

My phone wakes me at just past midnight, and I can't remember which room I'm in. The poster of Tim Berners-Lee's benign eyes ('THIS IS FOR EVERYONE') doesn't narrow it down much. I slap the phone to silence it, and when my disorientation passes, I slip out from under Zach's arm to talk in the hallway.

Barb is phoning me, crying, from the library. The results from her last essay were released onto her device at 00:00.

The mark isn't what she'd wanted.

"It'll be on my transcript for ever! I'll get suspended!"

I soothe.

"It's alright for you! You're going to get a First!" She wails for a bit: she'll starve in a gutter, she'll go on the game.

I interrupt. "If you come home and sleep now, I'll talk to your tutor with you tomorrow."

"Swear?"

"Print me off a copy of the version you submitted and put it under Zach's door. And don't write anything about it on your device—no messages, no notes, OK? See you at eight in the kitchen."

She is snottily grateful. I return to bed.

"What was that?" Zach asks, wrapping his skinny arms round me.

"Barb. Didn't get the grade she needed on Modernism."

"You're the good deed fairy, you are," he says, rambling, half-awake.

I feel his arms slacken in sleep. I stay awake, waiting for Barb to slide the essay under the door. I build the case for the defence.

•

Barb swipes us into the Tower and we climb the concrete stairs. I review my longhand pencil notes. She fiddles with her device. I want to remind her not to drop it; it's a nightmare to get the department to replace them.

We have a ten o'clock appointment with her tutor. Barb has drawn heavy lines round her big eyes. She'd better not use her wiles on him.

"What are you going to tell him?" I ask.

She starts her panic breathing but I grip her arm and she says: "That I did read a lot of critical material, and I drew pretty heavily on one source—"

"Who?"

"Mitchell, 1980. But I didn't understand how to reference it."

"OK. And don't ask him to change the grade."

"But that's what I need!"

"Yes, but it's rude to ask. Just say 'I'm worried about getting into trouble.' That means 'change my grade.'"

"He's going to flay me!"

"This is the least of your fucking problems," I tell her, to reassure her. She looks shocked, and I remember that I don't usually swear in front of her. I reach past her and knock on the office door.

I only catch a glimpse of him, as she enters: a young man in corduroy, elbows on knees and fingers steepled. Playing at being an academic. The name on the door isn't his; he's a PhD student borrowing the office. This year is the first time he's taught. I'm not psychic—this is all public information, if you cross-reference. He's under-trained and underpaid and scared that he hasn't got it right. Maybe the wiles would work.

I'm doomed for a certain term to walk the corridor and eavesdrop. I move far enough away from the door that they won't hear me speaking, and I listen in through Barb's microphone.

He has a soothing voice, impersonating other people who have taught him. "...but Barbara, it's a very respectable grade!"

"I'm worried about getting into trouble," Barb says, shrill in my ear.

When he speaks—"Why would you be worried?"—I know she's infected him with her panic. He's afraid he's failed to spot something, and there will be a referral, a process.

"Tell him about Mitchell," I say into her earpiece.

She tells him.

"Tell him you put it in the bibliography."

"I did put it in the bibliography!" Barb retorts, a loud defensive non sequitur, which is even better—no tutor wants to deal with a mental health crisis. Barb rephrases herself: "I mean, I did put it in the bibliography, but I didn't know how to reference it properly..."

The tutor sighs with relief and spends ten minutes discussing ways of acknowledging sources. He's pretty good. I jot some of his tips in my notebook.

"Make sure he's going to change the grade," I remind Barb. "You're still worried—"

"I'm still worried that I'm going to get into trouble."

"It's a fine grade, it won't affect—"

"Mention probation," I prompt.

"I'll go on probation and they'll make me work in the cells, and I can't, I'm claustrophobic."

"The cells?"

"I mean the Supported Learning Unit."

"Oh, I see. I'm not sure whether I can actually—"

I want to barge the door open and show him. I have to instruct him through Barb: "Tell him your friend had his grade changed."

Double puppetry: I work Barb, she works her tutor. "My friend's tutor put something, hang on, he wrote 'post-tutorial grade adjustment' on the—what? The online feedback sheet..." She dips in and out of fluency, sounds like she's possessed. I can't keep doing this. As soon as the procedure's complete, I yank Barb out of my ear and leave her to say her own goodbyes.

Barb catches me up on the stairs.

"Why did you give me a fucking A essay, anyway?"

"You wanted better grades."

"I wanted a C+! Maybe a B." That single A, in amongst Barb's Cs and Ds, would have triggered an avalanche of new anti-plagiarism measures. Hopefully, we've averted that.

"It was a B-, at best. Your tutor's a soft marker, doesn't want his students crying all over him."

She's glaring at me, but she still needs me. We have a pre-existing appointment that evening, because she owes the department an essay on psychoanalysis in contemporary women's fiction.

And it's fine. I don't like her, either.

The ones I don't like, I do everything for them. I run all the searches and don't show them how to use the databases. I steal their style and I tidy their grammar, but I don't tell them what a comma splice is or how to use a semicolon. They bob along. Sometimes they think what I do for them looks easy, and they try to write something of their own; their grades dip down, and they come back to me, begging. But their arrogance, their attempts to break away, keep them on the borderline between passing and failing. In their final year, around Easter, they realise everything hangs on their dissertation. They just can't risk doing it themselves. And by then, nobody else knows their style. By then, I am their style.

And I fleece them. If you've paid so much in fees, how much more would you pay, to not fail your entire degree?

It's not entirely personal. I like Isha, but it helps to have a lot of goodwill in my cover-house. I dislike Barb, but it also helps to have someone in my cover-house who's in as deep as possible. Not handy tips for the promise of a pint. The full service.

•

Barb is still glaring at me when we settle in her room for the evening's work. I have pages of handwritten preparatory notes. (Never type anything, never use a device. Never leave a trail. Electronic documents barely exist but they never stop barely existing.)

The log-in takes forever. Password and thumb-print and luminous face, suckers on her temples like extra nipples, and more passwords and a voice-check.

"It's measuring my stress levels, isn't it? How should I be? Should I be calm, or terrified, or..." She's nervous because she's cheating, she's calm because I'm going to write her an impeccable C+ essay. She's nervous because she's not sure if she's nervous enough.

"It doesn't test stress."

"Of course it does. Doesn't it?"

"How would they know how stressed you ought to be?" I imagine complex charts, with variables for parental income, bar job, caffeine and tranquilisers, with a slider to adjust for how close to the deadline the student has started typing. "It's checking your brain activity."

"Oh God, it'll know..."

"It's not that sensitive. We'll be fine. I'll explain it, bit by bit, you'll write an essay plan, then I dictate the essay."

She frowns. She wants it to be over quicker.

"It'll be useful if you understand the argument, in case they pull you in for a viva."

"They won't, will they?"

"They'll ask to see the essay plan, first. But they viva 5% of second year essays."

Barb looks sick, so I give her a pep talk: "This way, you understand what you're writing about. Which is good, because we want to learn, not just get the degree. Don't we?" A little humour, there.

The brain-rec is incredibly crude, and my precautions should fool it utterly. Its outputs look like crayon drawings. The detection tech always fails, and sometimes I think it fails because it's striving for the impossible, the philosophical. A sniffer dog, or an honest gumshoe, would ask: are there phrases which match other sources? Was this file originally created eight years ago, in the wrong country? Simple things.

Detectors ask impossible things. What does a lie sound like? How does an honest man breathe? They want to photograph the shadow as it falls across the soul.

I've reread one of Barb's essays to catch her style. I'll drop in 'furthermore' every page, weave in some multi-sub-clause sentences deliberately. But most of my imitation is intuitive artistry. I take on her crooked way of thinking, and her writing comes naturally to me.

I consult my notes. "OK, so: the phantom in psychoanalysis! The phantom comes back, but he doesn't want to set things right, he just wants to continue a cover-up."

I could write a better piece. I don't build an elegant argument, stack up unique evidence, deliver a killer punch. It's only a second year essay, and it can't be higher than a C+. I wish I could write more for the final-year students, but I can only write for the modules which are taught through large lectures. I'd be spotted in small seminar discussions, despite my boring hair and my boring clothes.

The polite term for what I do is ghost-writing. Sometimes I'm ghostly. When I creep into lecture theatres. When I need someone to swipe me in and out of buildings, to pick up their device, to type for me, as though I can't touch objects. When the lecturer says, 'Any questions?' and I'm bursting with questions, but I can't have a voice. When I see my face reflected in the screen of someone else's device and I pull away before the face-rec can catch me.

But the writing itself doesn't make me feel like a ghost. I'm shaping, knitting, hacking, building, and never more alive.

If there's a ghost in me, it's my conscience, which is undetectable by current tech.

Suddenly, Barb cries out. I peer over at the screen of her device.

Another window has opened, an image in moody blues with splats of mustard yellow. A blue figure solidifies out of the general fog, and another shrinks back and melts away. At the foot of the screen lie two twitching red blots.

I jump away from the screen and scramble towards the window. I wrench it open, and Barb is yelling, terrified, and springs up after me but is tethered to her device by her brain-wires and drags it half across the room. I wave my hands to keep her away from me. I lean out of the window as far as I can, sitting on the sill, out into the cold air, away from the device.

Because that screen—which I shouldn't have seen—was a combination of heart monitoring and thermal imaging. I didn't know the devices could do such things.

I signal to Barb, hand over my mouth, pointing to the floor: sit down, shut up.

She scowls. She points at me, then makes two of her fingers run like little legs, across her other palm and off the edge, peddling in mid-air. She thought I was going to jump out of the window. I don't let myself laugh in case the device is audio-recording.

I tell her with gestures to put the earpiece back in. I can whisper the rest through my phone from here on the windowsill. It'll be awkward, and annoying, and my arse hurts already from balancing.

When we're done, Barb pulls the sweaty suckers off her head, and I hobble out of the door before she can speak.

•

And Isha is haunting the hallway and she calls after me: "I know what you do. I heard you and Barb talking about it." The sound insulation in student houses is terrible.

She is shaking with indignation. Maybe she'll try to throw me out of the house.

"You need to write my Victorian essay for me, or I'll report you."

Sweet little Isha! The worm turns! She's been nervous lately, and her perfectionism drags her grades down.

I mentally review my portfolio. I'm running some students at another college, across town. They bring enough money for me to live on. But it would be a shame to lose Barb, and the other students at this University, before they mature—before the big pay-off from their dissertations next year.

"I'll write it, but you need to pay me."

"You're a cheat."

"And you're a blackmailer! Except I'm not going to write for free, so you're not even a successful blackmailer." I'm amused because it reminds me of an old joke—we've already established what kind of women we are; now we're just haggling.

"That's different!"

"How the fuck is it different?" She looks more shocked at my swearing than my ghost-writing. I've been a good shy swot. I try reasoning. "Let's start again. You don't want the person who writes your coursework to be pissed off at you. That's just—" Fuck-witted, I think, but I keep it clean. "That's handing me a weapon."

"You couldn't report me. They'd kick you out, as well."

"Kick me out of where?"

"The University."

"Bless you. I'm not a student here."

We've known one another for a year, practically lived together for the last six months. She counters surprisingly quickly. "Well, wherever you're studying. I'll tell them, they'll kick you out."

The solipsism of youngsters protects me all the time, but sometimes it's staggering. Knowing it means the loss of this whole house, I say:

"Isha, I'm not a student. I haven't been a student for years."

I duck into Zach's room while she's still blinking.

•

Linton got bitter. Academia was a pyramid selling scheme. We'd polished our PhDs, churned out scholarly articles which nobody read, and taught undergraduates for minimum wage. But there weren't any jobs for us. I had a couple of interviews for lectureships but—possibly because I looked so young—nobody took me seriously.

Linton would wake in the middle of the night gripped by new ways to plagiarise. He stopped thinking of selling his solutions, and planned to give them away for free, the keys to the ivory tower.

Meanwhile, I marked hundreds of essays in which the stolen sections stood out like dolmen on a dull landscape.

I stopped listening to Linton, because it seemed simple to me: the most rigorous tech couldn't beat slippery, dishonest flesh. But the most eloquent, creative tech couldn't persuade a human marker, either. It was stalemate. To write a convincing fake essay, you'd need to be human and on the ground. Attend the lectures, collect the hand-outs, read the lecturer's favourite sources. Remind yourself how students thought and sounded. You'd have to spend time with them, but that would be easy. Their social circles were passionate but weirdly permeable. In fact, if you hooked up with one of them, you'd have an instant sample group.

Linton's mania progressed so far that when his final submission deadline arrived, he had nothing to submit. I had to write his thesis. I wrote it with him, at first, standing over him, questioning him, kept him typing and talking. When he flagged, I wrote it for him.

We worked, night and day, for a fortnight, and then parted. He was rotten, or he wouldn't have let me do it; our relationship was rotten, and I had to end it. (I don't mean to duck the blame, but I still can't decide. Was I already rotten, or I wouldn't have done it? Or did I, during that fortnight—living a double life, over double-length days—bend too far, and become rather more flexible than before?)

"You could alter the students' genetic code," Linton woke me to tell me, one day in that endless fortnight.

"Shut up."

"You could make them fluoresce if their stress levels reached a certain point."

"Go to sleep. Some of us have to write your thesis in the morning."

"Turn them into human lie detectors. You could switch off the lights in a lecture theatre, shout 'who's been cheating,' and boom—pull in all the glowing students."

"Hang on—isn't that a detection idea?" I asked.

Concealing plagiarism and detecting it went hand in hand; Linton had been watching the detectives so he could design his dodges. When his fascination became all-consuming, he forgot which side he was on, and just marvelled at the fight. After he passed his viva, after we broke up, Linton got a job with one of the biggest plagiarism detection companies. He writes impeccably original copy for their publicity.

When I got my own doctorate, I went into the plagiarism business as well. I didn't have a vendetta, like Linton. I just wanted to keep learning, and writing, and if there was nobody who wanted to read my ideas, there were certainly people who wanted to buy them.

I'm smart. I have a small, high-speed processor, and access to huge datasets. I can pull in information, quickly filter it and tailor my outputs. But I'm also clever.

Students approach me warily, broaching the subject outside the library, and they always think there's a single solution: a magic formula, a cloak of invisibility. Managing their disappointment became part of my job, breaking it to them gently that the only way to write an essay is to write an essay.

•

Zach is sitting with his back to me, so it takes me a moment to see that he's unpacking my bag. He's heard me arguing with Isha. He's looking for evidence. Clever.

He's laid all the faces out on the bed, side by side. And of course they look creepy, like a decapitated choir. Which is unfair, because they're purely pragmatic. The face-rec is, indeed, stupid, and I can pop on a mask and pass as one of my clients long enough to type their essay for them. The faces are just colour photocopies, with pieces of elastic, not weird rubber masks or anything.

There's a trio of students from China; they pay huge fees, they're not used to this country's referencing conventions, and nobody's got time to explain it to them. There are four incredibly posh but not very literate finalists from the Home Counties. A couple of mature students. Each name is written in pencil on the back of its face.

"You've just been lying to me forever," Zach says.

I don't say: "No, it only feels like forever because you're, what, *nineteen*?" I'm sick of being Mr Chips and Mrs Robinson.

The truth is, students are so similar to one another they might as well have been cut and pasted. Someone is always sweet and someone is always melodramatic and someone is always nerdy. I can always half-live in a student house with them (retreating to Linton's spare room whenever I need to, because he'll owe me forever). I can pick up enough—words, clothes, gestures—to blend in. And I can pick up the kind, nerdy boy who's pleased to be picked, who believes I live with my strict parents who he can never meet. I'm a good girlfriend. And I'm fond of Zach. I've been fond of all my cover-boys. I have sympathy for him, for all of them, paying so much to get a foot on a broken ladder, with unemployment waiting for them at the top.

He's looking at me with disgust, though, and my patience for that is limited.

"How can you do this?" he asks.

It's only plagiarism. His friends and housemates have asked me to help them cheat. None of us are monsters. We're symptoms of a sick system.

And then his face crinkles up, as much as those super-young faces can crinkle, and he says, "I liked you."

He's angry about our relationship, not my job. That's fair enough, I was pretty despicable.

He asks: "How old are you?"

Which they almost always ask, and which is the least of their fucking problems.

Windows Into Men's Hearts

Sir Francis Walsingham to M Critoy
Secretary of State for France

I find therefore her majesty's proceedings to have been grounded upon two principles. The one, that consciences are not to be forced, but to be won and reduced by the force of truth, with the aid of time, and use of all good means of instruction and persuasion.

...her majesty, not liking to make windows into men's hearts and secret thoughts... tempered her laws...

but when, about the twentieth year of her reign, she had discovered in the king of Spain an intention to invade her dominions ... and after that the seminaries began to blossom, and to send forth daily priests ... yea, and bind many [English subjects] to attempt against her majesty's sacred person ... And because it was a treason carried in the clouds, and in wonderful secresy, and came seldom to light...

...then were there new laws made...

•

Journal of William Allen Founder of the English College at Douai

December 10th 1591

God be merciful—three more good men of ours taken, in the last six weeks.

Each of them was asked their profession, by officers, on arrival at a new town. All had rehearsed, with me, the most subtle dissimulations—and yet, all announced the truth! Treacherous truth: that they were priests, come secretly to England to restore the land and its monarch to the true faith.

All these men were arrested. One has been hanged, winning his soul's eternal exaltation. One is exiled, three rot in the Marshalsea.

I do not understand these fits of honesty! The need for equivocation troubles all of us. But these men agreed that some lies might be told in the service of Our Lord—or they pretended to me that they agreed.

I fear that these men—these novice boys—fix their minds too much on the martyr's rose, and the glorious deaths of Briant and Campion. Our enemies say our order delights in wasting the lives of young men. As though we flung them into England like coins down a well, hoping for good fortune. Unfair, untrue! But we have lost so many...

I must pray, and not succumb to despair, and recall that others of our order thrive. One such, Edward Shepherd, was held by an officer of the law. But when questioned by his superior, the officer confessed that Shepherd had done no wrong within his sight, and that he 'had the look of a good fellow.' Brother Edward was then set free—to preach, to travel, to minister to the faithful. Surely this is Providence?

•

Journal of Anne Barton

December 10th 1591

God protect us, we are to have a priest. Father told us yesterday.

We have had no priest in ten years—since old Father Rutter—and the laws have tightened a notch every year. Now, to shelter a seminary man means death.

"It is but for a short while," Father said. "And I will bear all the consequence."

That was little comfort! And untrue, for Mother could be taken also, and perhaps our home seized from *praemunire*. And I as well, despite my youth? I am fifteen years old, and Bedingfield child was charged with treason at eight. (Might a child not say "I hate the Queen", meaning no more than "I hate cabbage"?)

Mother bit her fist and spoke not. I hid my fear and smiled.

Our faith has been a private solace to our family. I wish most fervently it had not become the business of Princes.

December 11th

The priest is here.

Although he wore rough clothes when he arrived, he was soon dressed in a borrowed velvet doublet, and looked well in it (although he tugged at the collar frequently). He has dark hair and skin quite sallow, and deep-set wary eyes. He walked with Father and me in the courtyard garden.

The priest said, "A beautiful house, sir."

"It is the cloister of the monastery that once stood here," Father replied.

I know the family story: when the monastery fell, during King Henry's time, my grandfather applied to purchase a part of it. Grandfather was a true Catholic but a practical man.

The priest took my father's hands in his. I thought the priest's fingers seemed askew. "Do your father's deeds trouble you, Master Barton?" asked the priest.

"They do. Where I dine and sleep and raise my daughter, Anne, I know that monks should be praying. I think I hear the Matins bell.'

He had never said such things before.

"You will not be judged for your father's actions, but your own," said the priest. He released my father's hands and pulled on a pair of fine calf-skin gloves. I fretted that I had stared at his deformity.

"You must stay as long as you wish with us," said Father.

•

December 15th

Cheering news: Edward Shepherd is a guest in a house of some standing. He has all good things: a warm home, a horse to travel, and intelligence as to the roads and the dispositions of people. He will do much to kindle the zeal of Catholic families thereabouts, spreading like a fire in stubble.

And there will be no need for Edward to hide in a sewer, should the house be ransacked by pursuivants: his host has summoned our man Daniel Owen to build a hiding place.

•

December 15th

Owen the builder walked once round our whole house and clapped his hands in pleasure.

"Will it do?" asked Father.

"Very finely. A house such as this, which has served two purposes, may be made to serve more." Owen showed how my grandfather's work, to make the cloister a private dwelling, had left many hidden nooks and false walls.

Owen sleeps during the day and the servants call him a sluggard, not knowing he has been cutting all night with a muffled saw.

The hiding place is a curious work. A double plank of oak forms the door. If a pursuivant should rap on the oak, only a dull note will return to him, as though there is a wall beyond the wood. This weighty plank swings lightly when a certain floor tile is pressed.

I dislike it. As a child I had dreams where a new door in the house opened to a strange room, and they troubled me more than nightmares. Owen's work is another clever lie in the service of the truth. The wall is not a wall, the priest puts on the disposition of a gentleman. We are all outward conformity and secret heresy.

December 16th

I had thought the priest would need to hide away, but today we rode out openly to hawk. He wears his years of study invisibly, like chain-mail under his doublet.

He knows falcons well. He does not know me well, though. He questioned me on some dozen subjects I did not care to answer. "Do you love your father or mother most dearly?" he said, as he handed me onto my horse.

"I should be ingratitude itself if I did not love both."

"Was your Father Rutter a good priest?"

"I do not know, sir. He kept us in the faith."

"And have you friends in the village?"

I feared he might ride off to convert them, so told him I treasured no person above any other.

Chafing under his interrogation, I questioned him in return. "Do you believe your work will bear fruit soon? Will England return to the faith in five years, perhaps?"

"'Strewth, no!" Then he said hastily, "Forgive me. You catch me in a melancholy fit." He is a mightily uneven man, flustered and assured by turns. "Ask no more questions. I must not give you knowledge that would harm you."

He has been harmed. He wore gloves to ride, and a hawking gauntlet, but I saw his hands at dinner. His fingernails are gone, leaving thick skin like melted wax. He shames us. Our family live secretly, and attend the heretics' Mass in the village church monthly. We disdain to pay a fine, when others give all they have.

I could only find weak words for him. "I pray we may all speak and worship honestly, one day."

He cast off my Father's goshawk and we watched it ring up into the white Winter sky. "Might you travel to the continent, one day, and join a convent?"

I imagined it as the hawk circled: studying and singing with brave women in far lands. It would be good to be whole-hearted, to serve the Lord as the hawk seeks the rabbit.

But I could not imagine leaving my home, the fields over which the hawk's shadow was shooting.

"I might," I lied, and it made the priest smile.

December 17th

The priest said Mass for us today. I have read the liturgy to myself, in the years since our old priest died, but not remembered how it stirred me. *Kyrie eleison* has the cadences of mourning, *Gloria in Excelsis* rings like trumpets.

Then the *Agnus Dei*—"take away the sins of the world". I thought of poor Father Edward's hands, and the sins of his tormentors. Father keeps the worst rumours from me, but everyone has heard of Richard Topcliffe, the Queen's pursuivant. Was it he who hurt Father Edward? Was it blasphemy to doubt that the heretic-torturer's sins might be removed? Or was it blasphemy to pray for it?

The priest stooped to place the consecrated wafers in our mouths. I felt something thaw that had been frozen. I wanted faith to flow out of me into every part of the world.

We dined together afterwards, and I spoke to Mother. "It is good to hear the Mass again."

"Yes—and in our house again."

"Would it please you for Father Edward to stay past Christmas?"

"No!" She gripped the table. "He should go from here as soon as your Father allows."

Silence spread around the table. Mother's face bloomed scarlet. The priest looked over to us. "Mistress Barton, should I leave your home?"

"Yes, you should leave! You are a good man, but your goodness will be the death of us. I would sooner have poison in my cup than you in my house."

She put her hand to her mouth and fled the room.

•

December 17th

A sad sight came to Douai this morning—a man screaming as two men lifted him out of a carriage. Fortunately, on seeing the sky, he ceased to scream. He would by no wise come back under a roof, however, so we set up a screen in the gardens where he might wash and dress himself. His clothes were stiff and his hair a bird's nest from sea salt.

He babbled, then grew calm, and confirmed what I had suspected: that under his long and salted beard, he was Stephen Griffiths returned from England.

He asked that a bed be placed in the gardens also.

"There is no helping it," he said. "Father Garnet tried all ways but I cannot be within doors."

I told him the weather was too inclement, and assured him that we were safe here, not to be raided like English houses. But he fell into fits on the threshold, so we fetched out a pallet and blankets.

Father Garnet, the superior who leads the English mission, had told me of this poor man's condition—the pains in his head, and his terror of close places. I had not expected Stephen's cheerful frankness. He had drunk beer, to permit him to travel by carriage, and I questioned him before the weakness might wear off.

"What has caused this alteration in you, brother?"

"Oh, one of our order worked the change. One of my fellows here at Douai—my rival, if a novice may have a rival, aside from the world, the flesh and the devil. He was more zealous than I, more learned, more holy." He spat on the grass.

"He is your brother in Christ!"

"But neither good nor Godly, now. He met with us at the great gathering..."

I knew of this ill-omened gathering. Garnet brought together all the priests of the English mission, twice a year. Many of our brothers lived in dark attics, alone for days at a time. Gathering together braced their souls, Garnet said, and sharpened them for new battles. But a raid on such a gathering could destroy the whole mission at once.

"That rival brother of mine—he said the Mass for us all. Then the house where we met was attacked. The pursuivants battered down the doors. Ten of us crammed ourselves into one of Owen's nooks, trapped there for hours, while those foul men stabbed the beds and tumbled the furniture."

"Terrible." But some of our men have been locked for three days in a priest-hole, and not suffered for it after their release. "Did the confinement distress you?"

"Oh, no! I have had worse hospitality. But the priest had pressed some charm onto my tongue with the consecrated host, and I felt it winding into my thoughts. Carving out a channel, like a worm, or a chisel..."

This was a blasphemous fancy. "The other men—they did not feel this?"

"They felt it not, but it worked on them. They cannot tell a lie, now, if asked a question." He tapped his finger on his forehead. "A gate has opened between my mind and my mouth, dear Father. My every conversation is a confessional, now. And I cannot bear to be hidden, or disguised, or kept in any closed place. I must be open in all things."

It was a vile tale, and he drew from it a strange conclusion. But then I recalled the recent spate of confessions, among our men in England.

"Test me," Stephen demanded. "Ask me any shameful thing! Ask me if I have been a knave, a cozener, a lecher!"

But my first questions were clear to me.

"Who was with you at the gathering?"

He gave ten names. Half the named men have been arrested for their unusual honesty; two of them are dead.

"Which man said Mass for you, and them?"

"Why, Edward Shepherd did it."

•

As soon as my mother left the dining hall, a farmer's boy ran in, shouting that men on horseback were asking questions in the town.

I took Father Edward's arm. "I will show you the shortest way to the priest hole, Father." I snatched up a knife from the dining table as we left.

I stamped on the secret tile, let the false door-panel swing wide, and ducked into the room after the priest.

The secret room was as long and wide as a coffin. The priest went ahead of me.

"What have you done to my family," I asked, "that they are no longer masters of their own tongues?"

He showed no surprise. "I have worked a charm on them. I understand it not myself. Maybe our Lord means your family to leave off dissembling."

"This is not God's work." I spoke too loud, and feared discovery, and dropped my voice. "It is Devilry."

"Call it what you will," Father Edward whispered back. "I am caught on the same hook. Do you love your family more than your faith?"

I did not wish to answer him.

But my tongue flapped against my teeth like a bird in a panic. "Yes. My family is dearer to me." I pointed my knife towards him. "How do I undo this *charm*?"

"I do not know. No, put down your blade—I cannot speak more truthfully, Anne! For the sake of pity!"

He feared me. He was scratching nervously at the skin of his wrists, one hand scouring up under the opposite cuff. He had strength but, pinned in this tiny room, he could not use it. I heard, from elsewhere in the house, the scrape and crash of furniture shoved aside.

"Could you truly kill me with that knife?" he whispered.

"No, I could not."

The words sprang from my mouth unbidden. Father Edward struck at my hand. My blade clattered on the stone floor. We froze, and waited for the searchers to turn in our direction.

We heard only a blunt knocking, far off. Then louder, sharper, with others joining in: a martial drumming on every piece of panelling, moving closer and closer. Until staves pounded on the false door to our little room and it shook under their blows.

If one man were to step, by chance, on the tile that worked the mechanism...

The priest pushed past me, to stand between me and the door. To protect me.

And a hundred heartbeats later, the drumming passed us by.

We waited in silence until the cacophony ceased. My father called for us. Was he a tethered lure, bleating for the hunters? No, his voice was joyful.

I backed out of the hidden room, shifting the lever that opened the heavy oak door. The priest followed me to freedom.

I tugged the door hard against his head. I could not have stabbed him, that was true, but I only needed to intend this deed for a moment, then the weight of the door did all the dreadful work. He screamed, and I let the door swing free again.

"Leave the house within a week or I will find another way to harm you," I said.

"You cannot. I will ask you every hour whether you mean to injure me."

"Then I will plan a dozen ill deeds, and when you discover one I will find another. I will trip your horse, or push you down the cloister steps." I saw a simpler way. "Or I will ask you in front of my father if you have worked witchcraft on us, and you will confess it to him."

And then I was silent, because Father had rushed forward to embrace us both.

•

December 18th

I have tested Stephen. He does not lie—which is to say, he does not lie when he says that he must speak the truth. But can Edward Shepherd be the cause of it?

Letters stream in from England. More of our men have announced themselves to be priests. They are believed by crown and commoner alike to be a small cohort of a vast Jesuit army—when in truth, they form the greatest part of our mission.

All of them talk without torture. Some confess strong sympathy for plots against her Majesty's life, when our mission has sworn to take no part in such politics. Others declare that her Majesty is no true queen (when we have schooled them, time and again, to equivocate on that matter). Two priests—if reports do not lie—have announced that any man who commits treason against Elizabeth will win his soul's safe harbour for eternity.

The Queen's advisors beg her for action: to make death the penalty for all recusants, and to raise armies to attack France or Spain. They tell her she will by no other wise be safe. Our priests, my brothers, are shown to her as evidence.

The compass of the nation swings to war.

And all these garrulous priests were given Mass by Edward Shepherd.

I know not what to do. If I summon him to Douai, will he come? It is doubtful, if he now labours for another master. If he should remain in England, Catholic families will shelter him, and fall under his sway.

Stephen Griffiths told me his own plan: to return to England.

"I cannot waste myself here."

"You should ask my leave," I told him. "I am your spiritual director."

"I do not go as a priest," he said. "I go to kill Edward Shepherd, before he kills every Catholic in England, and—by fomenting war—half the men in Europe. I cannot expect your blessing, so I do not ask your permission. But I do ask for his whereabouts."

I did not sleep. His request racked me all night.

This morning I find he has already left, and stolen from me all of Edward's letters.

•

December 22nd

The priest has gone from my home. His new home is twenty miles away, a house so large it would take a year to search.

My family do not speak of the curse he has laid on us. We spend much time in solitary contemplation.

After Father Edward left, I sat in the cold cloister-garden, trying to discover how much he has altered me. I asked myself questions, but could not make my tongue wag against its will.

A young and pale-haired stranger entered the garden, picking his way around my mother's bare rose bushes.

"What is your name and business, sir?" I asked with courtesy, in case he was a pursuivant, but as he drew close I saw his clothes were all over mud and twigs.

"I am Stephen Griffiths, a Jesuit, come to kill Edward Shepherd," he said. Then he laughed. "And I say so grudgingly, of course. Curse the man. Has he lodged here?"

"He has." I found that I still must answer honestly.

The man plumped himself down on the ground and pulled up his feet to examine the soles of his boots. I could not believe him a murderer.

"I marvel that you can walk abroad," I said, "If you must announce your intention to any who ask."

"Oh, I travel by night. Sleep in ditches all the day. Is that man, Edward Shepherd, still in this house?"

"He has left here, an hour past."

"So close! Tell me in which direction he went? And if he has somehow locked up your tongue on the matter, draw me a map, or point. And give me a loaf of bread and a fast horse."

"I will give you the bread and the horse, but you need no directions. I will show you the way."

"You should not come with me. I am an honest villain. I mean to kill him, it is no sport."

I did not know if I wished to see the devil-priest dead. But I could not stay home.

"You need me. Your tongue is not your own." It was a lie of omission, for it hinted that my tongue was free. But no dire consequence descended on me. It was a great relief to find I could deceive, even slightly. I stiffened my spine to deceive even further, as we reached the door of Father Edward's new home.

"Sir—I would speak with Edward Shepherd? I hear he lives here and gives good Christian counsel."

I flattered until the servant turned back into the house, locking the door against us. Father Edward re-opened it, wearing another borrowed doublet, with a collar of cut-work lace.

"Anne! You have made my host afraid. He thinks that every man in the country knows he shelters a Jesuit. Why do you come here?"

Then Father Stephen stepped into his sight. Father Edward made the sign of the cross on his breast.

"Are you my death?" he asked.

"I know not. The hour of your death is not mine to choose, but God's."

"But have you come to kill me?"

"Oh, yes! You cannot doubt it, Brother Edward."

"I will not let you in."

"Run to your hiding-hole, then—but I remember this house, and could tell the officers where to find you."

"You need not threaten me, brother. No place is safe for such as you and me. We are leaky boats, who cannot reach safe harbour." I searched Father Edward's face for signs of devilish allegiance, but he looked bone-weary, uneasy in his courtly clothes. He stood to one side of the door, to let us enter.

"I cannot join you in there, brother. And you are the cause of it, so you must excuse me. We will talk in the open air."

Father Edward guided us around along wall of the house. He asked as we walked: "Why will you not come inside, Brother Stephen?"

Father Stephen looked confused and insulted. "To enter a house is a kind of deceit—like hiding myself away. And thanks to you, I cannot abide any kind of lying."

Father Edward seemed just as nonplussed. "It does not seem like lying, to me. I am not affected that way."

"Ha! You are a lucky devil."

"I do find it painful to disguise myself." Father Edward's hand crept to his lace collar.

Father Stephen sniffed. "You have my sympathy." We reached a garden of knotted hedges. "This is a pleasant place," said Father Stephen. "It will be a shame for Anne and me to leave it, and a shame you will never leave."

The priests took either end of a wooden seat, while I sat a little further off on the grass. Hedges grown to hide lovers now hid Father Edward and myself, and the snake I had let into the garden: Father Stephen, rocking where he sat and jesting at murder. I could not doubt his intent, but I could not persuade myself that it would happen. How would Father Stephen do it? Would he bid me leave, or make me witness it? Should I prevent it?

"Your soul will pay a high fine for murdering me," said Father Edward.

"Better my soul than all the souls of England. Our mission cannot thrive while you prosper, you gross carnosity. You are working for the crown?"

"I have been sent out as their instrument. But my heart is with the true faith."

"What, weasel? If you are not a turn-coat, then how are you their instrument?"

"I follow no instructions from them—I myself am their curse on English Catholics. Brother, what could I undertake to do, that would make you spare my life?"

"Nothing."

I watched their strange duel of words. Each had a weapon which could undo the other, and yet neither was the victor.

"How does it happen that we must speak the truth?" asked Father Stephen.

Father Edward smiled with grim relief, as though he had been waiting to be asked this question. He spoke in a confiding tone.

"Richard Topcliffe is a witch."

That man, Topcliffe, the Queen's pursuivant—I had thought of him during the Mass. I had half-way asked for his trespasses to be forgiven. I renounced that feeble-hearted prayer.

"He has a room for the torture of priests in his own dwelling..."

"But it is a felony to house a priest!" said Father Stephen.

Father Edward tightened his fingers into a fist at the poor jest. "I hung from the wall in that room. Topcliffe pushed my head up, but it would not stay, so he knotted my hair to a nail..."

"What did he then?"

"Drove his fingers into my ears, and drew forth my tongue with pincers, and he spat on it. And said, '*Ephphatha*'."

"What does it mean?" I asked.

"*Let it be open*." They answered me in unison, and Father Stephen winced, but spoke on: "It is mockery of Christ, who healed the dumb man. What then?"

"His spit tasted of dandelion stalks."

"What *effect* did it have, Brother Edward?"

"Topcliffe asked me questions. As soon as I saw that the truth would stream out of me, I tried to bite my tongue off. But he held my jaws apart."

"Better you had done it," said Father Stephen, but his voice was not steady.

"He questioned me for an hour. I told him the names of some Catholic houses, the ways to find their priest-holes. When he left me alone, I struck my head against the ground rather than leave myself in his hands. But I only lost my senses, not my life. Do you doubt me?"

I did not doubt him. I pitied him. I had wished Father Edward would suffer, for causing my honesty, and my family's suffering. But my wish for revenge was a shallow cup, and his past pains overflowed it.

"I do not doubt you," said Father Stephen. "But I am not compelled to pardon you, brother."

I should not have brought Father Stephen to Father Edward. I should have sent him down a false road. I would share the blame for his murderous deeds.

"Topcliffe returned with a man—wealthy, with a deep peak to his hair. Topcliffe asked me questions, and I spoke the truth. The man said, ***This man has been ill used, and will confess to anything.*** But Topcliffe swore my honesty. And the man asked me this and that, conundrums and paradoxes, until he was satisfied. A clever man."

"Who was he?"

"I know not. But I fear he was Walsingham."

I knew that name: the Queen's spy-master.

"He laughed and said that Topcliffe had done what God could not, and made men honest. He questioned him further—asking if a man under this charm might sign a treaty falsely, or do a thing against his nature. And they tried to make me sign a false document, and... other things. Topcliffe used all his old methods, then, to see if they could get a lie from me, when before he sought the truth."

"And *then* they set you free, to curse your fellow priests."

"Yes. I heard them fight over it. Topcliffe planned to enchant all Jesuits; Walsingham wished to keep the charm for use on other men. Foreign ambassadors, and the Queen's own advisors. He told Topcliffe to cease all experiments, and kill me, so that news of the charm would not spread.

"Topcliffe raged, and defied the spy-master by releasing me, that night—he had me dressed, and gave me a horse. And I met with you all for Mass—and knew not, when I took the Mass, that the charm could pass from me to you, by touch. And touch on the tongue, especially. I believed that I, alone, would speak the truth and die for it."

Father Stephen looked at his own hands, and at Father Edward's. I thought that Father Edward's words would change Father Stephen's direction, as the wind turns the weathervane. But Father Stephen gave no sign.

I spoke in desperation, to delay the evil moment. "Father Edward, why did you come to our house?"

"To minister to your souls. I hoped—God forgive me—that I might be a better priest, for my affliction! That the fears, or lies, that keep men from Our Lord might all be known to me. I am sorry, Anne..."

Father Stephen spoke. "That was spiritual vanity, brother."

"I know it."

"We should all listen to our spiritual directors in such matters. Not chase off on missions of our own devising." He was chastising Father Edward, but seemed abashed himself.

I pushed my point. "Father Edward, why did you not end your life, when you were able?"

"Oh, for I am a coward," said Father Edward. "Self-slaughter would mean Hell for me. And Hell would be an eternity of Richard Topcliffe's private chamber. So I have tried to continue our mission, despite my gift."

"Foolish," said Father Stephen.

"I know!" he shouted, then. "But you have saved me! I will make confession, and you will kill me. And *you* will go to Hell, in my stead, brother."

"I know it."

"You have never been put to the question, Brother Stephen, have you?"

"No."

"Then you would brave Hell for eternity, when you have not felt it for a minute."

Then Father Edward stood, and began to undo his doublet.

I knew not why. Had the dishonesty of disguise grown too much for him? He undid the dozen small buttons that ran down from the lace collar, shrugged himself free and stood in his under-shirt. His wrists and neck were red and chafed where he had worried at his own skin. Was he shedding his gentleman's clothes to die a priest, without lace or velvet?

He folded the doublet reverently and handed it to me. It was warm from his body, and heavy.

I saw his reason. Knowing that Father Stephen would kill him, he did not want his doublet, his host's gift, to be spoiled.

I laid the doublet on the bench and, lacking more words, I stood in front of Father Edward, barring Father Stephen's way.

Father Stephen called across me: "Edward! Why did you not leave this country and come home to Douai?"

"I could not cross the channel. I must speak my profession to any who ask it. I could only slope from house to house, on borrowed horses..."

Father Stephen rose to his feet, and came close to us both. He reached past me, but held no blade, and laid his empty hand on his brother's shoulder.

"I have left England, and travelled to Douai, and returned here. I have passed four days in England, this time, and not suffered arrest."

"Do you tell me that to taunt me, Brother Stephen?"

"No. Will you come home to Douai with me, Brother Edward?"

"You said you would not spare me!"

"I spoke the truth, but I am not a prophet. My heart has been changed. I did not foresee it."

Father Edward stepped out from behind me and let himself be embraced. "Have you money for our passage?"

"For mine. Not yours, Brother Edward, as I did not think to need it—it does not take a full purse to kill a man. But we might cut the fancy buttons from your clothes..."

•

December 25th

Two of my flock have come back to me.

I foresaw that one would die by the other's hand. Now Edward takes food out to the arbour where Stephen lodges, and they study together.

They say they will go to Spain, for the mild climate will allow Stephen to work despite his peculiarity. I have overheard Stephen say that their frankness may see them made saints; he does not make such impious jests in my presence.

Anne Barton writes that the charm weakens, but does not pass. Much can be achieved through misdirection, but questions from her parents still compel her honesty. I have sent letters to Edward's hosts, telling them this hard news. Perhaps the charm afflicts seminary priests most strongly because they have spent years in the consideration of truth. Those who know truth, but have not studied or disputed it, are less fertile soil. Stephen, who is affected most deeply, was the most scrupulous of novices.

Anne also asks me if there are convents with vows of silence. I will tell her no order would accept her as a novice until she is eighteen. It is a lie, to prevent a rash decision. The charm's hold on her may still lessen.

I have called home all the priests that Edward met—all those who survive. I pray they will return to me in safe silence, not lose their lives to feed a courtier's greed for war.

Soon we will have here a seminary of spotless honesty. All fear, all doubt, all jealousy will be seen clear as if it were nailed to the church door. We have survived another of the world's tricks; will we survive the truth of one another?

Sunslick

Yea, I fought to bring the sun here. Times change. My grandfather was a crofter, and I canna live that life. I've worked in oil instead, but there's a finite supply. We're pulling in gas from the Laggan-Tormore fields now: trillions of cubic feet, but we'll hae it all oot in twenty years or sooner.

The sun lasts forever.

I've no bairns, but I thought of my sister's peerie lass, Catriona, and how she'd need work one day. And I argued we should harvest the sun in Shetland.

Sun, in Shetland? I heard a lot of jokes. Soothmoothers axin, did we hae sun to spare? Could we sell off the wind, instead? We had plenty of wind, sweeping in from the neighbourhood of Iceland, roaring ower the treeless hills. And our islands do keep looking to wind power, but we hit snag after snag. Some sites, you'd need to sink the mast of each turbine through twenty feet of peat afore it hit solid ground. Then RSPB Scotland pop aroond and say no, the blades'll mess wi the whimbrel flying ower, and we shouldna risk it.

So no, we didna hae much sun. But *light*, yea. A lot of light. The simmer dim makes you lightheaded in June. You lose track of yourself in the evening and find it's three in the morning. You sleep and wake and sleep again in a kinda fuzz and you wonder at the cocky little digits on your bedside clock.

We wasna greedy. We wanted to balance oot the cruel swing of the year, the simmer dim and then the eighteen hours of dark in the Winter. If we could claw together some sunlight while it was plentiful, save it up to keep Winter houses lit, and make streetlights as warm and kindly as daylight... I heard that plan and I thought: we could lift a lot of folk oot of the doldrums.

My sister's bairn Catriona is smart, she'll go South for University. She's a teenager, and they all itch to see the world. She and her friends flock aroond that coffee bar on the Sea Road, buy mocha-frappa-whatnots and moan how every soul on Tindr is their ex or their cousin. They boast aboot what they'll do, soon as they step off the ferry—things I widna tell my sister.

When I was a kid, and I itched to travel, the oil work took me South to Aberdeen, London, Kuwait, across to Canada. But I came back. I wanted reasons for Catriona to come back, when she's seen the world. She loves to surf, she's lightsome on her board—that's good, that's something the islands can offer. She's got friends here, now, but they could fall away and scatter. She likes lasses, and I fret aboot her chances: finding a lass who wants to live here, too. She'll want a good job. She'll want the stuff that springs up when people hae money in their pockets, like coffee bars, and art films at Mareel, and festivals and fancy food... For Catriona, I wrote a shameless long shopping list.

So I fought for the sun, and I got to kaen a lot aboot it. As soon as the Council voted in favour of it, I got a job up there at the sun factory.

•

It wasna ordinary solar power. It was only the light we wanted, no the heat, and no need to convert it to electricity. We kept it as we caught it, raw light in big tanks of mirrored metal. Dozens of tanks, forty foot high, lined up above the cliffs at Sullom Voe.

Real daylight. I remember the first grey day I clanked up the stairs and stood at the handrail to look down on it. I saw great silver sheets, winding in slow circles. As I watched, the wind blew and a patch on the left side cooled, puckered like custard skin until the lively right side of the tank erupted right ower it. The whole vat churned itself back and forth like tilted mercury.

It was six in the morning, deep in November, but I wasna tired any more. Looking at that light was better than drinking espresso.

That first winter, Catriona surfed at the Voe for hours after the sun went down. The tanks glowed so it was never fully night. I'd take my break and walk down to the beach to watch her: balancing on her board, slicing a phosphorescent line through the dark water. The seals were awake and puzzled, bobbing aboot, turning their muzzles as she passed. Seabirds wailed as they zoomed towards me, hurrying ashore to nest because it was dark ower the waves. Then they saw the false dawn of the vats of light and flew oot to sea again. Poor befuddled bonxies, bombing back and forth; RSPB Scotland didna see that one coming.

At the end of my shift, I'd find my niece dragging her board up the beach, waving to me to hitch a lift home. She'd grin while she peeled off her gritty suit, like a selkie changing, and dump the slippery mess in my truck. *Pure dead brilliant,* she'd say as we drove away. She'd shake oot her hair, which had new blonde streaks. I was growing tanned. We sun workers were golden compared to the peelie-wally oil men.

•

We wanted the light, no the heat, but you canna hae one wi'oot the other. So when the main tank burst, and the light gushed down the cliffside, the sea boiled.

They told me a wall of steam roared straight up, like a geyser, wi thrashing beneath. By the time I'd driven up from Lerwick, a steekit mist hid the road. When I climbed down from my truck, I found the mist was warm.

It was half an hour after the spill, and the sea was still roiling. As I gawped, the sea wind drove the mist away and I saw the pools of sun: brilliance lying on the face of the water. Blinding, making ghosts float in my eyes. The edges of each pool sizzling like pancakes—you've seen the films of it. But you widna kaen the reek of salt in the air, and then the seared fish stink of it.

The crew had already thrown down booms to contain it. The sunlight had burned them up. The pools of light were racing South, vaporising the water and scorching the shore.

The foreman said: *Your sister's bairn.*

What aboot her? She was home in bed.

She was here, on her board. They've airlifted her down to the Gilbert Bain hospital.

I phoned my sister. *Dinna come down here,* she warned me. *You stay there and clear up your mess.*

I did. I worked wi the lads to shore up the other tanks where they were sagging. Sent up helicopters to chase the light and hose it down, break it up.

I could see so clearly in the spilt light: every pebble as it shattered, every tuft of grass as it withered and burned. Cooked fish were washed up wi the first tide and started rotting. Half a dozen sleekit otters barrelled down to the ebb, gorged themselves, then lay at the water's edge squirming in pain or ecstasy. Later, the gulls came screaming to peck at the seal carcases, some of them flying lopsided, white wings wi blackened edges.

My eyes ached. My mind churned. I worked for three days on the clean-up, and I never needed to sleep.

•

Catriona—well, she had her wetsuit on, and it saved most of her. Her hair had to go, but she says that short hair suits her. Her hands will work fine if she keeps up the exercises.

You widna stay here, will you? I axed her, by phone because my sister's mad at me. *You'll still go South?*

Yea, she said. *Why ever no?*

Because folk here kaen you, I thought, but a new place will be full of numpties axing you: what happened?

But the world calls to bairns. It offers the chance to get oot your nut and kiss a stranger. Catriona put her life in a rucksack, just like she'd planned, and unpacked it six hundred miles South. She sent me an email: *It's pure dead brilliant, here.*

I miss her. I'm awful glad she left.

But will she come back, now?

I'll stay, and clear up this scoodered stretch of coastline. I'll fix the baked mud and the cracked rocks. I'll make lightsome reasons for Catriona to come home.

A Marvellous Neutrality

A Poet had invited my husband and I to dinner.

"Must it be tonight, Mehmet?"

"He sent a message to me at the Museum! He wishes to talk about angels."

"I thought we might dine with your colleagues, first. It's such short notice." Or was it commonplace? We had only been living in London for a week but I had glimpsed a hundred differences between Egyptian and English manners.

"Amina, my dear, surely good manners matter less than good intentions? And his grandfather is a Duke!"

In the hansom cab I tried to bring to mind what I knew of angels. They are made of light. They do not eat or tire. Our carriage's jolting progress over the cobbles summoned up names: Jibrael, Mikael, Israfil, Malik.

I saw I was being unfairly jealous. Mehmet and I had spent every day together on the ship to England, and now he worked while I read guide books and wandered department stores with our maid. But I needed to share my husband with the world, for his happiness' sake—and my own, for how many other women had such opportunities?

We climbed out of the cab, and up the stone stairs of a great town-house. My husband tapped on the door.

Suddenly I saw that I, too, had been impolite. "Mehmet, love, I've not read any of his poetry! What is it about?"

"He wrote a wonderful verse-story about an unjust king. It's a little like *The Eloquent Peasant*."

"Good! What else?"

"Oh, he couldn't expect you to have read his recent poems. They are rather improper."

My stomach sunk. "Then how can it be proper for me to dine with him? Mehmet!"

His face crumpled because my sharp words had broken his unworldly heart and the door swung open before I could make amends.

The Poet's footman seemed loath to step out of the dark hallway. He leaned his long body around the door-frame and his head weaved as examined us. Copper stubble glinted along his pale jaw.

"Mehmet, my good fellow!" He swiped a hand out to clap my husband on the shoulder, and missed.

It was not the footman but the Poet himself.

•

"So, Mehmet. You've committed to our endeavour. I thought you were going to disappoint me."

"Not at all! May I introduce my—"

"You and I will speak with angels."

"I would be very glad to speak *of* angels. But I fear I—"

"Too modest, my friend! We will batter on the very gates of Heaven. Did you bring the necessary things?" He coiled an arm around my husband's shoulders and seemed about to drag him away. I coughed.

The Poet spun to face me. "Mehmet, you've cheated. You've brought your own angel with you. Not allowed at all."

Was that gallantry? It held no hint of welcome. My husband and I shared a weak smile. Our manners would not be the worst at dinner.

The drawing room he led us to smelled musky, as though an animal had rubbed itself about the clutter. The curtains were drawn, and by the gaslight I saw—oh, glorious things. Benin bronzes, brass Tibetan singing bowls, painted ostrich eggs, crammed onto shelves and spilling onto the floor. I was dazzled then distressed. Chosen for their rarity, these treasures were jumbled into a squalid equivalence.

A short old man with a beard neat as a brush stood among them.

"This is Professor Quixano," the Poet said. "You must get along well. Very friendly, no fighting. We're all people of the Book." He smiled at his own wit and hurried my husband into the next room. Mehmet carried the small suitcase he'd brought with him. It was full of books, I suspected, to consult and lend.

"I lecture in Hebrew at the University College," said the Professor.

"Pleased to make your acquaintance. Is your wife joining us?"

"I'm not married. Not yet!"

So I would be the only woman at dinner—improper, again. The poet's fault, but it made me self-conscious. I looked to the windows, to see if a breeze could be encouraged. The curtains glittered, beaded borders brushing the carpets. I recognised them as Indian sarees. For a moment I had the unpleasant notion that the Poet had stripped them off women's bodies.

"Mrs Basha? What is your husband's field?"

"He studies inscriptions. On tiles, at the moment."

"And are they pretty?"

"They are naskh and kufic script," I said, so that he would not condescend to me all evening.

Blessedly, he laughed. "Forgive me! It was an honest question, my own texts are often deathly dull to look at! You're from Egypt? It must be nearly as hot, here, at the moment."

"Almost." But England seemed badly prepared for such temperatures, by comparison. The buildings were sweltering and the parks had shrivelled. The clothes I'd purchased at Liberty—Summer dresses, they assured me—were tight-fitting and heavy.

"May I get you something for your thirst?" He held out a decanter. I wondered how the Poet had mislaid his household staff.

"Is there anything but wine?" There was not. I accepted a small glass to moisten my mouth. My Father drank, sometimes, when we had European visitors. The wine tasted vinegary.

"Our host must be delighted to have found your husband."

"How do you mean?" I had thought my husband more eager then his host.

"Our host asked me here to look at some writing in an unknown alphabet. He has certain books, by Dr Dee?" He said the name with glee and it rang like struck brass. "He asked me whether the writing relates to Hebrew."

"And does it?"

"Complete gibberish, as far as I could see. Now, your husband is probably my counterpart. I imagine our host is showing him the same writing, to see if it's Arabic. And if it is, all the secrets of the Heavens will be unlocked for our young Poet!"

"Goodness."

"So, the question is: how quickly can your husband deliver bad news? I like to dine before nine..."

I knew Mehmet would be in agonies at disappointing our host.

Professor Quixano misinterpreted my pained look. "I promise we won't talk business over dinner. But this Dr Dee is an interesting chap, very interesting—do you know anything about him?"

I made a guess, from what Mehmet had told me. "Did he speak to angels?"

The Professor's eyes twinkled.

"What a question! Did he, indeed? Dee was a sort of court conjurer for Queen Elizabeth. Horoscopes and alchemy, three hundred years ago. And he spoke to angels, maybe." Professor Quixano frowned. "Our host wishes to write a poem about Dee's talks with angels."

"Do you study angels?" The room was worse than stuffy. The air pressed me from different directions as if I sat in a slow-swirling current. I drank more, hoping to feel better.

"No, but I'm interested in the messages they can carry. Dee's angels spoke a language which was shared by all people, so they said. And they told Dee himself to share all his goods with his friend, Kelley. Now, our Poet host—" The Professor rolled his eyes. "He's very fashionable. What if he wrote a poem about how the angels *tell us to share*? Regardless of nation, or class, or religion? If he wrote such a thing, and did it well, I wouldn't think this evening a waste."

I couldn't hide my pessimism. "Could our host carry such a message?"

"Certainly, certainly! He's a rich man himself, of course, but that's an advantage—when a poor man speaks of fair shares, they call it sour grapes. And he wrote that doggerel about the tyrant king, which was half-way to Republicanism."

"But his reputation..."

Professor Quixano dismissed my doubts with a wave of his hand. "His nasty poems were only published in France. Most people haven't heard of them. Good job, too! They're piffling, ridiculous—"

And then the Poet returned.

My husband trailed after him, at his most apologetic. "Of course, if I could take a sample, or a copy, I could make more thorough checks..."

The mysterious writing had proved not to be Arabic.

The Poet clicked his fingers impatiently. "Come along, people of the Book. Get into that room, we need to prepare. Fear not. Hurry-scurry."

•

I'd hoped for food—I felt worse, from drinking—but the darkened room we entered was not a dining room.

Desks on either side held huge open books—covered in a strange cramped script, lines slanting across pages, forming boxes and columns and stars. This was the script which was not Hebrew, not Arabic. Peering at it frustrated me, this language that was shared by all people but which nobody could read.

"Make yourselves useful and light those," said the Poet, pointing at a dozen candles set around the books and tossing the Professor a box of matches.

My husband and the Professor lit candles together. I heard the Professor suggest that they should meet later that month and perhaps increase the connections between Museum and University. I was glad that some good would come out of the evening. To allow them to talk more, I moved further off.

At the head of the room stood a table covered with black velvet. Resting on the velvet were large purple quartz crystals, and between them, paintings—icons, small but with beetle-bright colours.

I saw the paintings were all of angels.

They each had a flimsy pair of dove-like wings. It seemed to me they would need wings both stronger and more numerous. Jibrael was described as having hundreds of wings. To come to earth from heaven couldn't be an easy flight.

"So very vivid," murmured the Poet into my ear. "And do you have angels? Where you come from?"

All four of us held some angels in common, I was certain of it: Jibrael became Gabriel, Mikael was Michael. The poet's ignorance annoyed me. "Oh, yes. Dozens. Should I have brought some with me?"

The Poet scowled. "Well, your husband has provided something useful, at least."

My husband's small suitcase lay open on the floor. The Poet stooped and lifted from it a small bundle of fabric. It seemed, for a moment, as though he reverently held a crumpled sock.

He unwrapped a bright crystal sphere, as big as a hen's egg.

"Dr Dee's shewstone!"

And from the suitcase, again, another object: this one round and black and perfectly polished, about the size of his face.

"And his obsidian mirror. Now we'll see something, for sure."

Light slid across the surface of the mirror as he placed both objects on the velvet tabletop.

My husband had brought these things with him in his suitcase. But neither object was ours. They hadn't come with us from Cairo. Where had he found them? I'd shopped in London, but he'd been busy working...

"You didn't bring the Seal of God," the Poet said.

"I am sorry—it is made of wax, it is too easily damaged. And I must take everything back tonight, of course."

Despite the heat, my skin turned cold. My husband had stolen the things from the museum.

"Let us all pray that the mysteries shall be known to us!" said the Poet.

I wanted to snatch up the objects, and my husband, and drag them home. How could he risk his job? And treat a National Museum like a circulating library? Was he dazed by the prospect of meeting a poet-aristocrat? A shabby man in a stinking house.

I watched the Poet stroking the stolen black mirror and muttering to himself. "Angel of the seven-pointed star, show to us knowledge of all metals! Come forth, Madimi!"

I couldn't bear this charlatan taking a share of my husband's admiration.

"I feel unwell," I said, loudly. My head ached. But I also hoped my beloved would take me aside—or even outdoors—where we could speak privately. It was not too late to leave.

"You're hungry," the Poet said, laying the mirror aside. "We should all eat. I have a cold collation, quite equal to the occasion."

My husband's eyes met mine. My clever husband, who had studied at Al-Azhar, begging me to dine with a drunkard.

But a wealthy drunkard and perhaps an influential one. I reminded myself of all I gained from Mehmet's curiosity and enthusiasm. My Father was kind and wealthy, but I would never have seen London without Mehmet.

And the theft was done and, I prayed, undiscovered. Little would be gained from leaving early.

We would stay. And if we were staying we should eat, to face the evening as calmly as we could. So I nodded to Mehmet and we followed the Poet out of the weird dark chamber and through the drawing room, into a far brighter space where a dining table was laid.

I had feared the food might be insanitary but it looked deliciously fresh. The cutlery shone. The tablecloth was spotless, apart from a plump bee resting on one corner. Windows were open onto a garden and birdsong poured in.

Why, then, did the sight of it unnerve me?

Because the meal had taken more than one person to prepare it but it wouldn't need a soul to serve it.

Our host had chosen this meal so he might send his servants away for the evening.

•

I began by taking a little of every dish, for the sake of politeness, then realised nobody cared if I was slighting the hard-boiled-egg salad in favour of the roast chicken. I could have eaten better if not for the bees. At my request the windows were closed, but it was impossible to rid the room of them. They droned past my face, blundered against my eyes and lips.

The men talked of angels.

"Why did the angels speak to Dee, in particular?" asked Professor Quixano.

"They didn't," the Poet explained. "His friend Kelley was the scryer, Kelley heard the angels. Dee wasn't sensitive enough. The angels won't speak to just anyone."

"And I suppose you're hoping you'll be a scryer, yourself?" asked the Professor. "Being so sensitive."

The Poet, immune to mockery, spread out his hand, as if to say, who else?

Then he jumped, startled by a sharp crack against the window-pane. A bee had banged against the glass, and now wavered away.

Beware of wavering, I thought, and then wondered why.

"One of the angels told Kelley, 'I am Prince of the Seas: I drowned Pharoah.'" The Poet sat back, satisfied, as though he had submerged Pharoah himself.

I thought of the waters rolling back over Pharoah's army. Rushing into the gap with relief, like a breath held for too long and then let go. Making the surface smooth again.

My husband looked nauseated at the mention of drowning. He'd been seasick, on the voyage here. To distract him, I asked the Professor to retell his story about the egalitarian angels.

Professor Quixano did so, with relish and embellishments, and my husband smiled wanly.

"How interesting! That sounds very—" He mulled over the correct word.

"Amiable?" said Professor Quixano.

"Amicable," said my husband.

"Animal," I said.

"I beg your pardon, my darling?"

"Amicable, as you said. A very friendly notion."

But for some reason, I had ceased to see sharing as a virtue. A hive shares all things. Does that make it virtuous? I thought of a bee angel, furred limbs in robes, wings not like a dove but made of veined glass. I swatted the angelbee away from my thoughts. Was the buzzing coming from inside my head, now? It was too dense in my head, too airy outside. I needed to get what was in my head out, to equalise the pressure. I had a sudden joyful vision of piercing my skull with a fork.

"Amina, my dear." Mehmet had placed a morsel of his own food onto my plate to tempt me. A bee had landed on it. Yet he still looked expectant.

"I can't eat that."

I saw my confusion mirrored in his face.

I looked down at my cutlery. In the bowl of my spoon, a dark shape was moving—not a bee, but a reflection. It slid around the top of the spoon, changing form: tall, then squat, then willowy again. It was a girl-child, walking across the room behind me.

A maid, come to clear the dinner? But the maids weren't home, and even in the indistinct and sliding image she seemed too young to be a maid. Perhaps some relative of the Poet—although who would trust him with their child?

Her feet made no sound, or maybe she was inaudible above the buzzing of the bees—the bees who were still increasing. They came from the other room. They came from the same place as the girl.

I stopped myself from turning my head to see where she could not be.

She whispered to me: "I will teach thee names without numbers."

"I don't want them."

"Perhaps a glass of water?" my husband said.

"Water?" sneered the Poet. He lifted a bottle of champagne and uncorked it, with a sharp pop and a splatter of foaming light.

•

I babbled excuses and escaped into the hallway, but the Poet followed me.

"Did you like my angels? The icons?"

"They're charming." But their wings weren't strong enough.

The pressure in my head, and the pop of the champagne cork, had helped me to understand it. A door is hard to open when the wind is against it; likewise, for the angels to pass over into our own world there would have to be an evenness on either side. An evenness of what, though? I didn't know. Of air? Of awe? Of everything?

I would not speak of angels to the Poet.

"You liked what the Professor said? About sharing possessions?" His eyes glittered. Had he seen how angry I'd been, at the purloined Museum artefacts? Did he mean to justify his theft by heavenly instruction?

I managed some bland words. "It is a sweet thought."

"Sweet as honey." The Poet's hand slithered up the outside of my leg. "The angels told Dee and Kelley to share their wives, as well."

I took his hand off my leg. I considered taking his hand off his arm, as well, with the blunt silver cutlery.

"Do not touch me."

"It is an English custom," the Poet lied.

"Really? My dear husband is very interested English customs, should I tell him of it?"

The Poet fled.

I considered this new angelic instruction. I was quite sure the angels had no interest in the sly fumbling the Poet was attempting. If they had truly told Dee and Kelley to share their wives, it was because the couples' fidelity, their specificity, was a kind of tangle, a density. The angel needed to make everything smooth, everyone one.

•

I re-joined the party as the Poet announced that we would now speak with the angels. My husband and the Professor shrugged and agreed. I saw my chance and excused myself.

My husband hung back behind the other two so he could hold out his hand to me. I squeezed it—dry, solid, warm.

"You aren't unwell, love?"

"I only need some rest." The evening would be over soon. And when we were home I would tell him everything. I would not share my husband with this ridiculous man again.

I sat in the drawing room. Through the closed door I heard them speak in unison but still with distinction between them: the Poet's high-pitched frenzy, Professor Quixano's mumble. My love's voice was fine, almost singing.

On a bookcase I found a volume of the Poet's French writings, a cycle of sonnets called *Melusine*. Women became snakes, women loved men, women loved women, some of whom were snakes. I could imagine the Poet cranking a handle to produce the tedious series of obscene combinations.

The buzzing in the room—or in my head—sounded more mechanical than organic, now. A treadle sewing machine running fast and hard might sound that way, punching a needle endlessly through the air.

I heard the Poet shout: "*Pactum factum!*"

I looked up from the poems and saw the girl again, walking across the room towards me.

Her dark hair floated like pondweed in the sultry air. Her dress was red, then green, then red again. She came to me, picking her way through the clutter on the floor of the room. No—the objects moved to allow her to pass.

"Beware of wavering," she said.

I begged her pardon. I begged her mercy. She recoiled at my uncertainty, the unevenness of my purpose.

I felt her attention turning to the men next door, and I sensed with her the Poet's arrogance and the Professor's amusement. And there, with them, my dear husband. His warm desire to please was waning because of his abhorrence of blasphemy. The dips and peaks of his temperament felt sweetly familiar to me.

The angels would smooth away all these things.

I knew the girl was only the tiniest tendril of what was to come. A wisp of smoke curls up from under a door when, behind the door, a furnace rages. When they arrived, they would not look like her. Jibrael visited Mary in the form of a man, but he was not a man.

They would not have wings, either. They would not beat their wings to carry them through the aethers. They would raze every obstacle, melt rocks like glaciers into smoothness. They would make everything even, everything the same, and slide over to our world in an effortless procession.

Share everything, make everything equal; these were not divine moral messages but practical instructions, as a ship's captain shouts to the harbour crew.

"I will teach thee names without numbers," the girl offered again. She showed me how much the angels yearned to cross over.

I said no.

The buzzing became a vibration that shook my bones until I thought the flesh would slough from them. I flung my arms around myself and gripped. My teeth rattled.

The girl stood in front of me. She opened her dress. I forced my chin down onto my chest and buried my face in my hands.

"Open your eyes and you shall see from the highest to the lowest."

"I don't want to."

I didn't want them to show me how they would make the highest and the lowest all alike.

I told her without speaking that I didn't want to know them, that I didn't want to speak with angels. That the Poet was the one who had called her.

I said: I cannot bear your messages.

And then the noise began.

It was a grinding, churning roar coming from the room next door. A wave surging over the longest beach in the world, dredging and inverting every pebble. That was how I heard it. But I understood it, with my mind and my heart, as a ripping apart of particles. It was happening to everything that was densely packed: the oak tables, the old books. All these things were being brutally evened out until they were all of one density with the dusty air.

I prayed. When the fear from not seeing grew worse than the fear of what I might see, I opened my eyes again, and the girl was gone.

I crawled to the door and opened it. How could I not? My love was inside.

Turquoise-blue light filled the room. It could have been blinding but it came from so far away that it was weaker than a Spring morning. And it was fading.

The angels had abandoned their attempt.

Inside the room everything had been made even, utterly shared. Furniture had been turned to the consistency of cloudy soup. Larger fragments drifted through this haze like dust motes—shreds of paper, threads of cloth. Some of them sparkled—grains of quartz crystal, I supposed. The fragments were drifting slowly to the floor.

My husband wasn't there. He had been an unevenness. He had been evened out.

The vibrations slowed to a long throb that ran through me and died away.

I was standing ankle-deep in a rising sludge made of everything and everyone in the room.

•

When the inquest is over, I will go back to my father's house in Cairo. I will never again share my husband, or this story, with anyone.

A marvellous neutrality have these things mathematical, and also strange participation between things supernatural, immortal, intellectual, simple and indivisible, and things natural, mortal, sensible, compounded and divisible.—John Dee, 1570

Since You Ask Me for a Tale

"There was something rum about it," said old Dr Haley. "I won't be drawn to speculate, though; it don't suit a medical man to speculate." The way he agitated his whisky glass suggested otherwise.

Mr Thurston, my solicitor, topped up the glass.

My forthcoming marriage had necessitated visiting my hometown, and my solicitor. Mr Thurston had suggested I stay for a drink, and invited Dr Haley (who had brought me into the world, and—when as a boy I had broken his greenhouse panes with a cricket ball—threatened to see me out of it again). Both men had regaled me with touching stories of my late father. But it seemed the stories would now take a mysterious turn.

"And of course, this all happened overseas," said Dr Haley.

"Ah, *abroad*," said Thurston, with a hint of mockery, to provoke Haley, who retorted with indignant specifics.

"It was on the Italian coast, twenty miles from Genoa! It is rather a perplexing tale—perhaps not one for a young man on the threshold of married life."

So then it was my turn to coax him to tell his story, and he settled down to business.

•

It had all happened some years ago, when Dr Haley was unmarried and able to roam. Every summer, he would exchange practices with an expatriate doctor in a coastal town outside Genoa. Dr Haley tended wheezy English patients, while writing a pamphlet on the effects of saline air on the bronchioles. When off-duty, he walked in the hills, wandering about the ochre rocks and poplar trees.

One day a middle-aged couple, English but not wheezing, called upon his expertise.

Lord and Lady Sherstock were deeply agitated. Their only child, Olivia, was engaged to be married to a local Count, a minor aristocrat of the type that pepper the Italian countryside. The parents had no objections; the Count was their coreligionist (the Sherstocks were Cumbrian recusant nobility).

"And Olivia has a sincere affection for him!" Lady Sherstock had volunteered, pressing her hand to her chest.

In the last fortnight, however, young Olivia's mood had changed. She had declined all visits from her fiancé, claiming fatigue. Lady Sherstock had sympathised, then jollied her, and was coming close to chiding her for poor manners—but you cannot chivvy a young woman into courtship as you might tell a child to eat their greens.

Day by day, their daughter became listless. The only activity Olivia undertook—which seemed to enervate her—was reading from a small book. She had slid it under her pillow when her mother asked after it, but the serving maid had carried it away as Olivia slept. Lady Sherstock now presented the book to Dr Haley and laid a hand on his arm.

"It is not one of *my* books. We have been a Catholic family from the days of Queen Mary." He heard in her voice the strength to sustain a belief through years of persecution. "But doctor, we have never been *morbid*, we have never encouraged any *excesses!*"

I thought of my fiancée Mary—as I did, when any lady's qualities were mentioned, in those sentimental days of my betrothal—and her own gentle tenacity. Thankfully we had not yet had a lover's tiff.

"Look, his mind is wandering," crowed Thurston, pointing to me. I must have been wearing a foolish smile.

Dr Haley cleared his throat. Like naughty schoolboys, we both attended.

When Lord and Lady Sherstock had departed, Dr Haley settled down in an armchair to read the book, a cheap thing with card covers, small enough to tuck into a pocket.

"I was shocked to recognise the place of publication," Dr Haley told us. "Some weeks before, walking through a nearby valley, I muddled up my directions. What's more, I had rather misjudged the heat. I'd become alarmed, but I saw in the distance a huge villa."

It had been a palimpsest of a building, modern brick stitching up the cracks in ancient stone. The closer Haley drew, the greater seemed its isolation; no sign of servants or household, and no windows in the external walls.

Dr Haley had staggered up to the great stone doorway, almost without hope, and knocked. A shutter had immediately snapped open. An old woman's face appeared, seraphically happy, in the centre of a crumpled white wimple. She placed a finger to her lips; unnecessary, as Haley had been startled into silence. The woman handed him a corked jug and a cloth bundle, and pointed along the wall.

Then the shutter had slammed shut again.

Bewildered, Haley had walked along the wall, which was spotted with lichen and incised with deep unreadable marks. He found a shaded veranda. A shelter, he surmised, so that the convent could do their duty to the poor without disturbance. The jug he had been given was full of cold water, the cloth bundle held bread and cheese. Fortified and rested, Haley had gone on his way rejoicing, back to the town.

Olivia Sherstock's confiscated devotional book bore the name of the convent that had saved him: Saint Rosalia. The book was a memoir of a quite conventional sort, of a young woman's early life and piety, her resolve to join the convent. The theology was not Dr Haley's flavour, but—remembering the words of Lady Sherstock—he found nothing that he considered morbid.

"But any book can become an obsession," he cautioned us.

At this dark remark, I glanced around Mr Thurston's study, where we were relaxing, to his bookcases: I saw legal tomes and detective stories. I thought of Mary's current fondness for accounts of polar exploration. I smiled at the idea of Thurston in a back-alley fight, or my beloved hiking across pack ice.

"It can, it can!" warned Dr Haley, as though by my smile I had contradicted him. "Young women can take a simple book and perceive some grand pattern, hid behind the lines…"

Dr Haley tailed off, staring at the fire as though it contained both the secrets of the universe and next week's Grand National Winner.

Thurston prodded him. "And the lady?"

Haley had visited the lady the following day. He had feared the house would be a gloomy purgatorial sort of place, but he found it plain and sunny. The daughter of the house was sitting in her room, gazing from the window.

She turned to him with no sign of lethargy: "You must be the medical man to whom Mama has spoken."

And for what reason, Dr Haley asked, might her Mama have summoned a doctor?

"Oh, only because I have been reading too much, and doing too little of anything else. But now they have taken my book away."

At this, Dr Haley produced the book. He searched the young woman's face for any sign of avidity, but she did not even reach for it.

"Do you not think the life of a nun to be an odd story," he asked, "For a woman about to enter the happy state of matrimony?"

"It is highly fitting for me to read of decisions, and thresholds, and dedication." She spoke lightly, but Dr Haley sensed an echo of her mother's steely resolve.

He turned (with the young lady's agreement) to a physical examination, He found no organic reason for lassitude, and told her so. She proclaimed it a relief.

"And will you now make an effort to go out with your parents, and meet your young gentleman?" he asked.

"I don't doubt it," she said.

"And might I keep this book? I did not finish it."

Then he saw it: a flash of fervour. Her eyes seemed to double in size. But just as quickly, she steadied herself. "I would rather you not."

"Then I shall buy my own," he said cheerfully. "Where did you get this copy?"

"I forget. My mother has many devotional volumes," she said.

But her mother had denied all knowledge of it.

"I will return it," said the doctor, "If you promise me you will eat more, and sleep more, and accompany your mother about the town a little, before the heat of midday."

Securing her promise, he laid the volume on the desk, and congratulated himself on a good bargain.

•

A fortnight later, at nine in the evening, an apologetic maid was knocking at his door. Could he come at once?

Lord Sherstock greeted him at the door. His daughter had not improved, not entertained her fiancé, and had developed a positive mania. But the doctor must see it for himself, Lord Sherstock would not prejudice him.

Dr Haley climbed again to Olivia's room, with the maid holding a lamp to light the stairs. The maid stopped to unlock the door, which gave him pause. "She is confined?"

The maid nodded unhappily.

"Is she a danger to herself? Why lock her in?"

The maid said that Sir would see for himself.

The young woman in the bed was very much changed. Her resolution was plain; like an outcrop of volcanic rock, bursting up from soft green English turf. But the doctor, at first, tried his old line. "You promised me you'd eat, and sleep."

"I was wrong to promise. I was forsworn."

"To whom?"

"To my vocation." She gripped in one hand the small card-bound life of the nun. "I feel it constantly, an undertow. I am meant for the convent."

"The convent of Saint Rosalia?" Dr Haley felt an instinctive revulsion at the idea of Olivia's interment. But he reminded himself of the cheerful face of the nun at the hatch. This was no anchorite's cell. "I have been there."

"You know it?" To the doctor's surprise, Olivia's voice held all the disgust he had suppressed. "I do not wish to! And yet, it is a terrible sin to go against a vocation. There is a voice at my ear, all the time. I think it is *her* voice."

A rattling knock, at Olivia's door; the maid had returned, to summon the doctor downstairs, where Lady Sherstock was clutching with trembling hand an unopened letter. It was addressed to her daughter, and the return address was the Convent of Saint Rosalia. Lady Sherstock could not bear to read it, and begged the doctor to do her that kindness.

The first line made clear that Olivia had smuggled out a letter to the convent, asking to take expedited vows. The doctor shuddered at her guile.

At this point in the tale, Thurston and I shuddered also. This was the time for Haley to play the hero. Might this steely young maid be rescued from the convent, perhaps even wooed and wed by Dr Haley himself? I racked my brains: what *was* Mrs Haley's first name? For the sake of the story, Olivia should be either married or shut up in a nunnery. I would accept nothing less, and being happily betrothed myself, I had a preference.

"But, good news!" cried Dr Haley.

The Reverend Mother had written that Olivia was welcome in the novitiate but could not take full vows until years had passed. She also counselled that the young woman might wish to discuss things first with a priest (she named a local English-speaking *curato*).

Doctor Haley gave a sigh of relief at this, and communicated the contents to the parents, who sighed in turn.

"We feared she might abscond," said Lady Sherstock. "Which is why her door is locked. Will you tell her the convent will not have her?" Dr Haley agreed, but first dashed off a note to an excellent Genoan mind-doctor, sending a servant to gallop away to deliver it.

Lord Sherstock had given him the key to Olivia's bedroom door, and he placed it in the lock and turned it.

But the door was unlocked, and swung open.

Most fortunately, Olivia (gazing from the window) did not seem to know that she was unconfined. The doctor was at a loss. He looked up and down the corridor but saw not a soul, stepped into the room and discreetly locked the door again behind him. He tucked his key into his waistcoat pocket.

Olivia took the news from the convent stoically. "No matter," she said. "*She* will find a way to bring me home."

And in the silence between two sentences, the lock of the door clicked open again.

Dr Haley did not spring up; the soft click had cast a spell over him. When Olivia finished speaking, he moved hesitantly to the door.

He prodded the door with one finger, and it swung free.

Olivia laughed. "You see? *She* will remove all obstacles."

Those words seemed to release Dr Haley and he raced into the dark corridor beyond. He stared wildly; what was that, in the gloom? The whisk of a white gown, turning a far corner. He chased after it, but hit his head against a sconce.

"With such force," he sheepishly admitted, "That I cannot swear to anything a few minutes before or after, such is the disarraying effect of an injury of that kind."

•

The following day, a summer storm settled on the town. The thunder-dark air smelled briny, and the doctor stayed at the Sherstock house while awaiting a message from the Genoan brain-doctor.

All day he spent with Olivia. While she woke, he tried gently to discover the roots of her obsession; he quizzed her about marriage fears, but she spoke of her betrothed as though she had loved and lost him a dozen years previously. "The dearest and best of men!"

While she slept he read the small, card-covered book. The room resounded with thunder as he concluded the volume, reading the sisters' proudest boast: that she was a fine recruiter for the convent, bringing over forty young souls to their path in Christ. He saw a stream of maidens walking into the silent valley, the convent door slamming behind them...

The doctor found he had dozed, or sat in a stupor. The sound he had imagined was not the shutter closing, but the click of the lock, opening.

This time, he sprung immediately forwards. Flinging open the door, he smacked his face into the chest of the figure who stood there waiting. It was not his dreaded opponent, not an incorporeal holy sister, but a very substantial bearded fellow. No nun, but the Genoan brain-doctor. And that brain-doctor hardly noticed Haley's assault, as he was gazing in puzzlement after a disappearing white-gowned figure.

"We must catch her!" Dr Haley shouted, over the thunder, and both men scrambled into pursuit.

Ducking under the sconce, this time, the doctor found himself closing on the white-clad woman.

A chill spread across my scalp. This was the moment of truth: what horrors would result when Haley closed on his spectral quarry? He had certainly survived, but surely anything short of death was possible.

The ghost put on an un-nunlike spurt of speed, but couldn't outpace Haley. They went neck and neck all down the servants' stairs. At the start of the chase, Haley would have feared to lay hands on the apparition, but the further they descended, the more tangible she became, with clumping feet and panicked breath, and as they tumbled into the reception hall, he seized her arm and found her solid.

"It was the maid, of course," sighed Dr Haley.

I gave a cry of surprise. Thurston raised an eyebrow at my credulity.

An interrogation of the maid had followed. The girl had been unlocking the door whenever it was locked, in case "Miss Olivia didn't want to be married." The maid had thought Olivia might seek sanctuary with an aunt, living not three miles away. She had not considered that Olivia might try to reach the convent.

Then the maid started to weep and blame herself, sick with guilt; for it had been her, you see, who had given Olivia the book, the nun's tale. It was a very delightful and spiritual account, the maid told us, and she and her sister had often read it aloud to one another. Nobody from the maid's family had ever wished to join the convent.

•

Of course, I was pleased to hear Dr Haley wrap up his story: the young woman agreed to treatment, and spoke to the friendly and reasonable curato. She had feared to admit she did not love the Count, even to herself, and all her troubles had sprung from that repression. The Count, stoic and charming, released her from all obligation. If her parents were disappointed by the rift, they bore it silently. Olivia married a different man the following year (sadly not Dr Haley) and her religious scruples were reduced to an interest in charities.

Thurston cleared his throat. "So! No ghostly, abducting nun?"

I defended Dr Haley—"A very chilling story!"—but I confess the lack irked me, also.

Dr Haley was a little hidebound, and it could be allowed that this was the most interesting thing to have happened to him in all his years. Thurston refreshed our drinks. But it rankled! Such a promising tale squandered: a distant country, a coastal storm, a beautiful young woman (Dr Haley had failed to say as much, but it was implied). A wedding imminent, but forestalled by fervent monasticism! And yet, the machinery around our heroine failed: the convent was not rapacious enough, the parents too reasonable, the aristocratic groom not cruel. The girl herself was insufficiently severe, and the worst of all, the ghost was just too tangible. Such a promising yarn, to end in a wrestling match in a stairwell!

Better if old Haley hadn't caught the maid, and had given us only the mystery.

I found myself eying his hair, and thinking: perhaps it turned white, all at once, on that fateful night! But then I remembered it changing, salt among the pepper, all through my childhood, damnit.

"Was the marriage a happy one?" I asked.

Dr Haley shrugged. "I rarely saw them. Three children, though!"

I'd wondered if some generational curse would fall on Olivia: for her to be doomed to celibacy, or childless, or to have a dozen daughters and they all become nuns. Well, that was a truly unworthy thought—what would I say to someone wishing Mary and I childless?—and I shook it off and raised my glass again.

Thurston sat back by the fire with a gleam in his eye, keen to step into the breach. "Speaking of unreliable domestics," he said, "I might have an account of my own in a similar vein. But as you said, Haley, perhaps not a story for a young man on the threshold of setting up his own home!"

Thurston was a younger man, and through his legal practice had surely seen more horrid affairs than a country doctor. I settled myself in for some proper shocks.

"It takes place in London," announced Thurston. "Where I lived as a young law student..." This was promising: the capital was alive with smog and criminality.

Thurston lodged with a crowd of bachelors, medical students and clerks, sharing only one servant: a housekeeper-cum-cook, ferociously strong, known to the boys only as "Mrs D.".

"Was she young? Old?" Haley demanded some colour to the picture, perhaps disgruntled that we'd not received his own story better.

"Certainly not young. Her face—in fact, her whole demeanour..." Thurston broke off, for thought, or for effect.

"Was it *curious*?" I felt bold enough to mock him. "Or *unheimlich*?"

"Not unless you find the humble potato curious," he retorted. "Her face resembled one spud, and her body, the rest of the sack. Her arms were like whole hams. You could have made a Christmas feast from her."

She lived off the premises, and was followed to work and home again by a dog like a sad skein of white wool, whose eyes were always watering. Mrs D. snarled at the world as she scrubbed it. Thurston became accustomed to this. He was more disturbed when, some time around Halloween, he handed over a shirt for washing and her potato visage split into a smile.

Thurston had been nonplussed. "Normally, she wished all us lodgers into the great hereafter, except in as far as our rent paid her wages."

Thurston compared notes with the other men in the house and discovered the reason: Thurston had expressed sympathy to Mrs D. on the subject of her terrible husband.

"She'd made the same complaints to everyone, but they'd all given her the cold shoulder. I'd said some commonplace thing—'what a shame, Mrs D.'—and won her devotion."

Thurston now got an extra sausage every breakfast, which was much envied. It wasn't all good, though. Mrs D. would often draw close and let slip some cryptic comment on Mr D.'s perfidy.

If she met Thurston on his way into the house: "Not like *some*, staying out until dawn."

If he was leaving the house: "Hard work and an early start! There's *some* who can't appreciate that..."

Mr D. himself, that maligned character, would appear at Thurston's lodgings, at the back door. For only a half crown, he'd deliver a letter or perform furniture repairs, but was usually swaying too much to take directions, or handle a chisel.

"He was a spud of a man, as well," Thurston told us sadly. "It is a regrettable mystery why their marriage wasn't more harmonious.

In November, Mrs D. gave hints of a darker hue. She scrubbed harder, ranted about ingratitude and her house being "like a mausoleum", and mused about moving East to join her sister.

"And Mr D.?" asked Thurston, tentatively.

"*Ha!*"

Over three more Sundays, the truth trickled out like lumpy gravy. Mr D. had *raised his hand to little Lulu* (the skinny-limp woolly dog). Mr D. had been cast out; Mr D. had not returned.

Thurston murmured some bromide about Mr D. finding his own way home. But Mrs D. had scowled. "I *know* where he is."

"Oh? Good?"

"A lot closer to the river," she muttered darkly.

Of course, it is hard, if you are an older housekeeper speaking to a young tenant, to mutter any other way than darkly, but Thurston dined out on it for days.

Just before Thurston departed for his family home, for the holidays, Mrs D. took him aside, and thrust a large package at him, wrapped in colours brighter than Mrs D. had ever worn, green trees marching across a scarlet ground.

The parcel squashed in his hands, having no stable form. He opened the paper, and coils of mustard yellow spilled into his hands and through them, cascading down to the ground. A scarf, knitted Aran-style. Cables twined up the length of it, making it oddly stiff. It would have looped twice round Thurston's neck and still reached his knees with both ends. But he did not wish to place it around his neck.

Thurston took a shaky breath, and I remarked (perhaps not sensitive to the mood of the story) that my Mary was a keen knitter.

"Then I hope to God," replied Thurston, "She never presents you with such a thing as this!" Mrs D. was tremendously strong, as he had noted, and the scarf was as one might imagine, made by someone with more strength than dexterity. The wool was coarse, like carpet wool, but also oily, and the hue reminded him irresistibly of bile.

Thurston tried to thrust the coils of it back at Mrs D., but she wouldn't take it. He said it was too dear; she said not to fret, she had remade it from old wool, a sweater of Mr D's that he'd never appreciated.

A sense of indebtedness crushed Thurston. He rushed up to his room, flung the scarf onto his bed, and scrounged around to find something to reciprocate. A box of fondant creams, intended them for his mother's gardener! He hurried back to Mrs D. and paid the tithe. She was delighted, but not more than Thurston, shedding the weight of obligation.

Thurston didn't take the scarf to his parents' house. It laid coiled on the bed, waiting for him. He didn't wear it on his return. But it hung from the back of his bedroom door. Mrs D. wasn't around to monitor its use, having gone to visit her sister for the duration of the holidays.

The sight of it as he fell asleep had a peculiar impact on his nocturnal visions. One night, it would appear to be a hose from an infernal mechanism, with a villainous purpose; at other times, a noose.

He slept so badly, and the scarf became such a monomania, that he wondered if the medical students who lodged with him had slipped nostrums into his drink for their amusement. He purchased new bottles of beer. But still he woke and lay paralysed, wondering: what was that rasping, pulsing sound? Was it the scarf, crawling across his counterpane?

"It was my eyelashes," he confessed. "Blinking against the pillow as I stared into the dark."

Thurston flung himself, in that colourless time between Christmas and New Year, into reading for his next term of study. A smog descended, of the same mustard shade as the scarf. His stocks of food dwindled but rather than go out into the evil air he pared his cheese and dined on crusts. He slept on a sofa downstairs to avoid the scarf. His bad dreams followed him and he thought he woke to find his guts unspooling from his navel, painless and endless. They were rough knitted tubes, mustard yellow.

He counted down the days until his fellow lodgers would return. On the appointed evening, Thurston grabbed up his coat in grateful haste to meet them in a pub on the river.

In so much haste that he snatched up the yellow scarf, as well.

He realised soon after locking up the house, and considered turning back. He even contemplated posting the thing back through his own letterbox, like an assassin with a boa constrictor. But that would be so cowardly. No, he could wear the scarf to meet his friends, and tell the tale and get a laugh from them. They'd put it in its place.

He wove through narrow streets down towards the water. He remembered Mrs D's pronouncement, that her husband lived a great deal closer to the river, now—which was sensible, as rooms here tended to be damp and cheap.

The scarf itched Thurston's neck. Half of the Aran pattern was knobbles. He recalled a story from a fellow student from Ireland, that the pattern of an Aran gansey varied for each family. The tradition had a dark aspect; that if a man were drowned, he could be identified by the pattern on his jumper, even if his face were no longer recognisable, from water-bloat or the bludgeoning of rocks.

Thurston walked on, slower now, as the fog was dirty yellow and stung his lungs. Grudgingly, he wrapped the scarf around his nose and mouth to keep out the foul air, resenting its oily animal smell.

He spotted the lit-up roundel of the station: taking an underground train would shave fifteen minutes off his walk, and allow him to remove the scarf. He dived down the stairs to the platform. The scarf flapped behind him.

Three minutes in a warm train should have raised his spirits, but it allowed him time to brood. He recalled what a housemate had told him: that the riverbed of the Thames, along which this tube line ran, was soft sediment, very hazardous to dig. That the builders would hit soft yellow sand with their shovels, and realise their error too late! Water would cascade in and fill the tunnel.

Thurston stared down at the cursed scarf around his neck. The knitted cables didn't seem to follow a purposeful pattern, diving under one another with more panic than logic. He tried to trace the paths with his eyes alone, not wanting to resort to shaking the thing out and following it with his finger. The errors of a novice knitter, or some deliberate chaotic scheme?

As his eyes followed the meandering lines, his mind worried at what Mrs D. had said about Mr D.. *Living closer to the river.* Had he left her, then, and would they divorce? Was hitting a dog enough for grounds of cruelty? Or maybe they would stumble on, shackled together, with Mr D. making calls for money when it suited him, until death did them part. Horrors!

And then Thurston remembered: not *living closer to the river.* Only *closer to the river.*

Mr D. had struck the pathetic dog Lulu and vanished. He never called at the house, now. And Mrs D. had been fiercely productive, since: tackling her work with those tree-trunk arms, and in the evenings, ripping apart the jumpers of Mr D., to knit them up again in a different pattern…

Thurston blundered off at the train at the next stop and thanked the Lord it was the right one, the last stop on the North bank, before the tunnel went under the Thames. He was the only disembarker. He looped the scarf again around his irritated neck and his face, then turned to check that he had left nothing on the train.

In the corner of his eye, something lumbered. He was no longer alone on the platform. Someone, something spud-like, was moving towards him.

The train doors closed on the ends of his scarf.

The train brakes wheezed, and the carriages began their inexorable departure. Thurston yanked at the scarf, wasted precious seconds trying to haul the thing free. He set his foot against the carriage door and yanked at it. The train's motion threw him onto his back, the scarf still clinging around his neck, and he was dragged along the ground. The scarf utterly cut off his breath. As his lungs spasmed painfully in his chest, Thurston knew his accelerating journey would end with him strangled and smashed in the tunnel under the Thames.

And over him, looking down on him, was a ghastly impossible face: the ghost of Mr D., stinking of spirits (as he had on the night he had died), animated with fury at his own murder. Come to drag Thurston to hell, for wearing his re-made stolen yellow jumper.

The ghost of Mr D. reached down and wrenched the scarf off Thurston's neck.

"Lord, the relief! I could breathe again!" Thurston cried. "My ear was burning agony, nearly pulled off in the rescue—but I could *breathe*, and I lay there in bliss…" He'd stared at the train sliding away, the scarf streaming harmlessly behind it like a ribbon.

And then he had stared at the visage of Mr D., who coughed phlegmatically, clearly wanting a half crown.

"And I gave him one," Thurston concluded. "I gave him a *whole* crown. I thought myself worth it."

Mr D. was not dead, and Mrs D. no murderer; Mr D. was, indeed, living (in rotten lodgings) closer to the river.

"But how on earth," old Dr Haley demanded, "Did he come to be on the platform, just as you were alighting, and in need of him?"

"Yes, how?" I echoed, sensing a deeper mystery.

"Oh! He was on an errand."

Mr D.'s role as Thurston's guardian angel had been purchased. Mr D. had recognised Thurston's friends in the public house; they had told him that Thurston was on the way (possibly to keep Mr D. from occupying their spare chair). Mr D. had promised, for half a crown, to find Thurston at the station and escort him to the pub, to make sure he didn't lose his way in the fog.

"My friends had not believed him at all. But they paid him to make him go away, and he had been as good as his word, and saved my life."

•

Dr Haley and I both toasted Thurston's survival, and the temporary honesty of the drunk Mr D., and toasted Mrs D. for having the foresight to not murder her husband.

And once again, I felt unsatisfied.

It was a good enough tale, and hemmed with danger. I imagined telling it to Mary, and hearing her complain: it was not an *eerie* story. It wrapped up too neatly. While refilling my glass, I took a careful look at both Thurston's ears, hoping to see his flesh still imprinted with an uncanny Aran pattern. No such luck.

I fantasised further: what if Thurston were to lean down and roll up his trouser cuff, to show us a mahogany shin and confess: that night, the train had *taken his leg...*

I caught myself wishing amputation on a dear old friend and felt nauseated.

Thurston perhaps sensed that his tale had failed to fill the gap left by Dr Haley. He shrugged. "It is a poor sort of thing, but I have no other. Have you a story or two?"

Both men looked to me. "No, none," I admitted. "Maybe when I've seen more of the world." Maybe on my forthcoming honeymoon, in Scotland, a great place for haunted castles and long-ago battles.

"I swear," Dr Haley declared. "I have not heard a true ghost story—concerning a friend, you know, or a colleague—in ten years."

That small remark fell upon the room with more force than any part of their narratives.

"That long?" fretted Thurston. "I swear, my cousin told me a corker—but no, that was ten years, at least."

I thought of my father's friends at Christmas, my college companions at All Hallows, the fellows of my clerkship at the turning of the year. All fine times to draw from one's memory a single inexplicable tale.

Had any of them recounted an experience which had *genuinely* filled me with dread?

They had not, of late. Any who had, the event itself had taken place many years before.

I was filled with a powerful desire to be somewhere other. Thurston's study where we sat had seemed perfect only an hour before, the epitome of gentlemanly ease. Now I could not bear its closeness and wanted cold air on my face. I gave Haley and Thurston thanks, and made my excuses.

"I hope we have not given you too much of a pessimistic view of matrimony," Dr Haley said.

"Or domesticity!" echoed Thurston. I reassured them both. They told me that I was a fine young man, that my father would be proud, and I felt cowardly to flee them so hastily.

Thurston's house faced a small church green. I stood under the stars, and they were remote, but not baleful. A row of pollarded trees stretched this year's whippy growth into the starry sky, black on black, but they were solid sensible shapes, no crooked fingers or tormented stumps among them.

I circled around the church itself. Goodness knows an old rural church, dating back to the time of the Normans, can be an object of curiosity; what paganism lingers in the carvings? What cruelty was exercised when the mediaeval church had absolute power over the villagers? But the church was neither squat nor looming. A dog trotted past me, concerned with scents among the graves, and did not bark at me or cringe from me.

I wanted something other.

I wanted to see my fiancée, Mary.

I hurried towards the centre of the town. My beloved and I had taken rooms at the Swan Inn. By the time I reached it, I was sorely out of breath. There in a first floor window was Mary, seated in an armchair in her nightgown, reading a book of arctic adventure, sipping her tea.

I felt no wild panic, no foreboding. In that soft golden light, her movements as she turned a page seemed infinitely sweet to me. But pressed with no unusual tenderness, no presentiment of doom.

I framed some phrases in my mind.

And that was the last time I ever...

But little did I suspect, at that moment...

But they would not stick. They were swept away in an instant by the bracing night breeze.

"Hi, Mary!" I called to the window.

She threw up the sash a little way. "What are you doing, Gregory?"

"Come down!"

She rolled her eyes, but in a few moments emerged from the door of the inn, wearing a coat over her nightclothes, and a pair of walking boots on her bare feet.

"Are you tipsy, Greg?" she demanded fondly, and slipped her hand through my arm. "This is very improper of you."

"Not tipsy! But very glad to see you."

"Have you had bad news?" Mary knew I had been drinking with a doctor and a lawyer. She supposed that one of them had told me that my heart was weak, or my inheritance contested.

"No, but walk with me..."

We strolled together to the banks of the river, a lazy meandering thing for much of its length, but compressed at points to flow strong and deep. We stood on the bridge and looked down into the rushing depths, but even they could not hold my attention.

"What's got you so upset, Gregory?"

I tried to explain the entertainments of the evening.

Mary laughed. "What, have the men been telling ghost stories?"

"Yes..."

"And they have unsettled you?"

"Mary, how long is it since you heard a *really good* ghost story?"

Mary drew in close to me while she thought. "I suppose, at school...?"

"And—my dear—we have never told such stories to one another." We had read Braddon and Butts aloud to one another, but never exchanged tales of our own experience. "Has anything happened to you, anything that you struggle to explain?"

She shook her head. "I saw shadows often, in my grandmother's pantry. But it was always a tree."

"The old men have a score of such stories."

She nodded, catching my drift. "But the girls at school only told stories from their grandmothers' time!" My beloved was the most intelligent of women.

We gripped each other. She raised her face to me, with hope in it.

"Wait, though—you have got me out of bed, not a week before our wedding, to hurry me through the streets at night! Surely you must feel something? Does..." She shook herself, stood back from me, and addressed me quite seriously. "Did some unseen horror push you onward?"

I could not lie. "No—only I wanted to ask, if you had noticed it."

She sighed deeply. "And even being disturbed like this, I feel only that it is some foolishness of yours, no cause for concern. There are no haunting owl's cries..." She paused for a moment, but none obliged. "Is it all gone, then?"

"I do not know."

I found it hard to answer, for the terrible loss choked me. Had I missed my chance? Would I never experience something to shake me to the root, which I would reveal to other fellows only in my cups? That like a contagion would crawl across their skin and mock at their sleep.

I would be a respectable banker, with the best of wives, a life with no crack in it.

Mary came close again and laid her head on my shoulder. "I had hoped..."

"What, my love?"

"I had wondered if we might stumble across *something*—on honeymoon, or holiday, or in a new house we had just rented. I thought *something* might happen to the two of us, and only us."

"I understand. Something which would make us doubt everything, and cling together." I had hoped as much, without knowing it.

"Something which afterwards, we told only to one another..."

It would have been sublime. It would have elevated our marriage, to share that vital tremor.

Mary pulled her coat tight around her. "Let us go back to the Swan."

We knew the landlady might evict us if she found us in the same room, but couldn't bear to be separated. We kicked off our boots, but Mary kept on her big coat. I curled around her back (for the first time), drew up the covers over us both, and put my arm around her, over that woolly carapace.

"Is there a reason for it?" she whispered.

I searched about in my mind. "I do not know. Maybe the penny posts and cheap newspapers. Or the war, or the wireless..."

Mary shook her head, her hair soft against my mouth. "I would like there to be no reason at all. I would like that to be the one inexplicable thing, if all the others have been taken from us."

I thought of all that was lost: how foreign lands had lost half their charm in losing their menace. How old manor houses would only be an unheated inconvenience, now, and why not swap them for a smart city apartment? People would become heedless and contented, and buy and build and travel.

Entire professions—the archaeologist, the archivist, the antiquarian—would lose their sinister intrigue. One might pick up a curious inlaid box from an antique shop, or an oddly shaped flint at an earthworks, without fear that you'd someday need to burn it, or throw it down a well.

By contrast, these would be boom years for the dull professions. I would thrive, for I would be a banker. Only ever that. And here, at last, I felt a kind of bottomless panic, the kind I had desired to feel hours ago as I listened to my friends—a intolerable pressure in my chest, as waves of fear battered me. But not from a nameless dread, but from fear of my clearly-labelled life.

The company of professional men, my friends, would be a satisfying thing, contained within wood-panelled rooms, never disturbed. My marriage—my much-longed-for marriage!—would be fine and light and wonderful, we would not cleave together from fear.

Mary stirred under my arm. "Are you awake?"

I hummed.

"Greg, I thought: if we were to have children, we wouldn't have to worry."

Since our engagement, we hadn't spoken much of children. I had felt superstitious and shy. But I grasped her meaning. Our children would never be harmed by—whatever had been lost.

My wife would never return home with a cradle of old oak, of peculiar significance to my family, which I had attempted to destroy but failed. I would never quash my fears to humour her fancies, and place our son in the oak cradle, only to see the child expire on the stroke of midnight.

We would never watch, powerless, as a sinking, crouching shadow went slinking under the nursery door. Our child would never be dandled on the knee of a friendly artist, then strangled by the vile spirit the artist had awoken from the crypt of our local church. I would never have to say to my child: *oh, this is a miniature of your mother, who passed long ago. No, I may not tell you the circumstances—perhaps, when you are grown…* And watch my child scamper away into the orchard to play, and feel dread clutch at my heart.

Or worse still, seek my children playing in the orchard, and ask my daughter, *where is your brother?* And hear her reply: *oh, the beautiful lady led him away down the moonlight path!* And never see him after.

I would be spared such horrors.

I had wished Haley white-haired, and Thurston one-legged, but I could not wish ill on my children. There was no charm to those visions and I gave them up willingly. I held Mary very tightly, and felt her answering press on my hand.

We were bereft of a terrible wonder, but by God, we were safer, and so we slept.

The Librarian's Dilemma

Jas's job was to bring libraries into the 21st century. St Simon's library hadn't left the 17th, yet.

Jas stood in a University quad. Butter-coloured stone buildings slept along each side of the huge square. The smooth lawns were quartered by paths, and in the centre spread a huge yew whose sagging branches almost brushed the walls. Ahead of his was the wooden library door, dark and nail-studded.

The house Jas shared with his mother in Leamington would have fitted comfortably into this quad. Jas felt his principles—the anti-elitist, democratic ones that drew him to work in libraries—should have soured the sight. But they didn't. He knew this place wasn't intended for him: too white and too wealthy. If it was queer at all, it was queer like an E.M.Forster novel, with upper-class Edwardian men supressing their yearnings. But Jas's objections were as muffled as the sound of traffic behind him, sedated by the sight of old stone dozing in the sun.

The oak library door opened. An older woman appeared in its shadow, straight-backed in dark clothes that swung about her like robes.

"Jaswinder? I'm the librarian for the Harrad Collection. You've brought a lot of luggage."

Jas was smuggling the future, in big suitcases. Digitisation equipment: expensive, and unique, and terribly heavy. They'd been hell to drag around on the long train journey (although had probably done wonders for his developing arm muscles). *The librarian hasn't asked for them,* his boss had said. *But you can change her mind. Just don't tell her you brought them with you.* "I wasn't sure what the weather would be like," Jas said.

"I'll send Fred to help."

She slipped back inside, and from the same door rocketed a figure in a suit, thin as a stick with thick-framed glasses and a mane of hair tossing around.

"Hand 'em over. I'm stronger than I look." A Scottish accent. "I do all the shelving. Up and down the stairs, too—no lifts, this place is too old." He grabbed a case, swung it over his shoulder, staggered a little. "Follow me."

Up a stone staircase, into a room overlooking the quad. Polished uneven floorboards, the yew tree pressed green fingers on the leaded glass window.

"Do I sleep here?" In a fairy tale, in a fantasy novel.

"Yep. Student rooms. I'm down the corridor."

"Aren't you a librarian?"

"God, no. Who'd want to do that?"

"I do." This holiday job was a decent start, but Jas planned (when he'd finished his degree) to get properly chartered.

"You're young. You'll grow out of it."

Fred lead Jas back to the library. A dim room, as long as one side of the huge quad. When the door opened, a knife of light stabbed across the floorboards. Tweedy readers cluster around the windows, desperate for the sun. Academics were strange. Any sane person would take a book outside, sit under the tree.

The librarian looked up from her desk near the door, shook back her bobbed grey hair.

"Jas. Call me Moira. Now, we have you for eight weeks?"

"Yes." *Or longer, if they need you,* Stella-the-boss had said.

"You're going to tag our rare books, and connect each book to our catalogue record. You've had experience?"

"I tagged the incunabula in the Founders' Library in Lampeter." A miserable wet fortnight in Wales, but useful for the CV.

Moira laid a book on her desk. "Show me."

Jas eyed the book, conscious of being auditioned. Nice leather binding, useful crescent-moon gap between the sewn pages and the spine. He took from his bag a small plastic box and a slim long tool, like a sparkler. *Talk them through it,* Stella reminded him.

"So these are the seeds." The box was full of flat beads, like white lentils. "And I pick one up..."

Dipping the sparkler in the box, giving it a theatrical stir, then tapping to dislodge all but one seed.

"Then we..." He slid the sparkler into the spine-gap of the book. Good: no knots of glue, no tearing threads. You wanted the invisible worm, from Blake's poem, to wriggle into the book and hide the seed there, in the spine or the cover. The benevolent reader would never notice, the malevolent thief would never be able to find the seed and remove it.

"And now you can never lose this book!" That was part of the sales patter, but Jas was heartfelt. In a traditional library books got lost, not just in a prosaic sense (like lost keys) but in a profound way (like lost souls). Misplaced, they became inert, never again to be useful.

This was a great time for a quick demonstration. ***Find an excuse,*** Stella had said. ***It'll hook them.***

"Can I show you..." Jas moved around the room, sprinkling seeds at different heights on the shelves. (They were fiddly, but you couldn't, *ipso facto,* lose them.)

This was the fun part. "Now, if you want to find something..."

Jas held his device up to the room. The screen showed dots of light sprinkled all around. Constellations. Jas knew why it worked: because librarians thought of themselves as being Gods of a miniature cosmos.

"Each light is a book. And when you know which book you want..." Jas turned off all the seed-lights except for the one he'd just installed. A single light remained, the star over Bethlehem.

"Hmm." The librarian seemed far from enchanted. "I suppose it could be useful."

Jas felt his smile congeal on his face.

•

"OK, let's do philosophers," said Fred.

"Plato."

"Ooh, a toughie. Ockham! William of Ockham. Your turn."

"Morris. William Morris."

"Sartre!"

"Emerson!"

At Moira's instruction, Fred was helping Jas to seed the books. Jas wouldn't have chosen him: he was beaky, frenzied, likely to jab a seed tool straight through a book cover. And he'd made it clear he was temporary: "I'm only working here until I get a post-doc job. I'm not going to be a shelf-stacker forever." Jas resented this slur on his vocation. On the other hand, Fred did help to pass the time with whispered word games. Without Fred, it would have been dull work; Jas never read the books he seeded beyond the title. He had to go fast, not get sucked in.

By lunch on the first day, they'd seeded a huge stack of texts.

"We need the catalogue," Jas whispered. "To match the seeds to records. How do I access it?"

Fred pointed to a beige terminal.

Jas read a peeling sticker announcing it had been inspected for safety. "Ten years ago?"

"Well, it passed the inspection!" Fred said. "What more do you want?"

When consulted, Moira searched under her desk and dragged out a laptop, maybe only five years old. "Don't take it out of the library."

It was ridiculously slow. The ancient kit was inexplicable, given that St Simon's was so well endowed. The library catalogue wasn't complex, you could run it on anything. Jas could load it on his phone, for goodness' sake.

After an hour of wrestling with the ancient laptop, he did just that, and the work went so much quicker he nearly cried with relief. He kept the laptop open in case anyone was watching.

•

On the dot of five o'clock Fred stood and clapped his hands. Every tweedy reader looked up, and half of them closed their books and donned their jackets. Fred the pied piper led them towards a pub on the seafront.

"Why do you want to be a librarian, then?" Fred asked Jas as they walked. "Isn't it a wee bit boring?"

Jas wondered if he was being tested. "There are radical librarians."

"Really?"

"Yeah, they campaign for access and freedom of information." Jas admired them for their principles. But his heart was stolen by their multicoloured hair, their facial piercings, and the fact that half of them seemed trans or queer. "Mostly in America," he admitted.

"If you say so. I'll get the drinks in. Professor Connell, tell Jas about your research!"

The Professor was an older man, a stocky black professor from Los Angeles. He nodded his bald head sharply at Jas. "Trauma! War, civil conflict, interpersonal violence."

"Oh. Wow."

One by one, the other researchers named their expertise.

"Fascism," said a wistful Italian guy.

"Madness," announced a wild-haired woman. "Sorry, I wouldn't call it 'madness' normally, of course. But I'm eighteenth century. It's all ***madness, lunacy,*** all that bonkers terminology."

"I suppose you could say... the occult?" A younger man wearing a pentagram necklace.

"Medical ethics. Well, mostly when it goes wrong." That was a softly-spoken person from Sweden.

They all looked at Jas, whose mind was blossoming with horrors. He didn't want to know more about any of the topics, but couldn't see a polite way out of it. He took a conceptual side-step. "So is the Harrad collection particularly good for what you all do?"

With a clunk, Fred set down a tray of pints in their midst.

Fortunately, that signalled a change of topic. None of the academics wanted to talk about their research as they drank. They wanted to complain about the library. Jas guessed that it had all been said before, because people took up one another's refrains.

"If I could take books back to my room..." mourned the fascism expert.

"And you're only working on the early 20th century, aren't you?" retorted the madwoman. "They're not fragile..."

"Not fragile at all! With the light levels, I get such sore eyes."

"I'm getting RSI. And the chairs!" The occultist rolled his tattooed shoulders. "No lumbar support. I have to lie on the lawns and stretch, five minutes out of every bloody hour."

They seemed such mundane complaints, when each of the academics, through their research, went willingly into a distinct and horrible world. What were pins and needles, compared to immersing yourself in fascism?

Prof. Connell murmured to Jas. "Hey, you're doing something technological with the library, Jas?"

"Yeah."

"Fantastic. Now, this place needs to open up a little, you know? An amazing collection. Should be available to people, 24/7. Are you going to shake things up?"

Jas, feeling shaky, nodded weakly.

•

When he next saw Professor Connell, the Prof. was reading a book while sitting in the yew tree.

"Stop this at once." Moira's voice ricocheted off the walls of the quad.

"OK, OK. Tell me which part I can't do. Is the tree the problem? Can I sit on the grass?"

Jas grinned, then un-grinned. Better not to appear partisan. Better not to be seen at all. He'd just arrived in the quad, and hung back.

"You've removed a book from the library. You signed a contract."

"Yeah, I'm not sure that contract's legal. Forgive me. Two months working in a dark room could make anyone a little wild. Cabin fever. Jas?" He'd been spotted. "Take this book while I climb down?"

The Professor leaned down from the branches to pass Jas the book: a slim gum-bound paperback from the 1970s. Then the Professor dropped neatly onto the grass, and walked back into the library.

"Good morning, Jas." Moira fell into step beside him. "You've done counter work, haven't you?"

"Sorry?"

"You've worked on library counters."

"Oh, yeah."

"You've probably had moments like this."

"Mm." Students hiding books down their trousers. Students tossing books in the air as they walked through the security gates, so the books sailed over the sensors. "I reckoned it was their job to push it as far as they could, and my job to bat it back."

"It's not symmetrical, though, is it? If half the time the thieves win, and half the time we win, soon there's no library." Moira held the door. "Jas, I want all the books seeded. Not just the older ones."

"Yes." That quadrupled the size of the project, at least. Stella would be delighted. But there wouldn't be time. "I mean—I'm studying, I start my course again online in October." Maybe he could stay here, study from here?

"What are your grades like? You could study here at St Simon's, perhaps, and work part-time in the Collection."

The casual offer, in the chill of the dark room, sent a shiver up Jas's spine. To *go to University*—to indulge in that old, expensive rite of passage. To drink in a student bar. To sit thigh to thigh in a lecture theatre, with rapt concentration, not watch a recording at home with your attention drifting.

Also, there was the added appeal of starting in a new place. His friends, his mother, had been a life support. But to begin again, where people had always known him as Jas, was tempting.

And to be a student *here*, in particular: to live year-round in a room with uneven wooden floorboards, overlooking a green and tranquil quad...

Fred had been eavesdropping. "So, she said you could study here? Will you go for it?"

To distract him, Jas asked: "What are you researching?"

"The Gothic." Fred widened his eyes, tossed his hair.

"Isn't that old-fashioned?"

"It won't die! It's big in America right now. I'm working on getting myself a Stateside post-doc. Going to become a genius."

"Can you—I mean, you can't *plan* to be a genius."

"You need more than brains. You need funding."

•

Moira was clearly embracing technology, so Jas decided to give her another demonstration.

"University of Salisbury—special collections. My boss designed this for them." Scans of mediaeval record-books filled the screen, so rich and sharp you could see the quill-strokes.

Moira prodded the images Jas's device, bringing up related lecture notes, an audio clip of two students debating.

"You could have something like this," Jas said. "Use work from the visiting researchers. Showcase what the library does."

Moira shook her head without taking her eyes off the device.

"This modernity," she said. Jas thought she was referring to something on the screen, until she continued: "This *modernisation*."

"Yes?"

"It happens, of course, but it's not inevitable. This project you're leading. It's incredibly useful. But it's not the leading wave of an unavoidable rising tide."

"Of course!" Jas tried to sound sympathetic. "Not every innovation suits every library." Which he didn't believe, but you had to be tactful.

"I hope you don't feel you're here under false pretences."

"No, no. I'm happy just tagging," Jas lied. "I just—I liked this." He pointed at the device, at the University of Salisbury's shining showcase.

"I like it too." Moira was faking regret. Dishonesty was contagious. "Perhaps if things were different." Then, sincere again, she held out a Post-it note. "Here's the contact for St Simon's admissions. I told them you'd be in touch."

•

"...your fatuous little *dictatorship...*"

Professor Connell had been shouting for a couple of minutes. Jas's hands had started to shake—he hated arguments—so he put down the seeding wand.

"What harm does it do anyone?" The professor was playing to the gallery, but getting no response. The madness expert shook her head regretfully, the occultist pursed his lips. "So that's it? No second chance?"

"You used your second chance weeks ago, Professor," replied Moira.

The professor scooped up his notebooks. Everyone found somewhere else to look as he stomped down the aisle, slammed the oak door behind him.

Jas scribbled on a piece of paper: *What was that about?* Pushed it towards Fred.

Fred mimed holding a box, squeezing: a camera. Except the Professor wouldn't have made that gesture—he'd have taken his snap with a discrete tap on his phone.

Back to America, Fred wrote. Utterly expelled.

•

"So photographs aren't allowed at all?" Later, in the pub, Jas was still keeping his voice down.

"Nothing's allowed." Fred pulled out a sheet of crumpled paper. "Here's the contract researchers sign. Check which ones you've already broken."

No stealing, no smoking. Fair enough. No photocopying, no scanning. Well, it might damage the books. But for every three reasonable requests, there was a big ask.

The researcher will not discuss the Harrad Collection in person or on social media.

Texts from the Collection will not be added to referencing apps or software including (but not limited to) Zotero, EndNote, RefMe...

Modernity isn't inevitable, the librarian had said. She knew about social media and referencing software, but had decided to ban them. She wasn't an aging dusty stereotype. She was well informed, and gatekeeping.

"I don't like it either," Fred said. "But I'm not going to climb a tree with a book up my arse to prove a point."

"I don't think anyone could expect you to do that."

"I'm out of here, anyway." Fred's exodus predictions had taken on a personal, insulting note for Jas. *This place that you want to get into?* Fred was saying. *I shun it. I'm better. I'm gone.*

"So you said."

Jas replied mechanically, thinking of other things. He'd been looking more at the books, while seeding them. Not reading them. But sometimes running an eye over the contents page or the frontispiece. They were all unfamiliar. They raised the spectre of forceful debates which Jas didn't have time to look into, full of rhetorical questions and ominous proclamations. His browsing hadn't enlightened him, had only left him spiky and off-kilter.

Fred shoved Jas with a bony shoulder, piqued by his indifference. "You should look into the founder, Lady Harrad. She had some interesting principles."

Lady Harrad had been born in 1890, Jas remembered vaguely. Victorian Values didn't feel relevant to the situation.

Jas felt Fred's hand fumbling with his own under the pub table. He felt a flush of embarrassment, then realised Fred was trying to slip a tiny object into his palm.

"Have a look at that."

"What—"

"There are more discreet ways to take photographs."

Jas remembered the thick-rimmed glasses Fred wore for reading.

•

In his bedroom that evening, Jas phoned his boss.

"Jas! Great work so far."

"Stella, did I sign a contract to work here?"

"The company signed one."

"Could you send me a copy? I want to make sure I'm sticking to it."

"Sure. Probably common sense, though."

But there was nothing common, or sensible, about the Harrad Collection.

Jas held Fred's gift. The sliver of plastic was almost weightless. He knew he shouldn't examine it. He'd lose his job, and any chance of studying here.

But a radical librarian had to be brave. Jas opened up Fred's gift.

The memory card held a dozen files, all photos of pages. Jas read a header at random: 'Unlike Other Women.' Intrigued, Jas read on.

The woman was Unlike Other Women because she wasn't a woman at all.

The page was from a transsexual autobiography. Jas knew the label was anachronistic, but the story felt so familiar. *I rarely found myself drawn to feminine ways, and as a child threw myself into games with hoops and trains.* The voice bubbled off the page. By the end of the first page, the narrator had become engaged but *could not rest while betrothed to Daniel, having no wifely feelings for him. I then lived ten years in Clacton under the name of Donald.*

'Lived under the name of Donald.' What a world of activity that sentence glossed over. How had he earned his keep, bought his clothes...

Jas checked the title of the book. *Accounts from the Patients at Woburn Sands.* Fred had also photographed the contents page, and there were twenty names: Constance, Jack, Alicia, Robert, JC. Were they all trans?

Published in 1878. A voice from history, a miracle.

•

Stella, in Jas's mind, said *slow down, hold back.* But Jas still cornered Moira the following morning for another demonstration. There were things in this collection too precious to stay boxed up. He'd known it objectively, but Fred's illicit snaps—Donald's story—had brought it home.

He needed to know where Moira stood.

Jas opened some images from the Lampeter website. "This was incredibly fragile, a Vulgate Bible from the 12th century." Everyone liked illuminated manuscripts. "We scanned it without even opening it."

Moira didn't dismiss it out of hand. "How?"

"Stella's inventions." He showed Moira pictures of the scanners. Sheets of graphene that slid in between pages, ultra-fast book flippers for the most robust texts, or ultrasound devices for the most fragile. "So now that book can never be lost, or destroyed, even if it's stolen or water-damaged..."

"Or burnt."

It felt wrong to mention fire, to a librarian. Like saying 'Macbeth' to an actor. "Yes."

"Interesting."

He would pitch hard, now, while he had her attention. "And with a collection like this, it seems such a waste for only the readers who are physically present to see it. I'm not saying you should throw it open..." He wanted that with all his untrained anarchist librarian heart, but he could haggle. "You would still absolutely be able to control exactly who has access to the texts." She'd like that.

"So you see digitisation as a way to *circulate* the texts."

It was such a basic question that it confused Jas completely. "Yes." Of course, why else?

Moira sighed. "Jas, you are a very diligent young man. That's why I hope you'll work here for a long while, perhaps study here. But please understand, I will invest in any technology that means I *know where my books are*." Tapping her desktop with a bloodless fingernail. "And which means they cannot be destroyed. Anything that makes it harder to steal them, to photograph them, to gain access to them without my knowledge—I want that."

She wasn't interested in opening the library up. She wanted to close it down. Maybe she'd misunderstood.

"We live in such an amazingly connected world, now," Jas said. "It's such a part of scholarship, and learning, and..." Vainly throwing keywords at the librarian.

"You're right. In fact, I've been speaking to Stella. She's agreed that you can advise me on this."

"Really?" A bloom of optimism.

"Building a security net, for a connected world. I'll tell you about some of the worst offenders of the last five years." Her eyes were bright at the thought of book thieves. Worse than that: library thieves. "You can tell me how you would have caught them."

•

"Yeats," said Jas. They were using famous writers for the game, today.

Each touch they give / love is nearer death... Jas had read that Yeats poem when he was learning about the librarian's dilemma. It applied more to books than to lovers. There were always two impulses in any librarian, any library, any collection: the desire to preserve a text, and the desire to make it available. Those two impulses were always at war. Each touch on a book lessened its lifespan.

But that was the marvellous thing about Jas's scanning work: now the whole world could read a book without damaging it, without even touching it. How many other professions, built around a central paradox, could say: we solved it?

"Wallace Stevens. Hey. Sleepyhead. Stevens."

Moira didn't appear to be conflicted at all about her collection. Preservation trumped access, for her, every time. She was committing an act of enclosure: taking things which could easily be in the public domain and building a wall round them.

There was a dark side to collecting books. A hoarding, acquisitive desire. To keep the books away from other people and their sticky fingers. You had to temper that desire, and use your knowledge to increase the knowledge of others. Without that, you weren't a librarian. You were just a hoarder.

"Stoker," said Jas. "Bram Stoker."

"Hey, not fair. That's my turf. Anything Gothic—mine. Anyway. Ayn Rand."

And now Moira wanted to set Jas's diligent young brain to keeping people out. Poacher turned gamekeeper.

"You coming to the pub?"

"Already?" The whole day gone, and he hadn't even tried to find the Woburn Sands book.

•

"All librarians are evil," Fred announced, as they crossed the dark quad on the way home from the pub that night. "You want to be a librarian, Jas. It's because they *make a difference*, right?"

Jas shrugged. There was still a light burning in the library. At lunchtime he'd emailed his best essays to an admissions tutor at St Simon's, and he wouldn't let Fred's ramblings damage his chances.

Fred rolled on. "But librarians are supposed to be neutral, right? You want a book about raising Satan, the librarian's supposed to give it to you. So how can you be moral *and* neutral? They want to *make a difference*, but they don't say what difference they actually make."

"But you gave me that book."

Jas hadn't intended to say it. He was tipsy. He wanted to check if he had someone on his side. "That made a difference, to me."

"Oh, that was just solidarity. Hope you didn't mind. I mean, I'm not assuming... Y'know."

"I thought you were agreeing with me. Showing me something that should be shared. Released."

"Nah. None of that hippy shit. Just a gift, just for you."

They climbed the stairs to Jas's room, and at the door, Fred said: "Hold on a moment." He reached behind Jas's head, speaking and moving so casually that Jas thought Fred was brushing fluff off his coat collar.

Fred laid his hand across the nape of Jas's neck and kissed him. His beer-tasting tongue parted Jas's lips and moved in a slow circle inside Jas's mouth. It was intrusive, but not unpleasant.

"Can I come in?" Fred asked.

"You're drunk."

"Have you met me? I'm always drunk."

They were both laughing. He could feel the upwards curve of Fred's lips, wished he could remember what Fred's face looked like, if he'd been attracted to him at all before this ambush.

"Look, come in, but not..."

"Not for that."

"Maybe not."

"But maybe?"

After all Fred's threats to leave, his sudden attempt to move closer was sexy. Sexier than his musty suit jacket. "Perhaps."

•

It was hard to plan the theft.

Jas found *Accounts from the Patients at Woburn Sands* the following day and read more of it in the library. It was too intense to read it in a dark public room during his lunch hour. It needed to be read on a windy beach, in a cafe in a city, on a bed, being charmed and buffeted by the voices from the past.

More importantly, it should be shared with the people who would be cheered by it, who were trying in the face of hostility to construct a history.

Jas checked the perimeter first: no door, no hatches. No means whereby he could slip the book into another bit of the building.

He argued with himself while he patrolled: I could get sacked.

I probably wouldn't.

This would be a ridiculous way to remove all hope of studying at St Simon's.

It's really important. It's the principle.

I'm a thief. When you steal from a library, you steal from everyone in the world. And all the future people of the world, readers as yet unborn...

That's such a pre-digital idea. A childish idea. I'm not a thief. I'll bring it back.

You'll keep it.

Shut up.

Jas looked at the windows. In most libraries, the perimeter was sealed, to prevent users from tossing a book out of a window and running away with it. If the library didn't have a central courtyard, the users were condemned to swelter. But here, strangely, the windows were left open.

Jas set his book on a wide windowsill.

Then he worked for another half hour, to make his movements less suspicious.

"I'm going for lunch."

"Mind if I join you?" said Fred.

"Oh, I need to do some things." It was tactless, after last night, to fob him off. "Sorry. We could meet later?"

Fred shrugged, all bony shoulders and nonchalance. "If you like."

Jas forced a smile. His footsteps down the library aisle had never sounded louder. Moira was in her office. His heart slapped insistently, *something is wrong, something is wrong.* Maybe the wide-open windows were a trap.

Jas opened the library door, turned hard right along the wall, to the window where, on the sill, his prize waited for him. He scooped it up silently, slipped it into his bag and kept walking.

In his room, Jas slid the book under his mattress. No, that was the first place people would look.

He turned round and round, eyeing every crevice and seeing no hiding place. What had he done? A sackable offence, definitely a sackable offence.

Better to scan it and take it back straight away. He popped the book into one of the slower flicker-scanners and watched it deftly turn the pages.

The door opened.

Jas shot up, tried to hide the device by standing in front of it.

In the doorway leaned Fred.

"Cheeky," he observed. "Oh, no, don't faint on me..."

Jas sat on the edge of the bed and waited for the room to stop spinning.

"It's not enough," Jas said, when he was calmer. "I mean, it's not fair for me just to borrow a book that I want to read. There must be other books, useful to other people..."

"Aye."

"What should I do?"

"Well, what can you do? You can't take snapshots of everything."

"I've got these scanners. Really good scanners."

Fred raised his eyebrows. "Moira wouldn't like that."

"Do you think we could talk to the Vice Chancellor of the University?"

"'We'? Leave me out of it."

•

For the next fortnight, Jas was remarkably productive in both halves of his double life.

He set up the online security net Moira had requested. First, he cross-referenced the Harrad Collection catalogue against other library catalogues to find the really unusual books. Then he set up alerts, triggered if anyone mentioned one of these rare books online.

"That'll catch them," Moira said. It was the most satisfied he'd ever heard her.

After work, Jas smuggled texts out of the library. He dived into the catalogue and searched every archaic term, every classical reference that might get a hit: inverts and urnings and symposia and myrmidons. He found a couple of texts a day and scanned them and returned them, too nervous even to read them. They went no further; he couldn't work out how to safely share them. It was a futile, miniscule act of rebellion.

Most evenings he ate dinner in the pub while Fred drank, and they slept in Fred's room together. And while Jas worked and stole and slept, he waited for an offer from St Simon's.

•

He woke up in Fred's room, colder than usual. Fred's warm weight was absent.

Jas wondered if he should go back to his own bed. It was weird to be here on his own. The pillows smelled of cigarette smoke—it had been exotic and sexy as he'd fallen asleep, but now he didn't want to rest his face in it.

Jas walked as softly as he could to his own room.

There was a light shining under the closed door. He flung open the door, hoping to startle whoever was in there.

The surprises came in quick waves.

To find Fred in his room, when he'd just come from Fred's bed.

To see Fred juggling very competently one of the graphene scanners, clearly having used the slippery and delicate thing before. A flicker-scanner fanned a stack of six books in one corner of the room, and the ultrasound machine hummed in another.

But mainly, Jas was startled by the scale of it. There had to be a hundred books stacked on the carpet. Fred alone had clearly carried them from the library, intending to scan and replace them tonight. Up and down the stairs, and no lifts. Fred was energetic, manic at times, but Jas had never seen him so industrious.

Jas realised that Fred and Moira both scared him. But at least he knew what Moira wanted.

Fred sprung towards him. Wrapped his pyjama-clad arms round him.

"You were right. Information wants to be free," said Fred.

"Fred, why..." Fred had been awake for hours, Jas for only minutes. He couldn't think straight, and Fred talked over him.

"You've opened my eyes," said Fred.

"You've nicked my scanners."

"Borrowed. Just for tonight. But something's better than nothing, eh? Send a few books out into the world, like doves after the flood." Fred tightened his hold.

Jas spoke into Fred's mop of smoky hair. "You need to promise—*swear*—you'll never do this again."

"Yeah, yeah."

"Have you shared any of it?"

"No."

"You have to wipe your memory cards, wipe everything. I'll help you put the books back."

Up and down the stairs in the dark. Barefoot on stone, so as to make as little noise as possible, so that each step was painful—like the little mermaid, he thought, as sleeplessness sent his brain off on strange tangents.

He was so bone-cold and bone-weary at the end of it that he never wanted to see Fred again. But so much of both that he let Fred creep into his bed and hold him.

"Promise you won't do it again." Jas knew his own lesser transgressions would have to end, too. Even though they were hardly comparable to Fred's efforts. No more scanning for either of them.

"I promise," said Fred.

•

An alert was triggered the next morning; something caught in the new security net. An academic in America boasting about working on a 'lost' Gothic novel. It could be a coincidence. Jas didn't report it to Moira.

Fred didn't turn up to work. Catching up on sleep, Jas guessed.

An email at midday from St Simon's made Jas an offer: a place on an undergraduate degree, starting that Autumn.

This was good, this was excellent. He'd work so hard, stay up all night in earnest arguments in the kitchen of his student halls. His claim to be here would be as good as anyone's. As long as they never found out about the scanned books.

During the afternoon, as he worked, he told himself: *this is good, this is good.* Until he said it out loud, without meaning to. He heard his own voice, furious and scared, and realised where his fear lay.

If he took up the offer to study here, would it be contingent on working in the library? At some point, the job had metamorphosed from opportunity to threat. Would Jas be tied to Moira, and to this archive, indefinitely?

•

As Jas was leaving the library, that evening, Moira spoke. "Wait, Jas."

She'd found out. About the alert Jas hadn't reported, or his thefts, or Fred's misdeeds. She was going to sack him, prosecute him, have him barred for life from all libraries.

Or she knew about his offer, and he was trapped.

"I've not been fair to you. Come with me."

Moira led Jas a long way into the library. Unlocked doors, revealed a dusty room. On a table lay metal guillotines, a pin-cushion stuck with three-inch needles. Moira was going to torture him. No, don't be daft.

"I do some small repairs, here. Have a seat."

She laid a book in front of him. Published in the 1940s, maroon cloth binding. He picked it up, automatically looking for the crevice in which to insert the tracking seed.

"The founder of the Harrad Collection."

Jas shifted his attention from the binding to the content. *A Life of Lady Harrad.* The contents page described the founder campaigning for women's suffrage; then for pacifism and the League of Nations; then against fascism, and in favour of self-government for India. An all-round good egg, Jas thought.

"Lady Harrad even saw the book burnings in Berlin. Including the archives of the Hirschfeld institute." Did Moira know that Hirschfeld would strike a chord with him? Did everyone know he was queer? "She thought them a terrible tragedy."

Surely, then, she'd want the world to *use* the damn Collection. Not for it to sit and moulder in a stone room in an odd corner of a small country. He phrased it as mildly as he knew how. "So she knew it was important to preserve ideas."

"She collected books to get them out of circulation."

Jas stared in disbelief at the frontispiece photograph of an Edwardian teenager, big eyes and swept-up hair.

" Anti-suffragette materials, fascist tracts," said Moira. "She boxed them up and sent them home to her mother and kept collecting."

Moira laid other books on the desk. Jas opened the covers carefully.

The Segregated City.

Motherhood in the Lower Classes.

Disordered Desire: Deportation as Solution.

"And the Collection kept collecting, after she died."

More volumes were added to the desk, modern ones. Virology, Anthropology, Economics.

It was horrible because the books wore all the trappings of legitimacy: smart fonts, cloth-bound covers, a familiar formal layout. Like a polite voice saying terrible things. And because Jas loved books, totally bloody loved books, it was like the voice of a friend in a nightmare.

Were all the texts in the Collection similarly awful? Had he been surrounded by walls crawling with malice, for weeks? But the book Jas had found, the book from Woburn Sands—had Lady Harrad disapproved of it? Why was it here? "There are good things, here, too."

"I don't doubt it. She didn't have time to read everything herself. And fashions change, in politics, as in everything."

Jas took deep breaths, looked away from the books. "So why keep them all?" he asked.

"For the same reason that we preserve the smallpox virus. They could be useful to study. That's why we permit researchers to visit. But the books shouldn't be allowed to spread."

Jas's head was swimming with objections. Paternalistic. Patronising.

"I suggest you take tomorrow," Moira offered, "To look around. Read the books. Talk to the researchers. Ask them about their work: the unethical medical experiments. The economists advocating enforced labour, and euthanasia for the unfit. The novels that are as beautiful as Proust but, oh, five times as anti-Semitic. See if they think *those* books should be available to the world."

She was defending herself heatedly against objections Jas hadn't even raised. "OK. I will." He needed the conversation to stop.

Moira sighed. " It's expensive to keep people out. Distance is a great boon. That's why Lady Harrad lodged the Collection at St Simon's. It's rather far from everywhere."

•

Jas walked on the beach for an hour to get his head straight. He imagined the horrors of the Collection, and tried to reconcile that with the dark, orderly library room. He heard the shingle growl as the waves dragged it back, then saw the surf roil and crash.

When he was exhausted he turned back towards the University. Across the beautiful quad, which his new knowledge still couldn't make ugly. Up the stone stair, opening the door to his room.

The sight was so much as it had been last night that Jas wondered if he'd become stuck in a loop of time. Fred, cross-legged on the bed, feeding books into scanners. More books, if anything, than before.

"Ah! Finally! You're back." Fred sprung up and moved from device to device, clicking out memory cards.

"You promised..."

"I lied."

"You've been here all day?"

"Yep."

"But you were up all night, as well. You can't have slept..."

"I've hardly slept for two weeks, Jas. I've been in here every night. I'm on uppers. Didn't you bloody notice?"

"What are you doing?" He definitely wasn't releasing books like doves after the flood.

"I'm taking everything relevant from the Collection and I'm going to America. Where I'm starting a post-doc. I'm not smart enough to get it on my own. No, no, Jas—I know my limits. I have to research a *unique* resource. And I have to bring that resource with me." Fred tucked the memory cards into his breast pocket. "Nobody's even heard of half these texts. They're nasty. Turn your hair white."

"This is all for your research?"

"Of course. Oh, and because information, it wants to be free, apparently."

"You set off the alarm I set up."

"One of my future colleagues. Got overexcited about one particular book. Idiot."

Jas tried to breathe evenly. He should tell Moira. But it was his own bedroom stacked with books, his own equipment (smuggled into the building) which had pirated them.

"Anyway, I'm off tomorrow," Fred announced. "But first: the final step."

"What?"

Fred's eyes sparkled.

"I burn the originals." Fred reached into his inside pocket.

Jas had a sudden vision of the room on fire, bindings blazing, leaded windows cracking in the heat.

Jas hit Fred.

He'd never done it before, and he did it badly. His knuckles jarred against Fred's cheek, instantly aching like they were broken. But at least he'd stopped Fred reaching for a lighter, or a bottle of petrol.

Fred reeled back, clutching his face. Laughing. "Good God, Jas, I'm not going to do that! Why would I need to do that? You're so bloody gullible!"

The side of his face was red, a spreading blotch, horrifying Jas.

"I wouldn't ***burn*** them. They're too bloody valuable. I mean, I've ***sold*** a lot of them. To cover my relocation costs. You wouldn't believe how much a neo-Nazi will pay for a—"

Jas hit him again. No ticking clock as an excuse, this time, just fury.

Fred fell, and lay on the floor, gulping.

"Sorry," said Jas automatically.

"Help me up, then."

Jas couldn't move. He could have helped skinny, frenetic Fred, the friend who was reaching up a hand to him. But Fred had metamorphosed himself into something untouchable. Revulsion welled up in Jas so strongly that it became awe.

The man at his feet was a library-thief. He had stolen from everyone in the world.

Red Kite Kindred

Footprints round my doorstone, when I came home. A strong woman, I am, and if someone has slunk unasked into my cottage they should be the fearful one.

My intruder I found bedraggled in a chair before the fire. How had the child wriggled her way in here? The only open window was high and small.

"You were out and it was raining," the child said.

"Wear a coat, then. Don't turn burglar." I didn't sit.

A settler child. Ten years old, maybe? Skinny drowned-animal-looking child, hair like a cawl.

"Have you brought me a problem, now?" Please, let it not be settler business. I could see the low-lying settlement buildings from my window, four miles from town, down in the valley. I oversaw trade with the settlers, and made it fair, rigorous fair. I was the Alderman. So my other job, the job with no payment, was to keep the peace with them.

I do not have overmuch peace in me.

"We need help." She spoke my language better than her Pa did, but something was sealing her lips. I wished Arak was home, she would know what to say. She liked kids. But she'd be out Devi way, looking for food and hoping for the rain to lift. "Can you explain it?" the girl said, lifting back her waterweed hair.

Her question was not to me.

A lump spasmed under the slick fabric of the girl's shirt. A dark snout appeared by her collar, then a whole black rat wriggled out.

It shivered itself from nose to tail, then fixed me with button eyes.

"Hello," it said. "Glad to meet you."

I sat, to save myself from falling.

A talking rat. A mockery. A monstrosity.

The furry parody waved its muzzle as it spoke. "It's a bit of a tricky problem." I watched his furred mouth form words, whistling on some syllables because of his split top lip.

I said to the child, "Get it out of here."

Thorny, she was, in an instant with fury: *you can't make me and it's not fair.* If anything showed that she didn't know what she'd done, it was her childish whining.

"We'll talk," I said, "Us two, but not until it's out of here."

A small voice of reason: "Maybe it would be easier..." The rat—the *rat*—was seeing the sense of it. So of course, she scooped it up and cradled it close-wise and cosy. Darling vermin, sweetest grotesquery.

"It's raining," she said. "He's not going anywhere."

Easy it was to grab the animal up, but then it was squirming velvet and I could hardly hold it. I shouldered the door open, kicked it shut behind me.

"Wait," said the rat. "Please. It's not safe!"

I looked up. Red kites over the cottage. Death to all small things, soaring in circles.

"Shut up!" Now I, a grown woman, was shouting at a rodent.

Hearing the girl crying indoors. Feeling the rat desperately shove with its rump, this way then that way, against my palms. I grabbed its tail and held it away from me, dangling and chittering. I could swing it out over the valley, let it go, never have to look on it again.

A familiar shadow passed over my head. I dithered. And the rat dived neatly into my jacket sleeve.

Arak was gliding over the cottage. Her flight feathers fanned like flicks of ink drawn with a fine brush. My wonder, my marvel, come home to this chaos.

"What, love?" Her croaks were so different from the rat's lisp. "Are you catching a rat?"

"Maybe."

"That's my job," she called down.

"It's rabbits you eat, love."

"Has it bitten you?"

The rat hadn't bit me. Why not? I felt it shivering, down around my elbow.

"Come out," I said. I held my palm flat and waited but it didn't emerge. Cowardly vermin, scale-tailed lily-livered thing. I wouldn't have actually thrown it.

I opened the door for Arak. She swished in past me. The wind from her wings smelled of rain and blood. Do I smell, to her, of earth and turnips? And yet she loved me.

Arak flew straight to her fireside perch. Which put the fear of God, of course, into the girl. I shook the rat out into the child's hands, and she clutched it, and after a while calmed enough to fuss and nuzzle it, but hardly took her eyes off my love.

"Why are you here, child?" Arak asked. Even with her rasp, she sounded kinder than me.

"I came to ask Annest for help. It's her job to help, but she won't," said the ingrate child.

"My job is to make for fair trade," I said. "Is it that you want to sell the talking vermin?"

The girl stroked the rat along its backbone. "It's your job. Pa said."

"Do you know what your Pa is?" I said. "He's a thumb on the scales. He's the scum of the earth. I don't have to help you."

•

The settlers had come sniffing here a few years ago, sent sharp-eyed charmers into the hills to trade trinkets for local treasures. What did they think to find? We were poets and dreamers; maybe we'd sell them the gold gods on our well-heads, and they'd leave within two years, rich cackling villains.

But the people who lived hereabouts had been forewarned. They'd sold the settlers next to nothing, and haggled hard.

I was not the least of the hagglers. I was not Alderman then, but I grew into it.

They did build a trade route, of the low-key ordinary sort: cheese and wool, and some lead, passed out of the hill towns and down to the cities. It was enough for the settlers to stay, but not enough to make them rich. They grudgingly grew food—vegetables from their home, which rotted in the ground. They bought our seeds and planted again. They didn't settle here as much as linger.

"What's your name?" Arak croaked.

"Lydia."

Did Lydia know her history? Or did she see her parents struggling, and blame the malice of the town? Settler children littered the hills, dressed wrong for every season. They knew nothing. Not from a lack of curiosity—they'd turn up, moon-eyed, at a shearing or a shoeing, even crept into the back of chapel. But their parents dragged them away. *You don't need to know that. We won't be staying here long.*

This girl must be one of the oldest of the lingering children.

I ran my mind deliberately over my calming things: clouds like mackerel skin over the sea cliffs at Gogarth, the Winter river in headlong spate near Pennal. I sat down opposite the child.

"How long have you been with this fellow?" Arak asked.

"Charlie? Half a year." Lydia smiled. She liked to talk about her talking rat.

"Busy few months," Charlie said. He clambered back onto Lydia's lap. "Super busy!"

He was a plain black rat, like the ones who live in groups under barns. But better fed and glossier. I knew talking animals. Horses, wolves. My mother's eagle. Even a fish who could more or less get her point across. But not a talking rodent. This child didn't understand the weight of what she'd done.

And I'd have to tell her. As my fury boiled away, fear flooded in to replace it.

"Lydia, how did you do this?" I asked.

"Terric showed us how."

Terric was a hill kid, showing off to the settler kids. Dangerous little idiot.

"But there weren't any problems until Will got a mouse."

"A mouse?"

"One of the kids has got a mouse." Charlie nodded to me. "Needs someone to take a look at it. Acting funny." His tone said: we're both grown-ups, the kid's upset, how can we fix this? I was being patronised by a rat.

"I'll fetch a blanket for you," I said, and stood, to buy myself time. A talking mouse. What would you say to a talking mouse? What could you learn from a pissing, nibbling, mite-riddled mouse?

Arak flew ahead of me into the bedroom, perched on the bedpost where she slept most nights.

"You can leave, if you want," I told her.

"Certainly not. You're much too angry."

She watched me take the blanket down from the big wood press and shake it out. "I don't like talking to the vermin while you're here," I admitted.

"Whyever not?"

"If I'm taking him seriously, I'm insulting you."

"A rat can't diminish me." She swept up onto my shoulder, let me rest my cheek against her warm breast-feathers, and had me carry her back to the fireplace.

"How many of you children have animals?" Arak asked Lydia. "Not just pets."

"Talking animals?"

"Oh, yes. Talking animals," I said. That phrase told me a lot. It shrunk down the whole bond to its least significant part. I threw the blanket at the child.

Arak tightened her claws on my shoulder. Meaning: *don't sneer, or the kid will shut up like a trap.*

I thought of wind on the top of Tarrenhendre.

"Maybe six of us. Is that bad?"

I reached up and gently ruffled Arak's head-feathers. Lydia scooped Charlie up and set him on her shoulder. We four faced one another.

"What other kind of animals do you and your friends have?" I asked.

"Foxes. Rabbits."

Rabbits. Did rabbits even have brains? Do you need brains to turn grass into pellets of shit, all day?

"And do your parents know about it?"

"They don't know how to do it." She paused and Charlie pushed his dark muzzle against her cheek. "Some of them think all the animals round here talk. But that they only talk to hill-people and children."

"Ha!" Children and hill-people, and they probably used a worse word.

"I can give you an answer," I offered. "It isn't nice. Do you want to hear all of it?"

Lydia nodded. Charlie pushed his way under her fidgeting fingers.

"When you join with an animal…" I tailed off. It rankled to speak to the rat, but it would be simpler. "Rat."

"Charlie," she said.

"Rat. Do you remember before you were Lydia's—friend?"

"Food wasn't as good. I don't remember much—but then, I wasn't very old!"

"Did you know words for things? Rat words?"

Charlie pulled a paw quickly over one ear, flattening it and letting it pop back. Nervous. "No? I knew smells, and noises, and movements…"

"Animals cannot talk," I said. "Not like we do. So when you join an animal, he has to take on your way of thinking. You give some of your mind to him."

"And vice versa," said my love.

"Very much vice versa. Then you have a companion who is part animal and part you." I didn't sing songs about it. I didn't say that every day was both the struggle and the reward. I did not speak of the awe, the startling combination of difference and proximity. I stuck to the practicalities. "And you are partly them. Now, most people join a bird, or a horse, or a wolf."

"A wolf?" Lydia gave a quick grin. I shouldn't have bloody mentioned the wolves.

"And those animals live a long time. And nobody takes on a companion before they're properly grown, see? I was twice your age before I met Arak. Because you have to be careful. Because when your companion dies, you do not get that part of yourself—the part you gave them—back."

Lydia sat very still. "What does that mean?"

"It means everything after your companion dies is much harder."

My stupid mind suddenly conjured it all up for me, until my eyes were stinging: Arak would be stiff on the floor one morning. I would lever up the grey slate doorstone and dig there, so that going out and in, I would think of her.

My love took pity and finished my speech for me. "So a companion should not be taken on lightly."

To be one of two utterly unalike things, who nevertheless become one another's better halves. That was worth the devastation of parting.

Missed the point by a mile, the child did. "You mean children aren't allowed to do it." She was scared, now, and turning angry to hide it. I knew the feeling. "But I did it perfectly well. It worked fine!"

I bellowed right back at her. "Gods, you don't get it!" Arka took off and shot up to the rafters. The scratches she drew on my shoulder just made me louder. "It's not about what you've done now, you fool. It's about later, when that bloody rat of yours dies. How long has he got? Two years, a year?"

Rain drummed on the slate roof. I'd shouted her into dumbness. But it was the pain in the eyes of the rat that stopped me.

How do you apologise to vermin?

I lowered my voice. "Nobody should have such a short-lived companion. Because..." Because it was an abominable waste. But Charlie was right there, mouth hanging open, and he hadn't done anything wrong. "Because you want as much time as you can get together."

Charlie turned around on himself a few times, embarrassed. "So what about the mouse?"

They both looked at me, expectant.

I thought: would the mind of a mouse not snap like a twig? "We'll come and talk to the mouse."

•

On the path downhill to the settlement, Lydia set her rat on the ground. "Would you go on ahead, Charlie?"

His head quested back and forth, sniffing the air, noting Arak drifting overhead. "Why?"

"I want to talk to Annest about something private."

It was a daft request—the wind was low, he'd have to go miles away to take himself out of earshot.

"Why can't I listen?" asked Charlie.

Now Lydia was the lecturing parent, and he was the defiant child. It amused me.

"It's just about me. I promise."

Lydia set him down on the path and he dawdled off across the slate chips and grass tufts. He'd learned spiky pride from her. Another reason to wait to join until you were older. The man is father to the beast, and vice versa.

"Will I be broken when Charlie dies?" asked Lydia.

I didn't want to lie. I didn't know for certain. I thought of my mother, after she'd lost her eagle. Less supple of mind, she had been, certainly. But she'd also been ground down by age, and ordinary misery.

"You'll still be growing," I said. "You might grow round the loss. And a rat!" I watched Charlie hopping ahead of us and pushed some enthusiasm into my voice. "You can learn a lot from a rat."

"I know. It's amazing."

Of course—Charlie had helped Lydia to wriggle in through my window. She'd made him stroppy, he'd made her twitchy and nosy. What mutual bounty. Absolutely worth the bloody risk.

"There you go," I said. "You'll keep that, you'll keep whatever you get from your companion."

"So it's not all bad?"

She was still looking for a way to be right. I didn't answer. Arak, above us, pretended not to hear.

On the grass ahead of us girl was sitting—younger than Lydia. A girl in green, surrounded by brown blobs. The blobs loped around her and she reached out her hands to them.

Lydia tutted. "That's Tammy. She has rabbits."

The rabbits hopped one by one over the kid's feet. I heard the child laughing. Rabbits.

"A whole pack of them," Lydia said, disdainfully. "But they don't live long, so she has to keep getting more."

I walked faster, my boot-heels grinding into the mud. Gods, where would it stop? "How many has she had?"

"Maybe a dozen?"

"And they were all her companions."

"Yeah, they all talked."

"They all *talked...*"

The child had gathered up three of the bunnies into her arms and was whispering into their soft long ears.

The rabbits spotted us first, to give them credit. As Arak's shadow fell on them, they cried out.

"Nooo!"

"No! Run! Nooo!"

The squeaking throng then tried to hide under the child's skirts. Arak swooped down to settle on my shoulder.

"The bird won't hurt you," I called.

Were the child's eyes were blank with fear, or a permanent malady? She scrambled to her feet and ran for the settlement. The rabbits ran with her.

"I thought Tammy had so many rabbits because she was stupid," said Lydia. "Do you think she's stupid because she's had all those rabbits?"

I watched the pale green fleeing figure, with its low-bobbing honour guard. If a young child lost a part of herself, what would she do? Reach out to things that had soothed her in the past. Get more rabbits. She'd feel unspeakable loss and a little bit of solace, again and again until her mind was gone.

"This is why my family are bird people," I said. "Not bloody mouse people or half-a-dozen-rabbits people. Go on ahead, find me the mouse."

When Lydia had run off ahead, I said to Arak: "We'll have to put the fear into the parents." She was running her beak through the hair above my ear. "Or they won't stop their kids from doing it."

"Oh, I don't know." Arak raised her wings to steady herself as I walked faster in a temper. "Maybe the settlers will do it differently."

Her wing-feathers tickled my ear. "No. How?"

"Maybe they'll have mice, as children..."

"And lose them." Shards in my heart at the thought.

"And bear the grief, and meet another animal when they're grown. Maybe they'll join with shoals of fish, and flocks of songbirds..."

"That is a real child, down there, with a real rat. A ball of mange that'll agree with everything she says and die in a year. You're fantasising!"

Her wings sliced the air and made me wince. I'd learned so much from her, but never when to leave an argument.

I'd thought she'd be appalled—a bond squandered on a rat. But then I remembered: she expected to die first. She'd never known a bird lose its companion, while I knew many people who lived on after their animals died.

I called up to Arak. "What can you even learn from a rabbit?"

"What can you learn from a bird?" she called down to me.

"Patience. As you know, my love."

"You can't learn it well, though, clearly."

"These kids don't want to learn. They want talking pets."

"No! They want to be here."

"They are here. See?"

We'd reached the settlement houses: built from old slate sheep pens, given wood walls, decently thatched. You couldn't skimp on the roof in this wet part of the world.

"Their parents tell them that this place is temporary. Yes?" Arak shot off again, zooming along the long line of hills, with the sun making the wet grass sparkle. Then returned to hover above me, still not forgiving me. "Imagine living here your whole life, and being told it's temporary. Children need more than that. When they join an animal, they're saying they want to stay here. They're trying to tie themselves to this place."

"By mockery and stealing."

"Strange theft. What do we lose?"

"I know, I know," I cried, to stop her talking. "I am intolerance incarnate!"

I hoped Arak was wrong. Because I would tell settlers they should leave. Because they treated every final agreement as an opening bid, and this was too serious to haggle over.

"The child is so stubborn," I said. "And prickly."

Arak croaked with laughter. "Of course! And of who does she remind me…?"

I imagined Charlie the rat wrapped in a handkerchief and laid tenderly in a hole in the ground. Poor Lydia. "She's tied herself to sorrow."

"She'll go far."

The thatch rustled on the nearest house. Two sleek and pointed heads popped out of the eaves and regarded me. Black rats, who live in groups.

"Charlie talked to us. He said you think we shouldn't be here," one of them accused. "Do we have to leave Lydia?"

More rustling told me that others awaited my answer. Of course, that is the first thing anyone would learn from a rat: the more of you, the better.

"No. You can go to her." They still hung back. "I swear the bird won't hurt you. Oh, and can you tell me—how smart is a mouse, compared to a rat?"

"Oh, really stupid."

"So stupid!"

They chorused their agreement as they poured out from the bushes and down from the eaves, forming a river of fur that wound ahead of me, down the path into the settlement.

•

In a horse shed, in the end, we found them. The horses stamped and stirred, resenting our intrusion. A child stood with its back to us, and he looked hardly large enough to walk, staring down at a dot that zipped to and fro across the straw-strewn floor. I heard words from it, I think: high pitched, half-formed. I had an unworthy wish that Arka would swoop on the dot and make an end of it.

"This is Will," Lydia whispered, pointing to the wobbling child.

"Can he catch it?" I asked.

"Can he call the creature?" Arka corrected.

Lydia stooped on her knees by Will to coax him. Her court of rats around her waited. She murmured a long time in Will's ear, and in the end, he piped up: "Come here!"

The dot didn't stop. It tightened its orbit, it zig-zagged less wildly, but it never stopped jittering. Circled closer and closer until Will grabbed up it and closed his hands around it.

Will faced us and his eyes were like a child in a fever that will kill him. What had he learned from the mouse? Endless hunger, and fear of every damn thing. What had the mouse learned from Will? Knowledge of its own insignificance, the strength of its predators. Even the glimpses that Will had of time, and distance, were of such great scope that the mouse could not comprehend them. Now the creature was strained to breaking, and Will was twisted up in its destruction.

"Give me your friend," I said.

He didn't trust me, or Arak on my shoulder, but he was too frightened to refuse. I cupped my hands, and he let the mouse drop into them.

It bumped at me feebly, not half as strong as Charlie.

I was holding a rodent. I could crush it, easy as kneading bread.

I was holding Will's companion. A cracked thing, but a thing still rational. Knowing that, could I destroy it?

I put my mouth to my hands as if praying, and spoke to the splinter of reason wedged in its tiny skull. "Small friend. Leave now, and find peace, and let Will go."

I counted my own heartbeats, up to nine. I felt Arak leaning in to press against me. The dot stopped struggling against my fingers. When it wasn't moving, it was almost too light for me to feel it.

As Will shuffled up to claim the limp scrap of fur, I looked into his face. He was heartbroken, of course, but was the rest of him intact? Lydia's face was stone, and her arms were crossed, and the beasts flowed up and down from her shoulders to her feet, trying to soothe her.

I should have said to her: You know why you chose me, you know why you brought me here. What you couldn't do, I did, quickly and kindly. Friends, are we, now, or are you my enemy?

But I was uncertain. Maybe the mouse had heeded my words, or maybe died of fear or suffocation. I walked out, and Arak took flight, and I followed my love home.

•

After I buried Arak under my doorstone, I did not wish to cross it.

After a week, she came. She did not knock, but paced across the room in her long gown with many pockets, and set down fresh bread on my table. "If you don't come to the market hall soon, they will make me Alderman in your place," she said.

"Excellent, you would be. How could any trader cozen his neighbour, when you have all your spies?" There were protests from her pockets, so I said it again. "That is what you get from rats. Spying. You have ears all over the town."

"I don't deny it. But have you known me to misuse it?" She looked me in the eye while the skirts of her gown twitched and billowed.

"In fairness," I said, "I have not."

"And that is not what the rats gave me," she said.

"Oh, no?"

"No. Fellowship, community."

"And fleas?"

She smiled. She was magnificent, always, but she scared me. Too alert, too canny. I wondered, whenever I saw her: was she a spectacular shell, hollowed out, grief by grief? Or had my love been right, with her pretty visions of a child harmlessly companioning a flock of songbirds? And now she was a fine young woman. I couldn't judge it.

"You can't make me leave that easily." She unloaded her bag of every kind of vegetable, oat biscuits and a round of cheese. The girl has done well for herself.

"I don't want all that."

"The biscuits are not for you."

From her pocket, she scooped two balls of fur.

After she left, I said to them: "Your names, then, what are they?"

"Bob."

"Jenny."

I sighed. "I am not good company."

I had never before seen a rat shrug. "We'll talk amongst ourselves," said Jenny.

Missing Episodes

Room 128 was full of zombies. John flinched, but pushed on down the corridor.

In Room 125 a three-armed woman swung a sword, while her friends tried to play a card game.

Room 139: a girl with kingfisher-coloured hair hissed *"My girlfriend's got a missing episode!"*

A missing episode! John's stomach fluttered. It was good to be back at a Con, where kids got excited about snowy clips from long-dead shows.

Room 142 was John's room. His stomach kept on flipping as he let himself in. John found it hard to tell his emotions apart, despite exercises from numerous acting coaches (*Where is it in your body, John? Sit with it!*). Excitement and stage-fright and lust—they all tugged at his guts and made him jittery.

Was he excited? He'd looked forward to this event for weeks, homesick for a hotel he'd never visited before. It was Con space itself that he missed, that temporary kingdom. John came to a convention at least four times a year.

Was he feeling lustful? Not for the zombies, or the card players, but for the trappings of the hotel room, the white towels waiting to be messed up. He distracted himself by unpacking. There'd be none of that, not at this Con. He'd even booked twin beds—no cosy double.

He felt a definite pang in his guts. Maybe it was food poisoning, from the plane.

John changed into a T-shirt that referenced a recent film, one that he'd not acted in—the fans liked to know that he was a fan, too. The shirt hung loosely around his chest. His roles these days weren't very muscular. He was cast as the librarian, the monk, the teacher. No critics clamoured for him to be the first black Bond. Meanwhile, bloody Adam was playing the action hero, the romantic lead. Would that change, since Adam's announcement?

John's stomach twisted viciously, and he realised the truth: it wasn't lust or botulism, but loss. Normally, Adam would have been at this convention. With John in the bar, at a tactful distance, and later in this room, at no distance at all. They only ever met at conventions, kissing in bland rooms like this.

But at this convention, there'd be no Adam. For the first time in his life, at the age of thirty, John had been dumped.

•

The lizard-woman staffing the check-in desk grinned as she passed John his lanyard. "Good to have you here!" It was nice to be liked.

John checked the schedule. He was booked for a panel tomorrow: "Queer Representation—Does It Get Better?" And he'd be doing a turn in the cabaret with another Crewmate, a guy who'd been on the show back in the seventies, George. They might do some tapdancing. Everyone loved it when actors danced.

The Con map showed a grid of boring conference rooms, rechristened with vivid names: *Mordor, Earthsea, The Hexarchate*. By the end of the weekend, the bland hotel would be a fantastical city, with distinct neighbourhoods and dodgy backstreets.

John wanted to feel that transformative enthusiasm. He steered back to room 139, to hear more about the missing episode.

"Mr Collins! John!" The blue-haired girl inside the room spotted him.

Her green-haired friend tried to quiet her. "Leave him alone, Violet!"

"He can always say no!"

"I can say no," John confirmed, but he already wanted to say yes. They were teenagers, one glamorous and gothic, the other sturdy and nerdy. Both of them were five foot tall, a butch-femme hobbit couple.

I'm Violet," said the blue-haired glamour-girl. "This is Morgan. She's got missing episodes of the Captain's Adventures. You're in one!"

"Great! I'll find a room. Let's have a show!"

Violet began hyperventilating with glee. Morgan seemed far less enthusiastic, but she swung her army-surplus rucksack onto her back and followed them.

John tried the door-handles of conference rooms until he found *Mordor* unlocked, and empty except for some half-drunk wine bottles.

"Hurrah!" cried Violet. "Bottoms up!"

From her rucksack, Morgan brought out a slab-like laptop. She stared at its screen with great concentration from under the fringe of her old-school bowl cut, while John plugged her laptop into the room's AV and set the projector humming.

Glistening white noise erupted from the room's speakers, followed by the Captain's theme tune. The lilting strings still gave John the tingles. The show was a nautical-infused sci-fi adventure—a space *ship*, do you see? So a spooky sea shanty had topped and tailed every episode, from the show's genesis in the 1970s, up to the present day.

The first voice he heard was his own, but soprano. "Heeeelp!" John tried not to cringe. The big screen filled with John's face (probably fifteen years old, but playing younger) menaced by stock footage of rats.

"That's *The Paws of Death*!" John exclaimed. First broadcast in 1998, maybe? The fans would know.

"Oh God," said Violet. "It's the one with the cave!"

She doubled over, and John knew why she was laughing. Halfway through *Paws of Death*, John and his Crewmate (played by Adam) got trapped in a cave. Rocks tumbled inwards, crushing them closer to one another. The scene held a sacred place in a lot of fans' coming out stories: *I was disappointed when they got rescued! Then I realised...* The original footage was missing, so fans had recreated and embroidered it in their imagination. It had been re-enacted wherever gay men on holiday found caves. At one Con, John had seen fan art for sale, with he and Adam aged to their twenties and stripped to the waist. He'd blushed terribly, and couldn't work out how to purchase it anonymously.

Violet nudged Morgan. "We used to play *Paws of Death* in the coat cupboard, when we were kids..."

"But you were too young to see it," said John. Maybe not even born when it was first shown.

"I had the novelisation," Morgan admitted.

"Skip to the saucy bit!" Violet seized the laptop controls. John let himself wonder: would the scene look any good? Had his (then unrequited) feelings for Adam lent it poignancy?

God, it was terrible. The budget had been low in those seasons just before the post-Millennium reboot. But John couldn't blame the cheap sets for his lacklustre acting: young John just looked like he might vomit. Would Adam (aged eighteen) do better? No, he was equally laughable, facing down death by tossing his floppy fringe as far as the cave's papier-mâché boulders allowed.

"Ooh, I can't *bear* the tension," wailed Violet.

John reflected that the sexy fan art had been an unearned compliment.

Then it hit him: there were no pictures of him and Adam as a couple, and now no chance to make any. But if Morgan had lost episodes, they would show years of him and Adam, mid-nineties to early noughties, growing up together on film…

"Where's the episode come from?" John asked.

"Morgan's got a listening device," said Violet.

"What? How does it work?"

"It picks up old signals." Morgan's pride overcame her reserve. "Echoes. I just get the device to listen for the theme tune. I walk around under the big transmitters: Crystal Palace, Emly Moor."

"But how…"

"It's just a hobby." Morgan was already closing the laptop lid.

"She's got a thing for enormous masts!" cackled Violet.

Morgan looked exasperated, but John understood: Violet was doing her girlfriend a favour, distracting John from asking questions. He took the hint.

Violet leaned in to John. "We could do a screening. Would you introduce it?"

It was nice to be liked. But it was perilous for his career to lean on his Crewmate years too heavily, to suggest that those shoddy moments were his glory days.

"I shouldn't," John said. "But—can I show a friend?"

•

George was at the bar, in a deep tan and a red suit, with a sprig of chest hair and a cat-like smile.

"I like the gear, George."

"John-boy!" George grabbed him round the chest. "John…" His voice was so bass that it shivered your timbers.

"I'm up to date on your latest season," John said. George had pottered around playing bit-parts for decades, but recently hit gold with a small cult show in the States. He played Satan, punching angels for the soul of a dewy-faced teen lead. At the age of fifty, he'd found himself with a following.

"You like it?"

Compliments were hard between actors. You told everyone they were marvellous, so you had to be specific to sound sincere. "Your voice is amazing! *I will destroy you, puny...*" He coughed.

"It's hell on the vocal cords."

"And I saw four people dressed as you, at London Comic Con." One kid and three dads, but George needn't know that.

"Oh, that's not my doing. That's the costume department, and the cosplay kids love anything in a suit."

George often scrupulously shared the credit, deflecting attention from himself, and John wondered if that came from his rocky start in the trade. He'd been a Crewmate of the Captain, and one of the first Indian characters on British TV—but not one of the first Indian actors. He was part of a Greek family, from Peckham. He'd talked about the brownface casting in interviews: "Big mistake, nasty, harmful. It was the 70s, I was twelve, it was my big break. Shouldn't have done it. Nah, I never watch it." He'd actively asked for the few extant episodes not to be released on DVD. Most of his current fans didn't know he'd travelled with the Captain.

"That reminds me, I saw a kid dressed as you, John," George said, "A moment ago. Good uniform. With his own little blonde friend..." George's brows lowered. "Are you alright, John?"

"Yeah. I've got something for you to see..."

"I mean, are you *alright*." George's voice sunk into a rumble. "I heard about Adam."

Nobody else had asked him that, checked in with him, laid a hand on his shoulder. John realised it was the first time anyone had treated him as an interested party to Adam's love life. Loss surged up and made him weak.

"If you need someone to talk to..." said George.

"No thanks. No need."

He'd told George about Adam, years ago. George had been maudlin about his marriage; his wife hated that George was always filming on location. John had spilled the beans in a moment of fellow-feeling. But George had been agog.

"You and Adam only get together at sci-fi conventions? But they're *months* apart! How do you do it?"

John had wanted to ask: How could you do it any other way? Lust was distracting and all-consuming. How on earth could you move around a set, deliver lines, when your body tingled and your mind was in the gutter? How could you integrate it into your life?

But Adam had bloody integrated it. Adam had got married.

Adam had come out, in fact, by releasing exclusive wedding photos through GQ magazine. Adam and his groom, some boy-band bell-end, wore dazzling white suits.

Because of that, George was offering his satanic shoulder for John to cry on. Loving the chance to sound older and wiser. Fortunately, John had a distraction prepared. “Come and see what I found!”

He dragged George back to *Mordor.*

“Oh my God Mr Lampros!” Violet held out her hand, and George bowed over it. “We’ve got an episode of the Captain with you in it.”

“Pleased to meet you. No, you haven’t.”

“It’s *Fate of the Skrandib*!”

George lowered his Mephistophelian eyebrows. “Prove it.” He picked up Violet’s wine bottle and agitated the dregs. “Well, it’s not worth leaving *that*...”

Morgan opened her laptop reluctantly, and John peered over her shoulder at the files. “Is it that one?” He dabbed at an icon.

The face that popped up on the projector screen looked like John, but it wasn’t. It was an echo, another teen boy in an updated version of the uniform.

“Hey, it’s that cosplay kid I told you about!” cried George. “I saw him, here at the Con.”

The kid was running through a ravine, feet slipping on the loose rocks, face contorted with fear.

“It’s a fan film,” said Morgan. “It’s nothing.”

She could be right. Anyone who wanted to could film himself running around a quarry. But then *whoosh,* the ship appeared, space-sails billowing. High budget for a fan film, or a clever blend with some official footage. A melodic whistle sent shivers up John’s spine. The boy was a Crewmate, he was being piped aboard...

The screen blanked. “Sorry,” said Morgan. “This is the right one.”

Now the screen showed George, small and bellowing, in the saturated colours of 1970s film and the corduroy flares of 1970s fashion. “Blimey!” George chuckled. “They liked to watch us scream, didn’t they, John?”

At least George had developed a jaw, since his childhood, and beetling brows—in middle age, he’d become positively saturnine. The round face of the child star was useful when you were fifteen-playing-twelve, but a hindrance afterwards, John found. (Adam had never been spud-faced, had always been handsome.)

Small George ran across a heath, chased by cat people, yelling, his accent somewhere between Calcutta and Camberwell.

"Put it away," sighed George.

"Mr Lampros, we were wondering about a screening…" Violet tilted her head and batted her eyelashes.

"Now. If you two are such big fans, you know why that's a bad idea."

"Told you so," said Morgan.

"But it's a period piece!" protested Violet.

"Look. I could say, let's keep this a friendly Con, everyone feeling welcome. But I'll admit it: I'm selfish." He caught Violet's eyes, his voice hypnotic. "I just wanna be the devil, this weekend. Not get stuck in the past. I'd consider it a *personal favour* if you didn't show that episode."

"OK, Mr Lampros." Morgan replied immediately, shutting down her machine and shoving it back into the rucksack.

Violet pouted. "But isn't there a way we could…"

"Call me George," said George. "Here…" He fished in his pocket. "You wanna dress up? Nobody else has got one of these, yet."

George dangled a chunky silver pendant on a chain, lowered it into Violet's palm. "You too, here you go." His big fingers unthreaded his own pentagram cufflinks and passed them to Morgan, who turned them over warily in her palm. George winked.

The two young women drifted out of the room as if mesmerised.

"That was generous," said John.

"It's only merch. Made out of tin."

"And sinister. Were you flirting?"

"No, I was bloody not! I was *performing*, Johnny, you should try it. They get a good story out of it, nobody has to watch that old rubbish, everyone's happy."

John felt reassured by his vehemence. George, of all people, knew when to move on. He wouldn't keep dredging up the past. He wouldn't keep grilling John about Adam.

"Actually, I had something to give you, too…" George looked around him. "Bugger. Left it in the bar."

"No offense, but I don't wear jewellery."

"Wait, John, don't go." George sounded uncertain. Was he going to get emotional, again? "I know you're busy, but would you read a script for me?"

"Of course!" Normally it would be an imposition, but as an alternative to discussing Adam, it was a relief.

"Great! You know I wanna direct? I've found a little online series. I need a second opinion, and you pick good projects."

"Do I?"

"Yeah! Your films aren't crap." George slid a sheaf of papers from his jacket pocket. "Ta! Where are you headed, anyway?"

"Back to the bar?" John began walking.

"Headed *professionally*, John."

"I'm in a fantasy film in Iceland, next month. I'm a monk."

George slapped his back. It was like being hit by a side of beef. "It's not the lead, is it? Is that what you want to be, Johnny? A bit-part monk?"

That rankled. Why was George dishing out professional advice, when his success as Satan had been so recent, so serendipitous? When he'd spent decades as a jobbing actor, just like John. "What's it to you, Beelzebub? You're not my agent."

"You're doing what I did, John: one thing after another, no plan. Don't you want to put down some roots? I bloody do."

John remembered, after the death of his father, asking Adam: do you want to meet for Christmas? He'd been thinking of staying in a hotel, not visiting Adam's flat, or hosting him. Adam had said no. And John had felt—bereft? Relieved? It was hard to remember an unspoken emotion.

"Are you chatting me up, George?"

"You're a sarcastic beggar, John. But you know I'm right. You want to try a TV series."

"Nah. " TV series could drag on for years, and they hung around, like the signals Morgan picked up. You got typecast. Better to be a one-off monk.

"Hey! Here's that thing I got you." George stooped to the floor between two barstools, scooped a plastic bag and proudly presented it to John.

Peering in, John saw cotton fabric and screen-printed letters. Like half the Con attendees, George was trying to communicate something important using a slogan T-shirt. It probably read *Satan's side-kick*.

•

Too early the next morning, John sat alongside his fellow panellists. The hungover audience facing them wore a lot of rainbow clothing.

John got many invitations to speak about diversity. At first, he'd discussed black characters and industry racism. More recently, and tentatively, queer characters and industry homophobia.

Adam hadn't liked that. But because Adam had never allowed any discussion of 'us', he had no vocabulary to object to John's new hobby. Realising this, John had become maliciously gleeful.

"But why do you care if I come out, Ad?" he'd mused aloud. "I mean, it's not going to reflect on you, is it? We're not in that kind of..." Adam had literally held his breath, as though John was pointing a gun that said 'relationship'. "...*thing*."

Adam had ignored him for a whole day. It had been worth it.

Now John felt less playful. The central question the chair kept asking—*are things getting better?*—felt like a dig. *Is John getting better?* He was never out of work. His work wasn't crap (thanks, George). But was it good enough?

Occupied by this personal inventory, John kept silent until the chair questioned him directly. "When you were young, John, did you have any role models?"

Was that a coded question about Adam? "It was like Fermi's paradox," John said. "If there were other black gay people, why hadn't I heard from them?" The audience chuckled—he'd thought they'd like that.

"Would you ever want to play the Captain?"

John gave the standard answer: happy times, never rule it out. He was surprised when his stomach fluttered. Anxiety, loss, stage fright?

Then he saw himself at the back of the room, a youthful ghost. It was the cosplay kid, that teenager who was dressed as young John. The kid whose face had popped up on Morgan's laptop, in the high-quality fan video. He had raised his hand with a question.

"Did you mind the way Adam's character was always bossing you around?"

Some sniggering broke out, but John shrugged, answered it straight. "He was older than my character."

"I always hated that, how the white kid gave the orders and you were always, *yes, no, straight away*. Didn't you ever try to change that?"

John hadn't expected the question to be so pointed. Don't get defensive. "No. It didn't seem strange to me. But yeah, someone cast us that way round, right? Could have had an older black kid, bossing Adam around."

He was passing the buck slightly. He'd loved Adam: older, stronger, handsome Adam. So he hadn't minded following Adam's orders. He wasn't going to tell that to the righteous fan. The kid whispered to another teenager sitting beside him, his friend, dressed as Adam with his iconic floppy fringe.

Remembering the fan video that Morgan had found, and working on a hunch, John asked: "Do you act?"

The kid nodded.

"Good luck." It was sincere, but it was also a jab back at him. Good luck with your ethics when you're trying to make a living. And when you're older and less cute—good luck then, too.

"Thanks," said the kid. "And sorry about Adam."

Man, that kid had nerve. John could feel his skin turn icy. Maybe the cold was radiating from the panellists on either side of him, who had frozen with embarrassment. The audience were silent and staring at John, mouths open. Whatever he said next would surely have to deny or confirm. He'd never done either, before. But why shouldn't he speak about it, now? Adam had never acknowledged their relationship enough to ask for John's silence.

The panel chair cleared his throat, prepared to change the topic. John looked down at his shaky hands. Loss felt a lot like a hangover.

"Hey, no," he said. "Congrats to Adam, right? He's come a long way. At least his hairstyle looked better, in that GQ shoot."

The audience laughed at that. Laughed at the breaking of the tension, but also laughed at Adam. Not at John, the juvenile sell-out, the grown man who'd never been in a proper relationship, who'd just been dumped by a film star.

It made John's heart swell. In the break-up, it seemed that he'd got custody of these fans.

•

What do you do, at the end of the evening, John wondered, if you're not going to have sex? He wandered the Con space, looking for answers.

The bar had been settled by bearded men discussing 900-page novels. John had privately dubbed it 'Fantasy Island'. In the foyer, kids in futuristic costumes were taking photos against a wall of mirrors. Board-gamers asked John to game with them. LARPers ran past: "Come and play football on the beach, mate!"

"It's dark!"

"It's OK, we set the ball on fire!"

Why wasn't this fun? It was usually fun: the easy drifting, the smiles without commitment. John would usually follow a quest or two, whether it was fiery football or a singalong or a deep chat with a stoned teen fan. But tonight, each nod of recognition felt like a parody of friendship.

John slunk away.

Outside 139, Morgan was lying on the carpet, head on her backpack.

"Lost your key?"

"Lost Violet. She's got our key." Her gaze wandered and her dull straight hair was ruffled.

John felt a flood of drunk sympathy. "Stay with me!"

Morgan looked unsure. Wouldn't anyone who'd used a device to track down the Captain's lost Adventures would know John was gay? Plus the idea of chatting up a teenager was appalling to John, but the Con probably had its share of lecherous older guys. "I've got two single beds," John clarified. "It's Con hospitality, it's a sacred obligation thing. I'm going straight to sleep, I'm wiped out."

She looked at her bag and then back at him. He thought he could read her expression: she didn't mind sleeping in a corridor, but she didn't want to risk losing her laptop. She stood up. "OK. Thanks."

Inside the room, Morgan placed her bag on one bed and lay beside it, and John flopped onto the other without turning the lights on. As soon as John's body was still, he felt his guts churning, hungry for something.

"Morgan, could we watch another episode?"

"No." It was dark, but John could picture her stubborn hobbit face. "I shouldn't have brought them, it was Violet's idea. I'm not showing any more."

God, he'd given her a bed for the night. Didn't she have any sense of community? "How do you get them?"

"It's echoes, I told you. I just walk around under the big towers."

"The receiver, the thing that picks up the messages—where did you get it?" Maybe John could do it himself, make his own secret archive.

"You can't have one, I made it." He could hear her wrestling to get under her duvet, wondered if the bag was under there with her.

"From a kit?"

"I invented it!" Morgan snapped. "God, this place! Everyone's wearing T-shirts with science-sounding slogans on them, but nobody actually *makes* anything, nobody even tries. They don't—oh, never mind."

Morgan had clearly wandered the Con and not found her people. Plus, her girlfriend had gone AWOL. John felt a flicker of guilt . Morgan wouldn't have told him the truth if she hadn't been pissed off. Well, he understood now, why she was so protective of her haul. If he apologised, maybe she'd sell him some of the old episodes.

"Sorry," said John.

"Don't tell anyone."

"I won't, I won't tell anyone."

Silence from the other bed.

"Got any plans for tomorrow?" John asked. Always a good ice-breaker question, at a Con.

A pause, and then an answer, less angry and more sleepy. "Giant squid mega-LARP."

"How big is the squid?"

"Really, really big..." Morgan started to snore.

John found his stomach pangs had lessened, and the urge to see an old episode, as well. It felt good to have a room-mate. It stopped him brooding on Adam's absence. And maybe he could borrow the receiver, or pay Morgan to make him one of his own.

As he drifted off, John imagined a transmitter astride a hilltop, like one of HG Well's tripods. Morgan walked beneath it, strapped about with dishes and antennae. John tried to reach out to take her kit from her, convinced it could direct him or advise him. But Morgan walked away from him, chasing the sea shanty on the wind.

•

The next morning, John left Morgan asleep, and took his fluttering stomach for a walk.

Across the foyer, he saw the boy. The boy from the panel audience with the awkward questions, who was also the boy from Morgan's fan film. He knew he had to speak to him. He started walking, finding justifications as he went: they could discuss acting, politics, casting! John could ask him about the fan film, how they'd done it, where they got the budget.

But as John moved, the boy ducked out of the big hotel doors, heading for the seafront.

Scrambling to follow him, John collided with everyone in the foyer. He smudged body-paint from a crowd of green Skrull, apologised. By the time he reached the door, someone's cape was caught in it. Finally outside, the sea-front wind clobbered him. He couldn't see the boy. Crashing around on the shingle, he discovered only dog-walkers. And what if he'd found the kid? No stranger to obsessive fan behaviour, John knew he'd blown it: this was no friendly chat, he was chasing a boy, his ghost, down an English beach in winter.

Turning back to the hotel, he saw the boy, hunched beside the main door. He'd been there all along, trying to spark up a cigarette.

John walked over, took George's script out of his pocket and held it like a windbreak for the cigarette. It worked—the cigarette lit.

"Thanks, John. You can go now." The boy grinned. "Joking! I'm Sean." He had chutzpah. How old was he? His spud face would let him play younger roles, but now John looked properly, he guessed Sean was somewhere in his mid-twenties. *Interesting*, said John's lust. John took a step backwards.

"I don't often see anyone dressed as my old character."

"My friend plays Adam. We've got a whole routine."

"Excellent. Look, this is weird, but I've seen that film of you. On the ship, and everything."

"My audition tape?"

Sean had auditioned? He could become a Crewmate! John felt excitement bubble up, on Sean's behalf. For all the fascinating work ahead, all the opportunities that would open up for him. John knew he should drop the subject, admit that he hadn't known about the audition, but he needed to hear more. So he nodded. "Just a clip."

"Damn! Are you part of the new series?"

"No, I just—a friend of a friend showed me. It looked good."

Sean sagged with relief. "OK. Do you know anything? I've not heard back yet."

"They must be impressed by you, to take you for an outdoor shoot."

"What? We didn't go outdoors. Was it green screen?"

"No, I saw..." He'd seen the gravel slipping beneath Sean's feet.

"Must have been someone else, then." Sean sucked at his cigarette. "Shit. They must have done another round. And they didn't ask me back."

Sean sulked and smoked in silence while John's mind spun.

When Sean stubbed out his cigarette, John managed to say: "Come with me. Just for ten minutes."

It was fun, to have a mission, and search the Con from dealer's room to disco, with Sean as his confused side-kick. Sean obligingly asked, "Where are we going?" and "But what are we looking for?", echoing John's finest lines from when he'd been a Crewmate. Morgan was elusive: not drinking in Fantasy Island, or posing by the mirrored wall.

John found her back in his own room, deep in a book.

"Sorry, John," she said. "Can I stay here? I needed a break."

"Of course! Morgan, this is Sean—he's in that weird clip you've got. With the ship. Can you show him?" He heard his own voice, trying too hard for a casual tone.

Morgan flared into incredulous anger. "No! I told you!"

"It was his audition tape! You should let him see what they did to it." Even as he said it, John didn't believe it. It wasn't Sean's audition, it was something else: a snippet of possibility, a clue.

"God, no!" She was standing, and hoisting her bag onto her shoulder. "It's not."

"Not what?" asked Sean.

"Not available." Her face closed up.

"But I need it!" It wasn't the past that he needed: not Adam, not nostalgia. That had been a temporary weakness. John knew, now, that what he really needed was a future. And this missing episode, this film of Sean, had a connection to the future.

Morgan barged past them to the door. "You don't get to boss me around. I only let Violet do that." Over her shoulder, from the corridor, she called back: "And I don't have it any more, all those files got corrupted."

Fair enough, thought John. If she was going to lie, he could cheat.

•

"It's a surprise, for Morgan!" John saw Violet soften as his flattery warmed her. "Go on, let us in the room for five minutes."

In the middle of the afternoon, John had spotted Morgan in the boardgame space, without her bag. He knew there was only one safe place she'd have left it. He should have felt guilt when Violet handed over her key, or when he tracked down Sean in the dealer's room, and the guy regarded him with deep suspicion. But John's body was ringing with lust, or excitement, or anticipation. In Violet and Morgan's room, as he rummaged under the bed for Morgan's laptop, it grew into an intolerable yearning.

He looked for the one episode that he'd played by accident. He saw a similar file-name, then another. God, there were dozens of them…

The theme tune lilted, the fuzz cleared, and the chase began. Onscreen, Sean hurtled across an alien moonscape like he was born to it, until he reached the ship and gasped the classic plea: "Let me in! They're after me!"

"That's me," Sean said. He sounded as badly shaken as his character. "But I never filmed that. Never." Sean slumped onto the bed, amid Violet's cast-off stockings. "I only auditioned last Thursday. It was in a studio, not on location. Is it CGI?" Sean started to laugh. "Why would they steal my face? I'm really cheap! What *is* this?"

It was a gravel pit, a hackneyed script, and a logical impossibility.

And now, on the laptop screen, Sean was inside the ship. John glimpsed another familiar face in the background of the scene.

"Could you keep a look-out at the door, Sean?"

"Nah, I'm not missing this."

The familiar actor, off to one side, looked like John's father. How? His father had never acted, and his father was dead. The man bounded centre-screen:

a big beard over a sleek uniform. John rubbed his own chin and wondered.

"Come, my Crew!" the man called, full of lively menace. He spun the ship's wheel and roared with laughter. He had a vessel, and a mission, and a twelve-episode season. He was the happiest man in the galaxy.

Sean peered over John's shoulder. "Oh, wow. It *is*, isn't it?"

It wasn't John's father, of course. The actor's hair was greyer than John's—artificially grey?—and his shoulders were broader. But it was definitely John. Not an audition tape, he'd never auditioned for this. Not a fan film, or a charity special. It was a fully-fledged episode which hadn't yet been recorded.

And John's heart went double time, because now he knew what he needed and he had no idea how to get it.

"Oh, God!" Over the swelling incidental music, he heard Morgan swearing. "You bloody arsehole!"

She nearly trapped his fingers when she slammed the laptop shut. He tried to tell her, *be careful*, but she'd already knocked the device onto the carpeted floor. As John watched, she brought her boot down on the lid with a terrific crunch.

"No! Wait!"

"I didn't want anyone else to see that. You *knew* I didn't. You promised!" She sat on the floor, pulled a screwdriver from her pocket and started to jemmy off the back of the computer, deft and relentless.

Sean, understandably, ran for the open door.

"Christ, do you have to do that?" John begged. All those possible episodes, destroyed. She was spoiling his quest, stealing his future. He wanted to shout: You're a friendly hobbit! You're supposed to help me!

"I have to." From the exposed innards of the laptop, Morgan yanked out a flat black and silver box, a couple of inches long. She considered it for a moment, then laid it on the carpet and speared it with the screwdriver until it splintered.

John cried out: "I need to see it!"

"Tough!" She'd stopped her methodical wrecking, and her arms hung limply. "You know what that stuff is?"

John knew. And he had the words for it, too. He'd had to deliver cheesy lines like this in a dozen films: *they're transmissions from the future!* But without a script, he couldn't say it out loud. "I know what it looks like."

"Then you know I shouldn't have them, I shouldn't have been able to find them." She was right. It was a ludicrous power for a teenager. What if she could follow a different theme tune, and pick up the lottery show, or news broadcasts? "I should never have saved them. It's dangerous."

Of course, she was a sci-fi fan. She'd knew what happened to amateur scientists. She'd seen films where armed goons break down doors, and the inventor backs away from his workbench, his white coat lit up with red dots from laser-guided guns.

"Why show me any of them, then?" John demanded.

"I just wanted to have something to share with people—the old missing episodes. Not the other episodes, the ones with *you* in them. Violet talked me into bringing it. But I shouldn't have." She sighed. "It's funny, I really like the show. But you're being a *dick*. And now, you're going to be *him*? The Captain? You don't deserve it."

That was when the shame hit him. John had played an autopsied corpse, once, and seen himself pried open. This felt worse, more exposing and more painful. He knew why he'd done it. He hadn't just needed a glimpse of the future. He'd needed continuity in his life, and community. He'd needed to know that he could build something new out of what had gone, make new connections. But the need had come so suddenly that he'd misunderstood, and snatched at it.

He'd treated Morgan like a side-kick. Worse than a side-kick. She was trying to be stoic but tears were rolling down her nose and dripping onto the glittering debris.

"I'm sorry," said John.

"You should go now," said Morgan.

Back in his own hotel room, sweaty and remorseful, he tripped over the carrier bag George had given him. He pulled a T-shirt from it. Blue, star-dotted, with a shadow-outline of sails. Words rippled across the rigging: *I am the Captain of my fate.*

•

The first step was simple.

"George! You're right. I need your help, and you're right." John cornered him in a niche in the foyer.

"Good. Let's have a drink, brainstorm what to do next. Your agent, for a start..."

"George, it's OK. I know what I want." The old devil looked less cocksure. "I read your script."

"You did?"

"It's good." It was competent trash: familiar enough to find a fan base, but original and well-written enough to hold it. One role was particularly strong. "George. I want to play the antagonist. The baddy, the Warden."

"John! I swear that wasn't why I asked you."

"Nevertheless." It was exactly the right part to change John's image, get him a cult following. So when what he really wanted became available, he'd be front and centre. Maybe he'd have to put up with George putting on airs, giving John unsolicited advice, but maybe some of the advice would be good. Maybe it would be nice to work with someone who cared enough to lecture you.

George sucked his cheeks in. "It won't be what you're used to. No budget. We're going to be paying off priests and sneaking into crypts to film this, you know? No fancy catering..."

"It's like you said, George. I need a substantial role." And it would mean working with a team for months. Listening to them, compromising, to create something together. That also seemed like something John needed to do. He'd screwed Morgan over—so what? She had no power over him. He never had to see her again. But it had been far too easy to think that way, to treat her like an object, like an obstacle. He needed to change that habit, quick. To think more, to step back, to grab less. "I can audition. If you think I'm not right."

"No, John, I mean: we can't afford you. We're crowdfunded, for Christ's sake!"

"Mate's rates, then! Or I could help you raise the money? Find backers?"

"Really? It's a deal! It'll be so good to have you on board, John..."

John steeled himself against the compliments. It was nice to be liked, but it would be better to deserve it.

•

The second step was less successful, perhaps.

John found Sean smoking in front of the hotel.

"Sean! That clip we saw. You were right, it was CGI."

"Really?"

"I asked my friend. They knocked it up, to see how you'd look." That was something else he could try to fix: stop the story of the future episodes from spreading.

"That's creepy!" Sean was too smart to believe it entirely, but canny enough to let it slide. "So, they liked me?"

"I guess so."

"So you must have auditioned, too?"

John thought fast. "You can't tell a soul. Seriously, you're not just a fan, now. It's a professional thing, like a non-disclosure agreement."

"Calm down, mate! Of course I won't tell anyone."

"Cool. I might not be in it for a while. It might never even happen."

"This business, jeez! Are they getting Adam back, too?"

The question sent chills up John's back, but he breathed through them. "Not that I know." John realised that the absence of Adam—from the show, from his bed—made it possible for John to go back to the Captain's ship. With Adam, it would have just been more nostalgia. Without Adam, the return trip became a journey forwards. "Hell, they couldn't afford him."

"Good. He's rubbish."

It was mid-afternoon but the moon was visible, hanging pale over the sea. "You never get to see space, you know," John said.

"What?"

"You never see space the way the audience sees it. I auditioned as a Crewmate because I wanted to see strange planets."

"Yeah, but I'm not as stupid as you." Sean smirked.

It was embarrassing to admit, but now that he wasn't the ghost of John's former self, or a talisman of John's future, Sean seemed a lot less attractive. That was a relief. After all, they could end up working together.

Hey, they'd be working together. Maybe it wasn't too soon to get started on that. "Hey, Sean, you know you and your cosplay friend—can you dance?"

"Why?"

"What are you both doing tonight?"

•

The third step was the most public. You can watch the convention cabaret, yourself. It was recorded on a dozen devices.

First, there's Sean, running on in his retro uniform, with his blonde friend. Sean's playing to the audience: 'Adam' keeps giving him orders, Sean keeps telling him to stick it. The fans are drunk, the fans are having a great time, settling old scores.

Then the kids get trapped in a cave.

The cave walls are other fans, clad in corrugated cardboard, and they keep shuffling inwards. Until Sean and 'Adam' are squished together, and Adam makes a lustful lunge at Sean.

"Leave it out!" says Sean, "You're a married bloody man!"

Laughter erupts from the audience. Then, salvation for the perilous pair! The walls are sundered (one of the walls falls over and has to be helped offstage). It's the Captain! It's—

It's John, in a makeshift Captain's uniform. He has a manic energy that the fans lap up. On the serious lines he gazes out at the audience, as though he's searching for someone he can't see, someone he owes a debt to, or an apology. Even his fans admit he's acting a lot better than he did in his last few films. He's throwing everything he's got into it. It's like he's auditioning.

(It'll be four years before the Captain is re-cast. The director swears that none of the actors involved in tonight's revels could have known.)

"Poor boys! But which despicable fiend trapped you here?"

"It was I!" A bass growl, a flash of light and a billow of smoke, and George Lampros swaggers onstage. "Your old nemesis!"

"Not..."

"Yes! I'm the Ancient Mariner!"

"My old nemesis!"

"I already said that, dear," sighs George.

"Mariner," says John, "You will be defeated! With the power of *dance!*"

George and John perform a tap-dance face-off that drives the crowd into hysteria.

"Enough of that bollocks!" Sean clicks his fingers to change the music, and conjures up a routine with "Adam" that receives wild whoops, while George feigns back-ache and John holds him up.

After they all bow, the compère can't resist quizzing John. "So, you said yesterday that you wouldn't rule out playing the Captain?"

"Oh, I'm afraid I've changed my mind since then."

The audience moans. John smiles, he *grins*, knowing that his words will echo and echo. The fans will spread the news faster than a transmitter mast.

"Now I fully intend to be the Captain." Then his arrogance wavers. Later commentators will say, of his uncertainty: ***this is what he brings to the role, this is how he elevates it above pantomime.*** "I'll try to be a good one."

Anxiety

Freud is dreaming. White wolves chase him along a royal road.

But I've analysed this dream! He thinks as he runs down the fine straight roadway. *I know its meaning.* Slipping because there's no grip on his leather-soled shoes. *The wolves represented the patient's parents! I solved it...*

A furred weight hits him hard in the back, knocking him to the ground. Grit in his mouth and a snarl in his ear: "We are not your parents."

He wakes in sweat.

For months, Freud's dreams have been troubled by animals. They are all familiar to him: last night, for instance, he was pursued by the horse that represented Jung's sexual drives. The week before, it was the vulture symbolising Leonardo Da Vinci's mother.

Freud is lucid in his dreams, supremely aware of psychoanalytic principles. Unfortunately, so are the animals. They are offended by his interpretations, and confront him with their beastliness: their oily fur, their yellowing teeth, their stink. Beasts trample and peck him and insist they are not symbols but horses, birds, wolves.

Freud rises from his bed, rinses the sweat from his high forehead and from the white hair of his beard, and decides that this morning he will go out for coffee.

•

As Freud enters the Café Central, cold wind rustles the newspapers hanging on a rack. The *Berlin Vorwärts* has already been taken. Freud spots it, shivering unread on the table of another customer, a limp-haired threadbare young fellow. He steps forward to enquire if he might take it.

Three women enter the café, getting in Freud's way and fussing until it's too late: the young man has pulled the *Vorwärts* towards him to read it.

"May we join you?" asks one of the women.

The jostling women have penned Freud into a corner seat. "Of course." He gestures politely, cursing inwardly.

"It's so busy!"

But the café is half empty. The woman smiles at her lie. Her smile is a work of art, with a sculptural curve to her slick red lips.

Fear plucks Freud's sleep-starved nerves. This is a trap. His enemies have sent these women to discredit him, they will say: ***Freud meets loose women in cafés!*** But the women are not dressed for show, and they have an air of respectability. One of them—not the Smiler—looks like his mother, her face is the same gentle oval. ***Freud accosts strange women in public, and tells them they resemble his mother!***

"Are the cakes here any good?" asks the maternal woman, sounding pessimistic.

"Yes. Excellent." Freud is polite but not encouraging intimacy.

"I'll order one for our sister, as well," remarks the Smiler. "She's too busy to choose."

The third sister has sat at the same table with Freud, but is turned away, facing the forest of pillars. She stares at that tatty young man, the *Vorwärts* thief. Freud can only see the pale edge of her cheek, but she is beautiful. More beautiful than the Smiler, he would swear: less vulgar, more timeless. He wills her to turn round, to prove him right.

"You'd rather talk to our sister," observes the Smiler, impertinently.

He wants to belittle Smiler. It's puerile to tease a man for such an obvious impulse, to look at a beautiful woman. "Well, I would like to be introduced. That's inevitable. She is the best-looking woman here." He must watch his tongue, his enemies would have a field day with this conversation.

"Not a good idea to talk to her, though, dear Siggie," says Mother. She speaks kindly, but he feels the reprimand.

Freud is still staring, but not in the hope the third sister will turn round.

His gaze has become a tribute. There is a compulsion about the third sister. It is fitting to desire her, to adore her, to fling yourself at her feet. To *choose* her. His innards flutter, from chest to groin. With lust rises his indignation: Freud is aging, his hair is receding, but he knows he is charming, cultured, well-dressed. Why would this woman sit down with him—impose herself on him—then twist herself round in her chair, to stare at a rough youngster?

"She's not much of a conversationalist," sighs Smiler.

"Some women don't need to talk all the time," he snaps at the Smiler. "That can be very peaceful."

Why is the third sister staring so long at the limp-haired man? Freud drags his eyes aside to survey the lad. Barely in his twenties. Fraying collar, paint-stained wrists. One coffee and four glasses of water on the table beside him, that cheapskate trick! The boy has even pushed the paper aside, crumpling it carelessly as though the content displeased him. If he's not even going to read it, he should put it back on the racks.

The young man is equally careless of the regard of the third sister. He hasn't registered her attention, while Freud is feeling a passion for her that goes beyond lust. It's more primitive, more elementary, more instinctual. He wants her to lead him—where? A tranquil place. "What does she mean, by coming here and shunning me? Is she doing it to insult me?"

"Of course not, darling," insists Smiler. "Use your big brain. What else is inevitable? And silent? And terribly peaceful."

Freud finally understands what Smiler is hinting. The beautiful third sister is—something else, too. Something that is the end of all things. Even knowing it, his desire lingers.

He turns to the Mother, the more sympathetic of the two, who will tell him the truth. "Has she come to take me?" He can't accept that his time has come, not yet. He has done good work, but there's more to do, and he has yet to secure his legacy...

Mother laughs softly and pats at his arm. "No, Siggie. She came here for *him*." The Mother nods to the limp-haired man. Freud feels another blaze of jealousy.

"He's going to die?"

"No. He's one of her supporters," says Smiler.

"A murderer?"

"Worse. A politician."

"Will there be a war?"

Mother beams. "You were always clever!"

"Not the next war, though," corrects Smiler. "One of the ones after that."

The man seems an unlikely candidate. Not a politico, only a twitchy bohemian.

"She is protecting him from harm," says Mother.

"Until he can harm others," adds Smiler.

Freud lunges, desperate to see the silent woman's face. Her sisters sway to block him.

"You're keeping me away from them both."

"Yes."

"So I can't prevent her...? No! It's so I can't treat him! You know I could help him!"

The sisters laugh, wholeheartedly, humiliating peals echoing around the vaulted ceiling of the Café Central. Freud stands up and shoves past them, out of the corner table, out of the café.

The cold air snaps at him, carriages rattle past. All at once, he sees it: he has been hallucinating! Starved of sleep, full of coffee, he has had a surreal daydream. Not even a terribly original daydream: mythological sisters always come in threes. But so vivid!

He had wanted to help that young man, the other customer. He winces at how embarrassing that would have been, to offer his professional services on the basis of a hallucination.

At least it showed his zeal. Indeed, the whole daydream doubtless sprang from his dedication. Freud fears for the future of psychoanalysis; he has no worthy successor, the movement may founder. Fear of failure has generated both this hallucination, and his recent dreams, every one of those troubled animals.

And both the hallucination and the dreams show not his weakness, but his profound commitment. He strives to analyse, even when dreaming, or hallucinating! That surely betokens success?

Satisfied, Freud strides home.

Now he has solved the puzzle, he will certainly not dream of animals—not horses, not wolves, not lizards with their tails pulled off, snakes, spiders. All of them biting him, telling him: *We are not castration anxieties, male members, phallic mothers, proofs of your victory. We are the animals who live in your dreams.*

But it is in vain that an old man yearns for the love of woman as he had it first from his mother; the third of the Fates alone, the silent Goddess of Death, will take him into her arms.—Sigmund Freud, 1913

Uranus

The *RMS Carmania* stood at dock, serene despite the gull screams and mud stink. Christopher had left me watchdog to three trunks and a brace of hatboxes.

A lad rushed over to earn a tip.

"I saw yer friend,' he said, as he loaded the trunks onto a trolley. "Are you two artists?"

I would be leaving England within the hour. A queer impulse prompted me to announce: "No. We are Uranians."

To my surprise, he grinned.

"What, is that like a Martian? Are you two from another planet?"

It wasn't even the first time I'd heard this witticism. I began to hate Mr. H.G. Wells.

•

Being Uranians has led Christopher and me to travel a lot. Never fleeing in disgrace. Not yet. Not quite. Few trips came as near the knuckle as our escape to Paris, ten years ago.

Christopher and I had met at College (Trinity) but we hadn't been the best of friends, only two of a group. As we lost good men to marriage, we grew more intimate. Not loving, not on my part. Perhaps had he been taller, less hairy, less like an anxious mole... But why would all that matter, you ask, when Uranian love is for the noble disposition? (Plato told Christopher so, and Christopher told me.) At the time, I believed that nobility would shine through in some physical way: graceful movement, sparkling eyes. So I would love my beloved's mind, but my beloved would also be beautiful. I was insufferable.

Christopher took me out every week for art or opera. He gave me Uranian pamphlets, which I forgot to read, and poetry, which made me melancholy. In his presence I felt, always, that I was failing an examination.

Until one night when he burst into my rooms, hatless and agitated.

"He'll be arrested this evening!"

We were admirers of Oscar Wilde (you could have known it by our neckties alone). Oscar's libel case had just taken a disastrous turn.

Christopher cried: "We have to leave England!" He then made the most eloquent plea of his life. His proposal: we take the boat train that night to Paris, to live where laws were more liberal.

I'd been torn between two idols, until that moment. Should I be a witty cynic, like Wilde? Or embrace the world as my brother, and find delight in every drop of dew, like Walt Whitman in his poems? I'd ricocheted between the two approaches, by turns aloof and sentimental. Now, Christopher was pushing me hard towards Whitman-ish optimism: freedom, he said, brotherhood!

While my man packed for me, I mused aloud: "If you think it's dangerous to stay, perhaps I should warn some of my friends..."

"Oh. Well, we *could*." He was right to be sullen, because I was lying. I wasn't thinking of danger. No, I was thinking: I could burst in on a friend, the same way Christopher had burst in on me. Make the same impassioned speech, steal all Christopher's best lines. Woo my friend! Win him!

And I would have done it. But there wasn't one man who stood out above the others. Uranian love is lifelong (said Plato-through-Christopher). So I couldn't accidentally shackle myself to a dullard. I'd been flitting about and fantasising, dithering over who to honour with my constancy.

The Waterloo platform was white with steam and swarming. Valets crowded the train corridors. Gentlemen sat in silent rows in every compartment, spines stiff with nerves. Nobody spoke. Half the Uranians of London were on the train.

Christopher's energy was spent, but I was exhilarated by our flight. I wondered: should I make a speech? *Brothers! We are travelling together.*

Once we reach Paris, must we disperse, like droplets in the ocean? Is this the greatest gathering of our kind since Athens? Surely, we should... We must...

I stood in the corridor by an open window, getting my nerve up. I looked into the starry night and told myself that the dark was as homelike and wholesome to me as the day. My brothers were beautiful (although not, I thought, all equally beautiful, and some couples shockingly mismatched). And somewhere up above us was our planet: gorgeous, mysterious Uranus. Pale blue, glowing from within, winding around the sun once every eighty-four years (Chris owned a small book on the subject). Unknowable, remote! My ruling celestial body!

"Everything to your satisfaction, sir?"

He spoke like a steward, but his bottle-green velvet suit put the lie to it.

"One shouldn't have all one's satisfactions satisfied," I spluttered, failing to be Wildean.

His face was sly and his nose was broken. Edward Carpenter the socialist said (via Christopher) that love may exist most purely between men of different classes. I wondered: who buys this lad's clothes? Who bought his ticket for this train? His arm pressed mine as the train jolted. It was all very sudden. Were we both under the influence of our heavenly patron?

"Sir," he said. "Can I kiss you?"

The last trace of my cynicism boiled away. I gave my passionate assent.

He pulled back and smirked. "That's handy to know," he said, and hopped off up the corridor, to boast to his chums.

I crept back to my compartment. I didn't make a speech to my fellow travellers.

On the ferry to France, I felt my purpose renewed. My lustful body was lost property. In Paris, I would be pure. No more self-deception. No more frittering my time looking for noble minds at tennis clubs. I'd been a terrible Uranian. We should be scholars, but I'd never stuck to any kind of study. I turned to Christopher.

"I didn't bring anything to read. Do you...?"

I wondered if he would produce *A Problem in Greek Ethics* and the deck would ring with cries of recognition. But he pulled out a slim tome from the Theosophists. I winced at the opening sentence: *Kamaloka as it is called in Sanskrit...* But then the tone altered. The author was speaking of something termed the *astral plane*. He assured me that the astral plane was absolutely *real*. As real as Charing Cross. I missed Charing Cross already. I was persuaded of his common sense.

I read about the astral body, a thing apart from the fleshly body. The concept gripped me. (Of course it did: I had more-or-less eloped with a man I didn't desire, and I wished to be so spiritual that his hairy hands wouldn't distress me.)

I read that my astral body could fly through the air, if I desired it. No, if I put my *mind* to it.

•

At our Parisian hotel Christopher slept. In my room, I prepared to make a further, audacious journey.

The book on astral travel had frustratingly little in the way of instruction. I lay on my bed, conscious of my sweating back. The boy from the train drifted into my mind, and I pushed him away. I pushed away all fleshly things. I pushed myself out of my body.

I left. I lifted. It had worked. I hovered.

I feared to look down on my own lifeless form, so I passed on, up, through the ceiling of the hotel room. I was naked. I was naked of *myself*, without a body. I wasn't cold. I could hear, faintly, the horses and the music of the Paris street. But my only crisp sense was sight. I saw Paris, a glittering mosaic. I took it in at a glance and then looked up to the stars. Could I go up, I thought, until the lights of the stars and the lights of Paris were of equal size, constellations above and below me?

How to move? Against what could I push? Should I flap my arms? I had no arms. I saw the moon. I thought: there! And leapt.

Such a pace would have made my stomach lurch but I had no stomach. I was gleeful at my lightness and speed. Nevertheless, I quailed at the prospect of the void between the planets. I'd forgotten most of what I'd read in Christopher's small book. Would it be cold or fiery? In a perpetual storm? It was calm as a millpond and almost empty. Dust, small rocks, passed through me.

The pockmarked face of the moon grew closer, whiter. I thought the surface would become less stark, but it remained without colour, and without grey shades; it was all white planes and black shadows. I was dazzled, I blinked, I did not blink, having no eyelids. Then why was I dazzled, having no eyes? I found that if I opened every part of myself to perception, I could see-perceive with other-eyes, and look straight at the sheets of lava, shiny as a japanned table, which had previously blinded me.

No living world, this. No greenery in the crevices and crevasses (and no plants of other colours, either, Mr. Wells). Severity everywhere in form as well as palette: sharp lava fragments piled like spillikins. I saw soundless avalanches rush down from the summits of volcanoes. I tried to listen with other-ears, and heard instead a great growling, like arguments shouted between nations.

Some of the lava and stones of this uninhabited land resembled ramparts and amphitheatres. I thought it an unsettling coincidence. Then I couldn't be sure: soaring over one plane, I saw beneath me a shape like a fortress, perched over a riverbed. I thought I saw arches, pillars, fallen columns, an aqueduct, even? But perhaps they were spat out by the thousand local Etnas, or whittled by lunar hurricanes.

I longed to know but I found I couldn't stoop or stop. I was exhausted.

As soon as my efforts slackened, I felt, attached to me, a sort of silver cord that I somehow knew connected me to my fleshly body. It tugged me like the kind hand of a good friend on my shoulder: *Come along, old boy, you've had enough.* I flew home. The moon was plucked from me, dwindled, became a coin in the sky.

The silver cord hauled me in. A good thing too, I thought, as I approached the rooftops of Paris: I'd not remembered where in the city I was lodged.

Snap! I woke breathless and chilled. In my murky brown bedroom, the memory of that austere landscape was like a slap. It had been the most terrific experience of my life.

•

"Sounds like Verne," Christopher said, ripping open a pastry.

"Like what?"

"That story by Jules Verne. Griffiths read it to us, at a picnic at college. In translation, of course."

I nodded. I blew across a bowl of hot chocolate. I was enjoying, supremely, being back in my body. Knowing it as only one of my bodies. It took me a while to think through the implications of Christopher's suggestion.

"Without eyes..." I began.

"What?" I'd interrupted him.

"Sorry—without my eyes, when I was travelling, I was perceiving through some other sense."

"And?"

"I was perceiving things too far from my own experience for me to understand them. So I translated them into familiar forms. Perhaps with practice, I could see more truly..."

"I expect you were lucid dreaming!" he cried. "I've always wanted to do that."

"What's that?"

"It's a dream state..."

"One travels in a dream state?"

He rolled his eyes. "One *thinks* one travels. You make things up, you direct your imagination while you're asleep. I'm impressed, how much you controlled your dream state!"

I watched a skin wrinkle across my hot chocolate while my heart thumped. Christopher thought me a liar. No, a self-deceiver of the highest order, impressed with how far I had pulled the wool over my own eyes.

"You should go 'travelling' again, ha!"

I was half outraged, half disconsolate.

But there were other things to occupy me. We had to find a flat, Paris demanded to be explored. And my cynical Wildean side sneered: really? Cities in space? Moon-men? Who are you, to explore the stars? Until the memory of my trip crumpled my chest like the end of a love affair.

I never had a firm opinion as to whether Christopher or I was right. But I didn't travel again.

After a year, he was calling himself Christophe. I slunk back, treacherously, to England. "Oscar isn't even released from prison, yet!" objected Christopher. But I missed Charing Cross. Christopher had made friends with French men, but I hadn't: my sense of universal brotherhood had ebbed, and I couldn't manage the vowels.

I thought, often, whether it would have been different if I'd made my speech on the train. If I'd allowed sincerity to conquer cynicism. I became, without meaning to, cold and distant. I was on a fixed path, unable to intersect with warmer men.

Christopher forgave me enough to take me, once or twice a year, on a trip. Each expedition had a fraction of the exhilaration of our Parisian exile: trunks packed, the funnel of a boat steaming. We looked for communities of Uranians in Sweden, India, Turkey, and (endlessly) Greece. My feelings of guilt towards my friend were as hefty as my luggage.

So now, as we found our cabins on the *Carmania* setting out for America, I bowed the knee to him again.

"I've forgotten to bring anything to read. Could I borrow something from your excellent little library?"

He drew out a pile of books. Amazingly, amongst them was the volume from our French trip, on astral travel. For sentimental reasons?

Once more, the book drew me in. I went to my bed as eagerly as a bridegroom.

•

It wasn't my annoyance at Mr. Wells alone that set my destination. I suspected that I had once travelled to the moon. I could reach, surely, for our nearest planet? A moment of hyperawareness. My itching nose. The crisp sheets. Then, up! This time, I was flying in daylight. The ship underneath me was a white toy on a blue sea, and when I climbed and I did so confidently the stars came out. Towards the great white face of the moon and past it. Its dark side was the first thing that really frightened me: craters the size of countries, with shadows so pitch-black that I hallucinated movement within them, squirming and sparkling.

I marshalled all I remembered from Christopher's small book and located the Red Planet. A red dot like a hot star. I set my course towards it and leaped.

And Wells was wrong! He was wrong entirely. I didn't even need to get close enough to see the surface of the planet before I knew it. The red of Mars wasn't caused by a weed, or any kind of plant. Instead, it was, as far as I could tell a property of dust. A hot and howling crimson mist, caused by ceaseless sandstorms. Like the haunted landscapes in the largest rubies: demon-chasms, their walls collapsing in, but never filling them, as debris is always boiling up out of them.

I sought a quieter spot: the long canals of Mars. I swooped down and hid in their cool, geometric shelter.

And there were others there with me.

They were near to my shape, seeming to be seated in a ring, but on no visible ledges or stones. I thought them inhabitants of Mars, at first. They were not tripod machines, nor had they oily tentacles. They were beautiful! Then I saw, trailing behind them, the silver thread that could take each of them home (so much more flimsy than it felt when embedded in one's own guts). Then I knew them to be thoughtforms, visitors like myself, gathered here. Possibly they lived too far apart on Earth to meet through ordinary means, or perhaps they wanted secrecy. I drew close and, under the howling of the storms, I heard them speak faintly to one another.

They had come to Mars to plan war.

last raid of the campaign, guys

need to synchronise

hell yes

mcneill sets up a bombardment

doing it already

eric, you send in your divisions to draw the initial attack

why mine

because we all had heavier losses than you last time

yeah, because I'm not an idiot

I had thought war would sound grander.

we agreed it already, eric

your divisions soak up the hits

eric you agreed

eric?

bathroom break

The form that had just spoken melted into translucence.

every time

has he got some kind of medical condition

we'll miss our window

Which of these tired youngsters was the General? Perhaps they were all civil servants. I moved closer. The translucent one became substantial again.

I'm back but my visuals are weird, anyone else?

ours are fine your machine's pathetic, eric

I can see right down the valley to the encampment

well I've got some crappy space theme or a desert maybe

so have I, now

it's really cheap-ass

One of the men of war turned and noticed me.

someone else just checked in did you invite him?

god no it's a closed group, isn't it?

who invited him?

he's the one messing up the visuals

this is supposed to be a private room

they're never secure

jesus get the mods to lock him out, I'll throw up some earthworks while we're waiting

A wall of Martian rock reared up in front of my feet. But it had no substance, and I stepped through it.

jesus

The men of war threw their weapons at me. Bombs flew, bullets whizzed through me. When their objects failed to touch me, they sent other, uncanny attacks. They blasted out their knowledge of past atrocities and it crumbled my bones. Like a disorientating cloud, I was surrounded by their indifference to suffering. I stumbled back.

But I also instinctively sent a scathing retaliation: flying barbs, then acid drops falling from the Martian clouds. I saw them flinch.

"I mean you no harm!" I called. Could men of war understand such a sentiment? The sound of my voice sent them into new confusion.

where's he coming in from

tell the mods to block his account

can't see who his provider is

this is a nightmare

we could change channel?

why should we have to go anywhere?

tell the mods to push him on

call off the raid?

we'll miss our window!

we've missed it, we're screwed

The men turned to steam. Their walls and bombs and clouds faded with them. And my silver cord pulled me back, because someone was shaking my physical body, hard. Whipping me back through thousands of miles of space. The air was sucked out of my lungs, but I had no lungs…

I opened my eyes and saw a crinkled face, bending down into my own. A hairy hand on my chest, shaking me.

"Oh, thank the Lord, I thought you'd died." Christopher sat with a thump on the bed next to my feet. "Did you take a sleeping draught?"

I found my mouth and tongue where I'd left them. "Sorry. I sleep deeply, these days." Should I tell him where I'd been? I couldn't bear him dismissing me again. "Where are we, please?"

"Fifty miles out of Liverpool into the Irish Sea. Heading for the Atlantic." His frown had lifted. He'd become more accustomed to exile than to England. We were both going to strange lands, but he was also heading home.

•

Later that night, as I approached Mars for the second time, I wasn't alone. "Christopher!" He flew next to me, wearing a vivid blue necktie I'd never seen in waking life. I was delighted—vindicated! I wondered how I'd brought him along. But his substance was different from mine, and different from the warmongers on Mars: crisper, brighter. Had he been here before?

"Oh, I'm not Christopher." He said it with absolute assurance, in his usual nasal voice. It was as eerie as if he'd said: "I'm dead, of course."

"Who are you?"

"I'm a mod, actually."

"A what?"

"A guide. Keeping the channels secure."

He made a little dip in the air and took my hand to tow me along. His hand felt warm.

"I don't..."

"I'm just steering you away from where you're not supposed to be." He smiled away my uncertainty. "Come on, I know this place better than you."

"Why do you look like my friend?"

"I don't look any way in particular. You're making me look like this."

Of course! The explanation I'd given Christopher, years ago—that my mind was interpreting what I could see. "Because you're the last person I saw? Or because I think of you as my guide?" I'd always been a passive traveller. It was Christopher who booked the tickets and read aloud from the Baedeker.

"It could be that. Or perhaps you're anxious? You've picked something comforting." He sounded embarrassed for me. "It really all depends on your settings."

We sailed over a waterfall of asteroids. Christopher's new necktie glowed in the reflected light of Mars. I was amazed that I'd remembered so many details of him as to make this charming waxwork.

"So do you have any relation to my friend? Are any parts of you actually him?"

"Well, what parts were you interested in?"

Flying together loosened my tongue. Nothing ventured! Although, perhaps, in this confusing cosmology, nothing could be gained. Could he answer a question to which I didn't know the answer?

"I'd wondered if you're happier, these days and how we stand..."

He laughed again. "How thoughtful!" If I was imagining him, was I mocking myself? "No time to talk, though. You're being bumped over to the next channel."

"I don't..."

Ahead of us reared a clean, silver planet, white caps at its poles. "One of the recreational channels. Have a good time there."

Morning star, evening star, bright beautiful planet. I somehow knew it would be more hospitable to life than Mars. More fecund.

"It won't be like the last channel," Christopher confirmed. "You can talk to anyone who takes your fancy, there."

"There'll be people?"

"Plenty of people."

"Venus-ians?" I shuddered slightly at the nomenclature of the dread Wells.

"Travellers. Like yourself."

"Will you stay and speak to them?"

He shook his head. "Don't think that would even work. I'm just moving you over. I'd best head off."

Venus was thick like soup with heat.

A cluster of figures stood not far from me. Again, wholly astral creatures. I extended my—interest? Sight? Soul?—to them. Several were women, the first naked women I'd ever seen and more naked than they could be in the flesh. But we were beyond reserve or modesty.

They turned on me. Their lust washed over me. The heat of it bubbled and blistered me. I was eyed up without eyes, handled without hands.

"Ladies!" I responded, to prevent a misunderstanding. "I do not desire you!"

The soupy heat of Venus grew chilly.

"I mean no offense! I am a disciple of another love, in which the female has no part!"

I was spat out. They turned their backs-not-backs on me. It was exactly like being cut at a party. As I made further protests, I was astonished to hear them refer to me as an arsehole, a complete cock, and other epithets.

My anger took form. I was more adept than the last time I'd tried it, on Mars; walls flew up around me, almost before I knew I was their architect. The women exploded the walls by flooding them with lava. I sprouted a pillar from the ground beneath me to lift me above the red flow, and I rained fog all over my opponents. The lava around their legs coagulated into greyish rock. I was quite merciless, scrutinising their agonised coils, reminiscent of those who perished at Pompeii. Their thoughtforms reached out to drag me down. I streaked away in disgust at myself and them.

The airs above Venus were far cooler than the surface. I became aware of other fliers, an escort surrounding me. Their forms were minimal, their greetings like chirping or cooing.

hullo!

who are you!

I introduced myself and asked, in wonder, who they were.

just mods!

"Like that vision of Christopher? But you don't look..."

who's Christopher? just here to keep the channel friendly!

had reports about you

losing us custom!

terms of service!

who's your provider?

A friendly hailstorm. A floating conscience, almost. How could I have been so violent, so cruel? I had been contaminated by Venusian feelings, of the body rather than the mind. I apologised profusely for my behaviour.

no problem!

where you coming in from?

"Earth," I said. Their giggles were icicles.

don't know your way around the channels!

not the right place at all for you

you'd rather be with the boys!

are we right? we're right!

try another channel!

They sprang away across space and I knew what they referred to. where I needed to go.

The luminous pale blue planet. My namesake. Far out away from the sun, but it might shed its own light, I'd read, and it might also be heated from within. I'd always hoped its colour was the blue of a year-round Spring sky.

Could I get there?

But fear prevented me, and I let the silver cord pull me back. Snap!

•

I had to hunt Christopher all over the ship before I found him in a bar with a crowd of other passengers, chattering in German and drinking schnapps. I thought it unfair he hadn't told me his friends would be aboard, but then I realised he'd only met them that morning. I sat on the edge of the group. An Englishman with a walrus moustache enthused about how there would soon be larger and better ships than this mammoth transatlantic liner. I, dizzy from another kind of travel, could not share his excitement.

I saw that Christopher had become more and more interesting over his ten year in exile, while I'd stagnated. Had he made peace with being a Uranian? Perhaps brotherly love was enough for him, the brief, intense connections that form between travellers. Maybe he was never tempted. Maybe he frolicked nightly with his chess opponents. I didn't think he was still grubbing around in Whitman's poems looking for a solution. Unlike me.

Eventually, I had drunk enough that my friend had to help me to my cabin and my bed. He poured me a glass of water. I was melancholy and I had to concentrate to remember that this Christopher hadn't steered me across the void of space. I'd never held his hand.

"Are you alright? Do you need the ship's doctor?"

"It's not that."

He was the spit and image of my celestial guide. My heart poured out of me despite myself.

"Christopher, if you have a great longing for a thing, a feeling of great kinship with this thing, and then you realise that it might actually be possible to see it, to *feel*..."

"What thing?"

But I could not speak the name of my planet. He would think me ridiculous, again. Or he'd enthusiastically tell me to dream, again, for dreaming was all I'd done. I tried to describe my dilemma in less specific terms.

"Chris, is it normal to feel wary to not even know if you should try to approach..."

I suddenly feared that he might misunderstand me, and think I was making a long-overdue declaration of love. Then his raised eyebrow deflated that notion. I blustered on.

"Because what if it's not the answer? What if you're stuck with being lonely, and not at ease, and it's not because you have any connection to this thing. What if it's nothing to do with...?"

He smiled and turned down my cabin light. We were used to helping one another when worse for wear. He wasn't waiting for my revelation; he had given up on loving me, years ago. But, I realised, I had not given up the idea that he loved me. He'd go back to his deck friends as soon as I fell asleep. I closed my eyes.

Brave again in the dark, I decided to tell him. I murmured: "I still want to. I want it. I want to *touch*..."

My knuckles struck the cabin wall. My hand had been foraging about without my volition.

Christopher had already gone.

Later, I went back, drunker, to the deck. I shouted: "The female has no part!" Christopher's friends stared at me. Christopher helped me to bed, again.

•

It was no hardship, the following morning, to leave my body. As soon as I was moving among the planets, my companions from Venus re-joined me.

you again!

we lost you!

we like you!

can't let you back in there though sorry!

Their feather-light push speeded me on. And I heard-without-ears the voices of my warmonger foes.

my view's gone fuzzy

it's him again

call in the supermod have him shut down

Christopher appeared, for a brief moment, in the air before me, waving his arms in warning. Overtaking him was something like a flock of carnivorous birds, or a rock fall that twisted in space to chase me. They called to one another in a grating crackle.

how is he moving across the damn channels

can't cut him off

provider's unclear

I sped on but the missiles dogged me. I raced them; they were hard put to keep up with me. I only need to outpace them for a little longer! We swung together around the enormous bulk of Jupiter, dodged between the rings of Saturn. I was out of breath, I had no breath, they were shouting behind me.

wandering all over

not a user, it can't be

only an error

clean it up

The blue planet came into sight. I knew at once that I'd been right: that it was a warm planet, a perpetual spring morning.

I went lower and dropped through the blue.

The planet wasn't featureless at all. There was a wood, a great greenwood, moss paths dusted with pollen.

where is it now

there, in that empty channel
looks busy in there
it's coming from him
he's populating the place

There was dew on the grass, and I delighted in it, and the dark in among the trees was homelike and wholesome.

we should lock him in
cut the account off
just disconnect it
lock him in there
yeah try it

And in a clearing of the woods was a college quad and the quad was the agora of Greece, and a crowd of young men smiled to see me come to join their conversation. My college friends, unencumbered by wives and children, stood with other men I had not yet met.

I felt pain all through me. The hideous mod-birds were above me, tearing at my silver rope with metal teeth. I knew they wanted to stop me from travelling. If I hurried, I could still use the rope, still let it pull me, and I might manage to get home.

I didn't want to go home. I'd come home. Christopher would understand. I took up the tight-stretched silver cord in my hands, near to my not-body, and wrapped it neatly around each not-fist. It would only take one quick—

locked him in
done it

Snap!

Raising the Sea Drowned

Julian, the CEO, looms too large for the tiny office. I look at his forehead, to avoid his intense eyes without seeming shifty, but am mesmerised instead by the sheen on his slicked-back dark hair.

"Thanks for coming, Dilawar," he says, and enfolds my hand in his, and I really feel like he means it. Posh boys are good at sounding sincere.

But he knows bugger all about the job he's interviewing me for. They want to recruit some kind of multi-skilled monster: someone who can do front-end, back-end, interaction design. Body of a lion, wings of an eagle, head of a recent Computer Science graduate. This hasn't reduced my interview nerves, because now I have to demonstrate my knowledge without showing up their ignorance.

"One last question, Dilawar," Julian says. "What did you dream about last night?"

That rattles me. I had a bad night, last night, and maybe it shows.

No, it can't be. They're asking daft pop-psych interview questions because they know nothing about coding. I can't tell them what I really dreamed (a proper nasty one, flavoured by my recent final exams: the question paper in Russian, the exam hall full of blood and frogs). I'd sound batty.

"I dreamed my database had flooded," I lie. "I was bailing it out."

Julian turns to the Chief Financial Officer, Nathan, and raises his eyebrows. I hope they have an understanding. I hope that exchange of glances means: "Check out this kid! We should employ him forthwith!"

Nathan has a cat-like face: wide with a pointy chin, amused and unreadable. He seems just as posh as Julian but more sly. "Anyway, Dilawar, we'll let you know."

I don't have high hopes. I'm a short brown kid from Yorkshire in a cheap suit.

That same evening, Nathan phones.

"We'd like to offer you the job of Chief Technical Officer."

The fact that they want me as CTO tells me that their company will fold within six months.

"Can I ask what the salary is?"

"What salary?"

"Sorry?"

"Just a joke. I'll be honest, we're not paying much at the moment, but you'd get equity. Shares in the company."

I've been on a student budget for years. I can keep scrimping a bit longer. I don't want money, I want to find my passion. I quite like sci-fi, and board games, but I don't have big enthusiasms (apart from coding, and that never made anybody more interesting). I need to make sure my job's fascinating or I'll end up really flipping dull.

Now this whole area, Silicon Roundabout, boils with enthusiasm. And this start-up that wants to employ me, it could be my passion. Couldn't it? It's got a charismatic front-man, in Julian; I could be the maverick back-room boy genius. I'd be working in Shoreditch. I'd have my finger on the pulse, or the bleeding edge, or some other throb-y, spurt-y place.

But they want me to build a social network. Does anyone want another social network? My Mam (keeping her fingers crossed and saying some prayers for me back home in Haxby) would rather see me in a bank. Somewhere with a bit of security.

"Yes. I accept. When would I start?"

"Tomorrow? Come in at eleven. Have a lie-in, do some customer research."

I don't get the joke. Then he tells me what they want me to build.

They're making a social network for dreams.

•

I retrace my steps through Shoreditch the next day. I'm just as nervous as I was for the interview. I wish Julian and Nathan weren't trying to sell dreams. I'm really bad at dreams. Well, I'm good at bad dreams. Constantly having nightmares, where I can't breathe or move, and dark things are approaching me. I used to take medication for it.

I brace myself and hop up the concrete stairwell, and re-enter the small attic office. Nathan wriggles out from behind his desk to greet me.

"Dilawar! You made it."

"Call me Dil."

"Ah. Call me Nate. And the company is called 'Sandpit.'" Nate says it as though he's picking a hair out of his teeth. "After the Sandman. But ***play***ful." I guess Julian the CEO chose the name.

Two desks are jammed in opposite corners of the room, but there's still hardly space to pass in between them. I wonder how the three of us fit in. "And what do I call Julian?"

"Oh, call him whatever you like. He won't hear you from here."

"What?"

"He has a job." Nathan waves southwards. "At Canary Wharf. He's in finance. His income from that job funds Sandpit. So he's not around much. Drops by in the evenings."

So we have a part-time CEO. That can't be ideal. The way Nate talks about Julian—annoyed, resigned—makes me wonder if the posh boys of the C-suite are also dating one another.

Nate starts scraping one of the desks clear of paperwork. He's wearing jeans. I won't wear this suit, tomorrow. When I told Mam I'd found a job, she sent me a hundred quid towards a work wardrobe. I can buy raw denim jeans and a couple of Doctor Who T-shirts. That's how a maverick CTO dresses.

Nate offers me a chair so luxurious, compared to the rest of the office, that I wonder if Julian's stolen it from his day job, ridden it across the East End on its tiny castors.

"Nice chair," I say.

"They're left over from the last company that Julian and I started."

I decide to ignore Nate's cynical asides. By noon, I've bent that rule, or I wouldn't be able to hold a conversation with him at all.

He talks me through the grand Sandpit plan. "So our users will record their dreams, read other people's dreams, share them, do *social stuff* with them. You'll have a better idea of what's possible."

I can make it function. Probably. Stick in all the structures, connect people up nicely. But will anyone want to use it? Aren't other people's dreams kind of boring? *I was teaching a class on Baroque music and my old boyfriend was there but he was my Dad, too, and the funny thing is that I don't know any Baroque music! Ha ha ha.* It's the ultimate 'you should have been there!'. You can't ever have been there.

I shouldn't say anything like that to Nate. It's my first day on my first job.

I say: "Do you think it'll catch on?"

Nate gives me a long, dry look. "Well, we certainly hope so."

"It's just... you know what it's like, when someone tells you about a dream they've had?" I wonder how to put it politely.

"You should talk to Julian about that," he says.

We start to sketch the architecture of the site.

I head out at lunchtime to explore. On the side of our 1960s office block, a spray-painted slogan straggles up the wall: *what you do today will transform the world.* Is that motivational, or menacing?

The office is in the heart of Shoreditch, a short trudge from Silicon Roundabout itself. It's a gold-rush town, a dream town, you can smell the optimism like sea air. I peer up at the windows of the redbrick Victorian blocks that line the roads. Where do the big-name start-ups live? The ones with headline sales to Facebook or Google, making their founders into millionaires? They can't be in these boarded-up buildings, graffitied with giant squid, and with weeds—no, *trees*—growing out of their roofs. If this place is so cool, why is it so scruffy?

I buy a cream cheese bagel from a twenty-four hour bagel shop. It is reassuringly solid and old-fashioned. When I bite into it, cream cheese squirts onto my shirt.

Julian sweeps in that evening, making the office seem even smaller. "Dil! Welcome on board. How's it going? Let's have dinner. It's on me."

He leads us to a Vietnamese café, hipsters lining the long canteen tables. I order the cheapest thing on the menu, to make a good impression, and spool noodles into my mouth as Nate itemises the territory we've covered that day.

I screw up my courage. "Julian, I was wondering about dreams. Are they the best thing to be using? I mean, when someone tells me about a dream they've had, it's..." I consider my next words carefully: Banal? Embarrassing? Icky?

"It's amazing, isn't it? Such an insight. It's got everything the Internet's missing at the moment: imagination, intimacy, yeah? It's big, Dil, but I know you can handle it."

Past Julian's shining eyes, I see Nate smirking.

•

I work from eight to eight, at least, every day. London buzzes all round me, but I'm oblivious. I could go to clubs I've only ever heard of: Popstarz, or Kali. Or a gay gamers night! Somewhere out there, cute boys in Threadless T-shirts are starting a round of Netrunner. But I don't. Even supported by my luxurious chair, I start to ache. I hammer out the structures of the Sandpit site late into the night. I never see sunlight, creep home each night to my box room in a rowdy shared house. I dream really badly: mainly vertigo and smothering.

I'm following my passion.

I get better at everything, but Nate and Julian don't know enough to notice. I resent Nate in particular, because he's right there, and I can hone my disgruntlement. Julian is absent too much for me to resent him. One time he drops by to hand me a little brass Lord Ganesha, the size of my big toe.

"Because you're removing obstacles, Dil," he says solemnly. I feel like I'm going to cringe myself inside out.

"Oh. Ta very much." I don't know what to do with the statue. I'm not going to Blu-Tack him to the desk. I pop him in the stationary drawer as respectfully as I can. Meanwhile, Mam asks if I'm coming home for Diwali, tuts when I say no, and tells me they'll have to let me go for Christmas, won't they?

We don't have any dreams yet, so as I build my first version of the site I fill it up with printer's Latin, the traditional place-holder text: ***Lorem ipsum dolor sit amet*** and so on. I get curious and look up what it means: ***no-one seeks pain for its own sake.***

One day, I come back from lunch and there's a woman a bit older than me with an afro and heavy-framed specs, sitting at my desk. "How do you want it?" she says. "Cheeky, friendly? Commanding?" She sounds deathly serious and isn't talking to me.

"Ah, Dilawar." Julian's squeezed in next to Nate. "This is Monifa. She's going to give us a *voice*." He's so sincere, so thankful. "We want it to be neutral, Monifa. We're not appealing to any demographic."

"But..."

Julian cuts off Monifa's objection. "Neutral. Everyone has dreams!"

When Nate and Julian go out for lunch, Monifa rattles away on Nate's computer. After ten minutes, she says: "There's no such thing as a 'neutral' voice, you know."

"Fair enough."

"'Neutral' is an elitist myth."

"Oh, aye?"

"It's true. I've got a degree in sociolinguistics but they never listen to me."

"What will you do, if you can't do 'neutral'?"

"I can knock something together. I know what Julian likes."

We've only just met, but it's a relief to speak to someone apart from the founders. "I think they think they're 'neutral'. Julian and Nate, I mean. I think they haven't noticed they're..."

"Rich? Uh huh. You know I did a bit of work for their last company?"

I try not to feel excluded. I won't ask what their last company was. "Was that neutral too?"

"Like porridge. It's a shame, I really need to write something distinctive. Put my stamp on a brand, use it as a calling card. Are they paying you properly?"

"Not much. I've got shares."

"Ha. Bits of paper."

"I think, to be fair..."

"Fair?"

"...they're not even bits of paper."

Monifa winces with sympathy. "Poor boy. I remember last time..."

I give it a bit of Silicon Roundabout bravado. "Last time they didn't have me."

"Huh."

I wonder about the proto-me, the coder they employed last time.

Monifa hammers away for a week or so, dutifully drafting dozens of boring messages to our future members. Letters to nobody. My skeleton site feels like those ghost cities in China, built for a boom that's waning.

Monifa's there, peering over my shoulder, as I show Nate our first bits of functionality. The dreamstream: a continuous feed of other people's dreams, selected by keywords. The dreamscape: a cluster of images, pulled in from other sites, to illustrate users' dreams.

Nate says, "Won't that be wall-to-wall spiders and celebrities?"

"There'll be a box for users to tick if their dreams are nightmares. So other users can avoid them." I've made that up on the spot, but it's a good idea.

"Or ask for them specifically," Nate says. "Settle down with a takeaway. Chicken jalfrezi and death by carnivorous toads."

Monifa says, "You'd better have a good harassment policy in place."

My heart sinks. "Sorry?"

"Well, there are laws, aren't there? Can dreams be defamation? Or stalking? Or revenge porn."

Nate gives her a thin smile. "We're working on all that."

"Copyright, too," says Monifa. "People might try to pass published stuff off as their own dreams."

That's simpler to solve. I make a note to create a plagiarism filter, matching against other online sources.

When Monifa leaves the office, Nate says, "Damn. I'll get legal advice."

"Right you are." I feel a bit sick. It works so nicely, as it is: Tim User is friends with Iman User, and they admire one another's *lorem ipsum* dreams. I don't want to let in strangers to ruin it.

"Can you set up anything to prevent it? All that stuff Monifa mentioned?"

"I don't think so." I don't have the ingenuity that comes from malice. I remember a computer game I had as a kid: the players couldn't physically attack one another, so bullies herded my avatar into a corner and built a wall round me. "What we really need," I say, "is a load of complete bastards. Let them loose on a test site and tell them to ruin it."

"But this is Shoreditch, Dil. *Shoreditch.* How could we find these digitally-literate arseholes?"

We cross the road to the Reliance, a dark old East End boozer packed with Silicon jetsam, underemployed, here for the buzz. Nate gazes around the gloom, holding a silent audition. Within half an hour we've hired the anti-testers. We can't give them office space, so they take our money and shove off to someone's house.

I sleep even worse, that night. My usual visions of paralysis and approaching teeth are inter-cut with scenes where drunk testers abuse my lovely site (which appears variously as an empty mall, a walled garden, and my Mam's flat).

They send a report in the morning describing their creative attempts to break laws and social mores. They've circumvented my blocking protocols and harassed one another with glee.

I am not in love with any of this.

•

When my city's built, we open the gates, and launch Sandpit in beta.

The dreams trickle in all day. Epics by exhibitionists and notes by minimalists. People dictate their dreams into our app, and the dreams are converted to text (if you're shy about your voice, or hiding your identity) or uploaded as audio (if you want to show off your mellow tones). Or you can type, if you're old school.

I don't have time to read any of the dreams. I fix and patch and note further problems. I eat at my desk—I can hardly swallow—and watch the total words in the database swelling.

"More than *War and Peace*," says Nate. "That's good."

"Why?"

"Good sound-bite. Monifa's writing our press releases. She's got a list of classics; I'm keeping an eye out for when we overtake them. 'Twice the length of all the Harry Potter books', 'Four times the Bible'. Maybe not that. Too blasphemous. How long would it take to read the dreams, so far?"

"I dunno." I doodle hastily in a corner of a spreadsheet. "Six years. No, hang on. Seven weeks?"

"Damn it, Dil..."

Nate would never misplace a decimal point. He has infallible spreadsheets, calculating the possible revenues for different numbers of users and hits. Dollar signs spin in his eyes. Behind him hovers Julian, more suave but just as avaricious.

At the end of the first day, the three of us blink at the stats. Is it enough?

"How many users do we have?" Julian asks.

"Twenty times more than we estimated," says Nate.

My chest swells. Is this pride? It feels like panic. "That's amazing."

Julian echoes me. "Amazing, yeah."

Nate sighs over his spreadsheet. "Pity. I was hoping for 'cocking unbelievable'."

•

Sandpit is a hit. We trend. We're mentioned on other social networks, and we spread: like contamination, like wildfire, like something that's nicer than those but faster. Like friendly fire? Maybe thanks to Ganesha (who is, to my shame, still in my desk drawer).

All that weekend I dream of falling.

Julian strides into the office on Monday morning and slaps a sheaf of London free papers and colour supplements on our desks. I weed through the usual scare stories (*Croydon kids in drugs death plunge*) to find the fluff. We are the fluff.

"We can get some decent ad income, now," says Julian. "And we need a better office."

We move into part of a converted Victorian warehouse. Its facial recognition lock won't bloody acknowledge me, but once someone lets me inside, I have an L-shaped desk in a big sunlit room I share with Nate.

Floorboards, potted plants, a complicated coffee machine. Julian has a separate room, with a door. He shuts it.

I buy some proper shirts, with collars. I actually take leave, and go north for a long weekend with Mam, eating chips and scraps out of paper on the bank of the Foss together. In my old room, under a *Matrix* poster, I dream of falling. On the train back down from York, I see one of our users in the wild, mumbling into our app.

The press call us The Dream Team. They say we're following our dreams. Julian encourages this, and it infuriates me. I still find dreams half trivial, half horrible. The headlines—'living the dream'—keep confusing the categories: wanting something a lot isn't dreaming it; working to create something definitely isn't dreaming it. I resent the comparison of my hard grind to our users' weird nocturnal spurts.

One reporter wants to title his interview "They Have a Dream." I beg him not to.

He asks me what my account name is, on Sandpit. I don't have one. I didn't even think of starting one. But the founder of Twitter's on Twitter, right? The problem is, I can't make my dreams public. Lately, I've been waking at four in my pitch-black box room, and I can't bear to fall asleep again. I stumble down to the lounge, praying that there'll be someone still awake, playing video games. Someone human.

If Julian insists I get a Sandpit account, I'll pay Monifa to ghost-write it for me.

The press want to know what dreams are. We show them some dreams. They say: but what *are* dreams?

"Get Monifa to give us a briefing," Julian instructs.

Monifa comes to the new office, and tells us about neuroscience, psychoanalysis, mysticism. She shows us slides. It's good stuff. I latch on to phrases, hoping to get a real enthusiasm for dreams. *Dreams work by compression, substitution and metaphor. Dreams are the Royal Road to the unconscious mind.* I'm not sure I like that last one. What things might leg it towards you, down a royal road?

"Dreams are also politically radical," Monifa tells us. "Allen Ginsberg said that consensus reality was a coercive tool, so the individuality of dreams is a form of resistance."

"We're not political," murmurs Julian. Monifa gives him a heavy stare from behind her heavy spectacles. "Sorry, do go on."

"I'm done."

"Thank you!" says Julian. "It's good to know these things." He squeezes Monifa's shoulder. What the heck is that? He's turning into a patronising dad. "But Sandpit is not going to hold an opinion on what dreams are."

"No?"

"We can't tell people what their dreams are about!"

"Hard not to develop an outlook, though." Nate is getting prickly. "That's like selling eggs and pretending we don't know what eggs are." We're not *selling* dreams, but I don't get in between them when they're fighting. "Even a child would have an opinion on..."

"Keep it to it to yourself!" snaps Julian. "This is important, guys." He paces back into his room, shaking his head.

"Give it a rest, Dad," I mutter as his door closes. Nate smirks, and Monifa invites me to the pub.

•

"It's like they still want to be as bland as possible," says Monifa, as I hand her a pint.

"Aye. It's a brand value. Not having a position is our most strongly-held position."

"They did that in their last two companies. Didn't save them," she says darkly. She wants me to ask, so she can show off her insider knowledge.

I change the subject. "So, are Julian and Nate dating?"

Monifa splutters into her pint. "Why? Do you fancy one of them?"

"Give over! Why is Nate still working with Julian, if he gets so pissed off with him?"

"His CV looks shit. They've had two companies fold, so Nate needs this one to work. And Julian's got the money to support it."

"Oh. Well, we've got some possible income, now. Adult advertising, porn and that. Your wildest dreams!"

"Oh, Dil. They can't do that. There's no point in having a ***neutral*** style if you're going to put tits on the front page."

I see her point, and I say I'll try to change Julian's mind. I rehearse arguments to myself, but I keep tripping over *double entendres*: we shouldn't hold a position, we shouldn't take a stance...

Then I feel grubby, and I don't want to talk about Sandpit any more. I look around the pub for people I know from the other start-ups. Everyone round here is working on terrible tat. Gadgets that quantify the user's every nap and side-dish (which are supposed to help people change their ways, but just help them sharpen their anxieties). Services that make you feel creative without doing any work. A watch that will tell you if you're in love. A cushion that really likes to be squeezed.

I'm tearful. I've been working so hard and I'm not sure that Sandpit isn't terrible tat, too.

"You OK, Dil?" asks Monifa.

"Bit knackered."

"Have you been looking after yourself?"

"What d'you mean?"

She ticks the basics off on her fingers. "Exercise, therapy and/or spiritual practice, nurturing interpersonal connections."

"None of the above." I think of the calmest person I know, my Grandad, and borrow ideas from him. "I could light some incense. Do some deep breathing."

"That's more like it. Want to get some chips and watch a film at my place?"

This is the night I fall in love.

•

I end up sleeping at Monifa's house. Her roommates all crochet, so I'm under a kind of woolly net on the sofa.

I dream of Atlantis, am captured by fish-men, and speared by a trident. I wake when I fall off the sofa and hit the floor, trussed in the wool net and thrashing.

I can't sleep again. I want to hear a friendly voice but I can't wake anyone. I pull up my laptop, put in my ear buds and turn on a dreamstream of audio files uploaded by our users. I tinker a bit: search by keywords, set up a sea-themed dream-stream to soothe away the nightmares.

I filter out the fears of drowning, and enjoy the joys of swimming. Exploring and floating with no need to breathe. There's a lot of marine-themed material on the site. Perhaps it crops up so often because dreaming itself is like an undersea world: different laws of physics, unknown currents, weird inhabitants. You submerge yourself in it each night and clamber back up the beach each morning.

I set my laptop on the floor and lie down again.

To enter the dreams is to fall into a whirlpool. The voices are a variety of pitches and accents, but they have a curious similarity of tone. It's the kind of uniformity Monifa helped us to achieve as a company, but I don't know why it's worked out that way, when there's no style guide for dreams. The tone is detached but intense. It is like a witness report of a crime. It's compelling.

I doze. I don't have nightmares. I dream of a sea that's misted, milky, which churns and churns. What's stirring it? Some thick sinuous agitator whipping back and forth in the depths. Don't look too closely. Look at the ocean, instead, and its creamy waves, because marvellous things will arise from it. Really sweet things...

Monifa, hair in a morning halo, peers down at me. "You look happy."

"I slept really well."

"That's a really good sofa. Want some coffee?"

The dreams meander on.

It's then, in that half-waking daze, that I fall in love. No single dream is enough to lure me in, but together? Absolutely. It'll be so gorgeous and so massive. I don't mean money. I mean the database, and its possibilities: the shapes and truths I can draw up from it, the paths and webs I can create within it. *What you do today will transform the world.*

Lying on Monifa's sofa, I also love the whole of Silicon Roundabout. Every shoddy start-up. The trains passing overhead on concrete viaducts in the dark, flashing and clunking. The promise of the infinitely quantifiable, connectible, social-local-mobile perfectible world.

"Monifa, why do the dreams all sound similar?"

She tells me, over breakfast, how groups of texts establish norms. Problem pages, suicide notes, graffiti slogans. When you come to write in a genre, the genre guides you. I'm too sleepy to understand. It's like a fairy-tale bedtime story: the magic book, that writes you as you read it.

"It's odd, though," Monifa says. "I wouldn't have thought your users have had time to learn from one another."

Monifa leaves me again and I listen to the dreams: words without weight, passing like sparks.

Why do I fall so wholeheartedly? Why now? Only the previous week I'd thought about how Silicon Roundabout was originally a joke name, and that Sandpit was probably a joke company, hitching itself to a joke boom. But I get sucked in despite that. Perhaps I fall to justify the sunk cost: I tell myself I wouldn't have worked so hard, for so little pay, if I didn't believe in it. *No-one seeks pain for its own sake.* But I *have* worked that hard, so I must believe in it, right? I must love it.

And falling in love gives me the energy I need for the next long slog.

•

Love carries me forwards faster but it doesn't smooth the path. I sleep so much better; as long as I listen to other peoples' dreams as I drift off, I don't have nightmares. But my improved sleep just allows me to focus better at work. I love Sandpit, but my general love for Shoreditch evaporates, reverts to cynicism; like most people round here, I've become a monomaniacal arsehole, who knows that my start-up is excellent, and that yours is tragically bad.

Julian keeps pushing me to enable cross-platform integration, so our users can share their dreams across social networks. One afternoon, as soon as Julian leaves for lunch, I scoot over to Nathan's desk.

"Nathan: *nobody wants* cross-platform integration."

"Is this an excuse? I mean, if you can't do it..." He's peeved that I talked Julian out of running the adult ads.

"Nah, I've implemented it. But nobody's using it. They don't tie their Sandpit account to their Twitter, or Facebook, or Grindr..."

"It's social software," Nate says, with panic in his voice. "Make it socialise, Dil!"

But I can't, and I freak out, until the morning that Julian drops a newspaper into my lap. "The *Guardian* compared us to an STD check."

My gut turns over. I'm going to be fired. There's so much left undone.

"Great work, Dil!" *Clunk* on my desk. Julian's giving me a bottle of whisky.

I run my eyes over the article. It tells me: sharing your Sandpit username is the new step in personal intimacy! Third date, or earlier? Before or after the first kiss?

I drink some of the whisky that night and think about my beloved, my dataset. What is it *for*? Screening partners, social ritual? (Imaginary Julian nods in full-on Dad mode: "We can't tell people what dreams are for, Dil.") Is it perhaps not for sharing, at all? Is it just shouting into an abyss? (And letting the abyss, presumably, shout into us?) I let the dreamstream massage my ears while I ponder. I listen to dreams most of the time, now. I use more piquant keywords for when I'm working, for a pick-me-up. But tonight, something spacey to help me unwind. I find a lot of the dreams are talking about collapse, things falling apart. Sometimes you get a run like that. I chase the feeling from dream to dream.

I don't fear the dreams, now. I remember how squeamish I used to be, but that's all gone.

I pour a third glass. It tastes vile to me, but knowing Julian, it's expensive.

What a waste. Could I swap it for something cheaper that I actually enjoy? I'm amused by that idea. Really amused, chuckling at my own cheap tastes. Maybe I'm drunk, maybe I'm vain. Or maybe everyone's smug about their quirks, their Unique Selling Points.

I make a leap sideways, a connection: maybe the dream database is about knowing yourself better. So we don't need to hook up to the social networks. We shouldn't want to! We should integrate with the other tools of self-knowledge: the exercise armbands, the mood quizzes.

The next day I create a dashboard of correspondences and coincidences. I start off with graphs, but they're too dull. I pester Monifa by phone to come in and work on it.

"Is there money involved?"

"There's prestige! It's cutting edge!"

"There needs to be money."

"Nate, can we have some money?"

Nate coughs up, and Monifa writes outputs in a conversational style: "Did you notice you dream of [dogs] whenever you visit [Glasgow]?" "Your dreams are less [anxious] when you [jog] [an hour] before you go to sleep."

I invite a few select users to connect their dreams to other parts of their inner lives.

They love it. They rush to hook up more of their personal devices to their Sandpit account: their e-readers, their cookery blogs. "You dream of [running] after you read [zombie poetry]." "You have more [adult] dreams after you eat [chilli]."

(Some of the rumours aren't true. Nobody's dashboard ever said, "You're happier when you drink more.")

The users are delighted.

Julian is a proud parent. "Marvellous. This'll help with the revenue stream, eh, Nate?"

•

"God, people are so literal," says Nathan.

He's researching possible sources of income. Julian's been yanking us in two directions, lately: *we need to invest, expand, make sure the product's right. Oh, but we also need to make money, right now!* Often, it becomes a straight split between Nate and me: *Dil, take all the time you need to grow the brand. Nate, where's my cash?*

We don't want to go for a funding round, because we'd have to give up some equity in the company, and the two of them are hanging on to that like grim death. We want the big buy-out, we want the yacht. But we need income right now.

So it's back to the ads. The companies willing to pay a premium for our unique proposition aren't classy: cheese manufacturers, mystics offering dream analysis, the makers of sedative teas and anxiety meds. Mattresses, both memory-foam and the old-fashioned amnesia kind.

"Doesn't anyone want to be a bit more creative? Like, actually *work* with the dataset?" I ask.

"We had a clothes company. They want to find out what a 'dream dress' looks like."

I crack open a laptop and search the dreams for "dress". *She was wearing a white dress which turned out to be a sheep, it was eating her.* I click on one of the user audio files, instead. A woman's voice, a Swiss accent. *"I was wearing a red dress, with seed pearls along the bodice..."*

"That's her dream dress," I say. I'm charmed and cheered. It seems magical to pull an object across from the dream world and make it tangible.

"I was dressed that way because I was to be shot. I was pushed up against the sooty wall and the octopus-soldiers..."

Nathan slams my laptop shut. "So. Three guesses why I don't want to talk to the dream holiday company."

"What about dream weddings?"

Nathan shudders. He returns to his angry research, fingers on his keyboard rattling like machine guns. He's stressed. I'm affronted. Why is nobody asking my database the right questions? What would those questions even be?

•

That month, we have two kinds of interest.

One is, at worst, only unprofitable: the art students.

"We've got invitations to private views," says Julian. "Slade, Central St Martins and Goldsmiths."

I can't wait to see what they've done with our dreams.

On a hot summer night, I step into the converted chapel and I see the texts of dreams projected onto curtains of swaying metal chains, elusive and protean. Then, a poignant high note calls me away, and I stumble into a dark room to find students chanting dreams as they writhe in bright yellow heaps of spice powder. Elsewhere, an artist has inscribed dream words onto paper flowers and is burning them.

Drops of cool water hit my overheated head. It is a miraculous indoor rainfall.

Klaxons shriek, and I realise: it is the sprinkler system, triggered by the idiot with the flower bonfire, and we are all evacuated.

Weird weavings hang down the outside of the church, and Julian is taking the opportunity to be photographed next to them. He beckons me over and pulls me in: family photo time.

"This is fantastic, Dil, isn't it? Super creative. Stand next to Nate."

Nate is talking through a gritted grin. "But it doesn't make us any ***money***. It doesn't get us any closer to the sea-drowned."

He's lost it. "To what?" I ask.

"Seed round funding! Art doesn't help us..."

Julian shushes as though Nate is being vulgar, as though Julian won't demand a revenue report from him the next morning.

I stand in the hot night outside the packed church-cum-gallery and I'm exhilarated. These projects are the equivalent of crude beakers made from river clay, but now the idea is there, someone will invent thrown pots, and discover firing. Someone will use my dataset elegantly. Someone will make bone china.

I pick up a glass of red wine that nearly turns my mouth inside out, gulp it down. A waifish woman artist with shining eyes tops up my glass.

"You're with Sandpit, right?" she says.

"I am." I'm CTO, baby! "That's me."

"You're the people who predicted that earthquake in Tokyo."

I feel a wave of annoyance. "That's a myth." A couple of weeks ago, an earthquake hit Japan. A genuine tragedy. Real people, actually dead. Then someone decided death and tragedy ***weren't enough,*** and looked at Sandpit and embroidered a lot of pseudo-scientific cobblers. We'd predicted the earthquake! Our users had ***felt it coming***. Big fights among conspiracy theorists, fat headlines in the worst tabloids, office phone ringing all day. I'd asked Nate: "Can we put out a statement?"

"Yes, how about 'fuck off, you fucking vultures'?"

Julian had understandably vetoed that wording.

But the waifish art woman is insistent. "People found patterns in your dreams, though, right?"

"You can find anything in dreams."

She tuts and moves away, and I realise she might have been chatting me up. I'm numb to advances. There's flesh on show, in the art and around it. The students like the sex dreams. I tell myself that I am married to my dataset. But I realise that no, I am the dataset's nice-guy chum, giving the death-stare to its suitors, whining that ***nobody understands its potential like I do***.

What *is* its potential, anyway?

I hear the high sweet note again, and follow it to a dim corridor, enjoying the quiet and the coolness. The corridor stretches into darkness, into the body of the chapel, and I can't see the end of it. It's an artwork in itself, it makes me feel (lightheaded from wine) that it might end anywhere or nowhere.

Something shifts in the dark, something rough is dragged against the stone floor. Then a wet slap. Slide-slap, slide-slap, a lopsided mime artist. Coming nearer. I'm ready. I've seen all sorts of things, at the other student art shows. I don't speak. I reckon it's polite to stay quiet, for this kind of performance.

The corridor smells of salt. The wall is damp. I move to one side and feel a squishing mass, like wet peat, underfoot.

It's too dark to make out the performer, although there's movement low down, things flickering and flailing.

I feel fear hatch in my stomach.

Well, it's a good show, then, I tell myself. A very effective piece. Congratulations to the artist! shouldn't I be able to see the artist, by now? Is the darkness deepening at that end of the corridor, so he stays in the dark even while he advances? A lighting trick. It's messing with my balance, too, as though a magnet is tugging me down the corridor.

Perhaps it's not part of the show at all, just an art student with a limp. Silly to be judgmental, stupid to be afraid of a perfectly ordinary person, who just...

I can't finish that sentence, and another thought fills the gap: it's not a person, though, is it? It's not human.

And fear claws up from my gut and into my throat.

More dragging sounds, now. Pattering, as well as slapping. More than one set of feet.

My wineglass smashes on the floor and that breaks my paralysis. My legs stutter, but they're back under my control, and I run from the corridor and out of the church. I push through the crowd.

I vomit pink bile into a university rubbish bin. I wipe my face and check around me, that Julian hasn't seen, that none of the artists are filming.

When I've stopped shaking, I get pretty scathing. The art's derivative tripe that's only interested in sex and nightmares, that has to terrify the viewers to have any effect. I wish I'd thrown up on some of the exhibits. It looks clever but really, it's not doing anything with our dreams that couldn't be done with Shakespeare, or the words from the back of a cornflake box. There's a true potential in my database and it's not even been touched by these self-centred shock-merchants.

On the train on the way home, I decide to do better. I'll teach myself data analysis. I will make myself into the suitor my database deserves. It's a mad vow, because when do I have time to do that? But I swear (on the many bird-headed naked anime women I have seen tonight) that I will rescue my dataset from shit art.

•

The other kind of interest we get is actively hazardous.

Julian has been hinting at a new investor. Big money. And a whiff of—power? Influence?

The morning after the art show, I get a call at seven a.m. I'm not at my best, but I'm a trouper, so I'm nearly at the office. "Spend the day out of town, Dil," says Julian.

Then I see journos surrounding our office doorstep, adjusting their cameras.

I carry my fragile head back down the road to Old Street Station, duck into the tube, make my way up to Stratford and take a train to Southend-on-Sea. Why not? I've never been, and nobody would look for me there, on the beach.

Julian probably expects me to find a seafront chip-shack with Wi-Fi and keep working away on my laptop. I rebel: I'll walk the pier, I'll ride the donkeys. I'll have a bloody day off. It's been long enough.

But I don't stop thinking about Sandpit. I see patterns of data in the breaking waves, the milling tourists, the swarming starlings when dusk finally comes at nine in the evening. I run nightmares through my earpieces as I ride the Adventure Island rollercoaster, listening to deaths by drowning and hurtling towards the sea.

There's only a small picture of Julian in the evening newspapers, and his statement: "Sandpit has not been in discussions of a commercial nature with the government. We have, however, talked with ministers about how to support thriving, innovative small businesses."

Julian's been paddling in deep waters. I wonder if Monifa wrote that for him. I phone her. "What's up?"

"Oh, Dil. Where are you?"

"Southend. You?"

"Julian promised me a hundred quid if I left town and didn't talk to anyone. I hope he pays up, I've been in a pub in Brighton most of the day."

"You should have called! We could have had a day at the seaside, together."

"Hmm."

"What's going on?"

"It's Tokyo. The government wants to know if it's true."

"The earthquake?" I'm pricked with annoyance, again. Third-rate shitty mysticism, obscuring the possibilities of what my database could actually do. (My own doubt mocks me: *Aye, but what can it do, Dil, really?*) "Tokyo was bollocks, though. Wasn't it? I mean, the idea that we knew anything about Tokyo was bollocks."

"Then it's an excuse. For the government to get involved. Use Sandpit for tracking, monitoring...."

"Oh. Well, that's better."

"No it's not! It's worse! God, Dil." She talks about Ginsberg, and the fascism of consensus reality, and how I can't have been listening when she did her presentation. I drift off a bit, thinking that she should be the one working out why my database is useful. She's clever about politics, psychology, all that. I mostly just know code. "The government's probably cross-referencing our users with all the personal data they hold on them. Extending their surveillance state to the bloody subconscious."

"I suppose," I say. "But how? I mean, really?" What on earth would the government do with my dataset? Use sweet dreams as an index of national contentment? Count the number of nightmares about immigration, swinging their policies to the right because of a rash of night-sweats? Call in drone strikes on seditious dreamers?

"I bet Julian didn't see a problem with it, either. I'm getting pretty fed up with being Sandpit's unpaid corporate ethics advisor, Dil."

She hangs up on me. A moment later, I think: *We can't work with the government! We'd scare away all the cool advertisers.* If I'd said that to Monifa she'd have been furious for months.

•

At least my day off has made our next step clear to me.

"Nate, we need to hire a data visualiser."

"Can't you do it?"

"No."

"Can *I* do it? Probably not. Look, I'm supposed to be raising revenue, not wasting money."

"And I'm supposed to be growing the brand! This is a brilliant innovation!"

"OK, boy wonder. Julian! Can we afford a data visualizer?"

Julian leans out of his office. "Why do we need it?"

I try to phrase it in Julian's terms. "We've got Monifa for the words. But words aren't the only language, Julian."

"Aren't they?"

"Dreams are pictures. We need to be pictures, too, yeah?" He's too easy to impersonate. I mustn't overdo it.

"I like it. Nate, see if we can spare a few grand."

Nate eyes me with hate.

A new desk in a corner of the office, and a data artist called Angharad (Welsh, wearing floaty scarves) takes up residence for a month. She adds an awesome visual dimension to my dials-and-words dashboard. New ways of perceiving: dream-data as waves, dream-data as clouds of starlings.

It looks so sweet, so sunny. I show Monifa but she sniffs at it, suspecting a deliberate attempt to hide sinister purposes.

I build sinuous links between dreams. We don't need crude tags, now; a phrase, or a mood, can spark a chain of connection. I watch users follow five, ten, twenty links suggested by us, into unknown dream territory. I create links led by dream logic: compression, substitution, metaphor.

It makes me embarrassed about our previous functionality, as though I've been peddling art-show cheap red wine when I could have been mixing sophisticated cocktails.

My new work attracts a potential income stream.

"Julian's got someone visiting." Nathan frantically sweeps his desk clear of accumulated crisp packets. "In ten minutes' time. Someone might want to give us money."

"Crap."

"Get the pitch deck ready," Nathan says, and I'm so nervous I forget what it means, and wonder where on a ship you find the pitch deck.

"Who is it?"

"Daddy won't tell me."

Julian and Nate fight all the time. It makes me nervous. A "good fail" would be one thing; I could work elsewhere. But to have all this potential pissed up the wall by bickering? That would be a disaster.

The doorbell rings and Nate springs to answer it. Into the office, graceful and smiling, walks a particularly fine specimen of posh boy. Cream linen suit. A few character lines in his face, floppy blonde hair.

Julian ushers him in and shuts the door behind them.

"You should have helped me bug his room," says Nate.

We're summoned half an hour later. Julian is fizzing. "Now, I'll talk numbers with Nathan, and Oliver..." The posh boy nods hello. "You'll chat with Dilawar about technical implementation. Dil, Oliver likes the visual presentation of data."

That sounds promising. Oliver sits in Nate's chair. "So, who are you representing?" I ask. Please let it not be another start-up. I've seen start-ups get locked into unprofitable entanglements, mutually reinforcing one another's delusions and avoiding the restaurant bill.

"I'm sorry, I can't share that. Confidential."

He enjoys saying that. "Fair enough. What do you need to do?"

"Well, my client..."

That's a neat phrase. I should say "my company" instead of "we". It would make me sound less co-dependent.

"...my client wants access to the dreams, of course."

"How much user information do you need? We have to protect our customers' privacy, but we can give you ages, genders...?"

"Yes! That might be useful," he says, as though it's only just struck him.

What kind of company doesn't care about its potential customers? I'd have thought he'd have a long list of demands, and we'd need to haggle. I could tell him that most of our data's self-report, and a lot of people lie. And some of them plagiarise their dreams. If I did, would he jump to his feet and yank his funding away?

"I'd need to know where and when the dreams happen," he says.

"We can do that. Get the data from the phone app, if the users have enabled it."

"And I want to search keywords. And this is informal, it's not a deal-breaker, but I love your visuals. They're so intelligent."

Jesus, I blush at that. "Angharad does the artwork. But we can definitely set up custom displays for you. Rather than just dropping all the data in your lap every morning."

"Oh, that doesn't sound bad either." He's flirting. Isn't he?

"It would help if I knew what you're planning to do with it," I tell him.

"Top secret things, I'm afraid."

"They're the only things worth doing." What a feeble joke.

Julian calls me in, and I explain that this is about the cheapest request, tech-wise, we could have. Then we play musical chairs so Julian and Oliver are closeted together again.

I want to phone Monifa and ask if she thinks the mysterious new income stream is flirting with me, but we've hardly spoken since our nearly-a-row about the government. I can't just call her to pick her brains. It would look selfish.

"Psst," says Nate. When I look his way, he mouths: *it's so my monkey.*

"What?" Is he saying the deal's dodgy? Is it Eton rhyming slang?

He scoots over on his chair and whispers, "It's so much money!"

There's a double surprise: the idea of riches, that old mirage, actually within reach.

Also, Nate's chest brushing against my arm makes me want to hold him.

He pulls away. He hasn't noticed. I don't want Nate, ugh. It's just a recent sea-change in me: on the train this morning, I nearly rested my head on another commuter's shoulder. I've been living in my mind for too long. When was the last time I did anything with my body? Probably the rollercoaster at Southend.

I put in my earpieces and press the random dream button to soothe myself. That intimate-distant feeling, and the confetti of images. One dream is nothing. You need three or more to resonate together. With a hundred, you can do anything.

I'm being dragged into the quicksand

I'm fighting with my brother

I've forgotten about my goldfish and they've had so many babies that the whole tank looks like marmalade

I'm kissing Nabokov and I tell him it would be weird, and my boyfriend would mind. His lips

Julian's laugh booms out behind his office door and I click away. That was an adult dream. I usually exclude them from my streams. Not safe for work.

But dreams *are* my work.

I can hear Oliver's light pleasant voice from inside Julian's office, but the words are inaudible.

I listen to a dozen filthy dreams. You couldn't use them as porn. They're explicit enough, but they erupt into weirdness too often; you'd need to keep your free hand on the pause button.

I realised I had bitten through his leg.

I had to concentrate hard to keep her from changing shape, and eventually I was just stroking a large Labrador.

Julian bursts out of the office, all smiles. "Lunch?"

To me, 'lunch' is a bagel, plus badam burfi from a Brick Lane sweet shop if I've got the time. So it's a struggle to look nonchalant while climbing into a taxi with Julian, and scrambling out again at a restaurant with real tablecloths.

Oliver sits next to me, but we don't speak much. Julian monopolises, Nathan supports, Oliver and I laugh in the right places. When Julian goes to pay the sizeable bill, and Nathan goes to the toilets, Oliver says: "I rather hoped we'd go somewhere in Shoreditch."

"Oh, Julian wouldn't take you to a ten pound noodle joint." I shouldn't be so informal with him, but thank goodness, he smiles.

"I'd wanted to see some of the famous hipsters." Wistful, like a tourist talking about the Northern Lights.

"I'll be in the Reliance tonight." A statement of fact and yet also a bold offer. "From six." I'm gambling that Julian and Nathan have drunk enough over lunch to leave the office early.

I shouldn't be messing around with an income stream. I'm living in a box-room in a shared house. I don't have anywhere to take a posh boy. I'm getting way ahead of myself.

•

The Reliance is a tricky place to flirt with someone I shouldn't be seen with. It's packed out and ridiculously loud, so I have to shout my witticisms as though I'm trying to charm a political rally.

"You came!" yells Oliver. "I thought Julian might make you work late."

"God, he's not my *dad!*" I get the teenage tone right, and Oliver throws his head back to laugh. He has a really good Adam's apple.

He tells me all about himself and at the end I'm none the wiser. As far as I can make out, he circles the globe like a migratory swan, doing inexplicable jobs for unnameable people. He says 'you know how it is' a lot, and I *don't*, and I think he knows I don't. I hope he's teasing me, not rubbing it in.

My life feels very short, by comparison. Shamefully, I borrow scripts from my industry to describe myself, talking about angel investors and big sales and Incredible Journeys.

I can't keep it up, and in the lull, we both look around the pub.

"There you go, those are your hipsters," I say.

"Marvellous! You've not grown the beard yourself, though?"

"Not likely. I'd get strip-searched every time I visit an airport." Bit heavy for a first date, but he smiles. "Anyway, I'm tired of hipsters."

"Ah. Are you also tired of life?"

Is he offering me a suicide pact? Oh. Yes. I get the reference. Tired of London.

I talk about the database, because what else do I have to say? At least I'm passionate about it. I'm not just a Shoreditch boaster with one eye on the lifeboats.

I tell him about The Night Before Christmas, the big push we ran. We were still in open beta, then, and scared that our users would put their phones away at Christmas. If they visited their parents, they'd be pestered to *get your nose out of that thing* and we'd lose them. We told them to update their dreams from bed before they got up, before they opened their stockings (Monifa wrote some really persuasive copy). We managed it: nearly as many log-ins as usual, and rich, weird, seasonal dreams.

And with answering passion, Oliver tells me what he wants to do. He's looking for keywords, but also for complex patterns, resonating across different fields: time, location, dream precedents. He wants to find order in complexity; not rigid uniformity, but agile, lively outputs. He's the only person who's close to understanding my beloved site.

In the end, my box-room doesn't matter, because the posh boy has a hotel room in Islington.

Our progress through the marble lobby, up the sweeping staircase, has the surreal quality of a dream. Oliver in his linen suit is the White Rabbit and I'm chasing him. Not from lust, but from dream-logic. Follow your passion, I catch myself thinking.

And later: is this my passion? It's passion. Is it mine?

•

When I leave the hotel it's a misty grey morning. At least the cold prickles help me shake off the dreams of drowning. I wait in the doorway of Marks & Sparks until it opens, buy a new shirt. I struggle into the shirt in the work toilet and I'm looking suave at my desk (with a crease over each nipple) when Nate arrives. "Morning!"

"Dil. Don't fuck it all up."

I resent the remark, but I know what he means, and I won't. It's not part of my dream right now. We're on the cusp of success, and it's another six months? Or a year? Of hard work, but I can do that. I can't start a relationship with anyone.

I don't contact Oliver before he comes in the following week. We don't shake hands, and we work hard all day, and then he asks me for dinner at Vanilla Black because he noticed I ordered vegetarian food the last time we ate.

"I admire what you're doing so much," he says, over ***pied de bleu*** souffle. "Making something new from new things. I'm a superannuated parasite by comparison."

I'm putty in his hands.

I lie awake that night, with Oliver a drowsy weight draped over me, and I think: *What are you up to, Dil?* He literally went to Eton, for heaven's sake. He's from the same set as Julian. Oh no. I'm having sex with Daddy. I've got to stop.

My phone pings on the bedside table. Oliver's head is resting on my shoulder, but I manage to stretch for the phone and open my email without waking him. It's Julian, announcing that with this new income, we can all have a raise.

I think straight away of a one-bedroom flat, maybe just off the Columbia Road flower market, a mile or so from work. So I can work late and walk home. Maybe an alcove, so I can bring Ganesha back from the office and set him up properly. A sofa bed, so Mam can visit me (and stop complaining that I never visit her).

Not so that Oliver can stay with me, when he's in town.

•

I build such a supple, gorgeous dashboard for Oliver. He wanted keyword searches; I go far beyond that, weaving a web of semantic sensitivities. When he's searching for "dog," he won't just be offered a tedious list of synonym searches (include hounds, puppies, pups?) but a delicate investigation into everything canine. The quintessence of dog.

I work with Angharad to make Oliver's dashboard unique. An antique look, with outputs on tiny brass dials, flickering from green to red. Hourglasses, with the sand flowing back and forth.

I work with Monifa on the words. I'm glad to have her back in the office. I buy her doughnuts.

"What's this Oliver person doing with the database?" she asks.

"I don't know." Damn, I should have said it's confidential. "I don't know *everything*," I add, too late.

"And you're OK with that? You're going to let him have all the info when you've got no idea—"

"He's not doing anything dodgy."

"He could be a middleman for the government."

I don't reply. I expect her to double down on me, but she sighs.

"You're always plugged in, Dil, whenever I see you. Listening to those things."

"The dreams? Lots of people are, these days." It's true. People use the dreams to get to sleep, to cheer themselves up. We have star users, big name dreamers. This grime kid from Lewisham called Morf grabs his favourite dreams, weaves them together and raps about them, a couple of times a week. He's got five million followers.

"Do you ever think that's weird?"

I think it's weird that Monifa already knows the answer to this, because she wrote it. Other people have accused Sandpit users of being voyeuristic, exploitative. Julian asked Monifa for a statement we could use in response, which she reluctantly assembled. So I'm going to mutter Monifa's words back to her. "It's all public information. The users put it out there."

"I'm not worried about the users, Dil. Sod *them*. It's what it's doing to *you*. You're just so immersed." She sighs. "Do you ever try letting go of things?"

"I haven't even got hold of things, yet! This is why I came to Shoreditch, to find something to be passionate about. I want to want something." I sense she's gearing up to give me a lecture with slides: *detachment as a therapeutic and/or spiritual practice*. I feel a bit indignant because I *know* all about that, I just don't *do* any of it. "And I'm young, I'm supposed to be learning things. I'm not supposed to be letting go of worldly stuff, going off to live in the forest." I think fondly of Grandad, who is probably right now either praying or walking the Yorkshire coast-path in waterproof trousers. But that's not the life for me, not yet.

"And how's the deep breathing going?" Monifa asks.

I scowl. "I've not got round to it, I've been doing something else." My face feels hot.

"Oh my God, you've slept with that posh bloke!"

I knew she was smart. "I was nurturing my interpersonal connections!"

Monifa snorted with laughter.

"I was really lonely! I never meet anyone—it was like I was drowning and I just—"

"Grabbed a buoy? No wonder you don't care what he's up to."

She agrees to write the text for Oliver's dashboard anyway, and I'm pleased she can't afford to have principles and has to come down off her high horse. Which is messed up of me, but I'm still a bit angry at her.

I don't need her approval. I've got Oliver and the dataset. I show Oliver his dashboard and he's gratifyingly enchanted.

"Oh, that's—you didn't have to do that. That's adorable.'

I am so smug I might burst.

Oliver takes me to the opera. It's not something I'd do off my own bat, but it's not bad, and I'm not paying, so I'm not complaining. Then he comes back to my new flat and admires the kitchen/living room, the tight spiral staircase, the new double bed.

•

After Oliver leaves, the next morning, I lie in bed. My dreams have been turbulent, not quite nightmares, but full of skirmishes. Maybe sex or maybe fighting. Which is a pretty transparent metaphor for my situation: I can't have a boyfriend, I haven't got time for a boyfriend, and I shouldn't date a source of funding.

I crank up my version of Oliver's interface and watch the dials quiver. Is he observing them, on his train home? What does he get from them?

The site's pretty quiet at night, while the dreams are happening. Then from seven a.m., the needles dance as people dictate their dreams over breakfast. There's another boost in the evening. The peaks are smoothing out as we go global—we're big in Japan but we've not cracked America.

I've started to upload, myself. Just fragments, posted to a throwaway account. I want to get the full user experience. Today I dictate some odds and sods about thuds and struggling, and I feel better for doing it.

One of Oliver's dials is climbing into the red. It's labelled *against*. It's the one which reports on dreams about conflict; all the cognate terms are hooked together to create a net. And this morning, in the net, there's something heavy.

I pull up the archive: two-thirds of them are flagged as nightmares. But when I view the dreams, there's no pattern, just the usual jumble.

Oliver's other dials say *heat, cut off, incoming, shaking, sea* and others. I don't know what any of them mean. It's part of our flirtation, him teasing me and me feigning a lack of interest. I open a few of them up—*visitors, angels* and *beasts*—to see the associated common words, from today's dreams. *Tea, inspectors. Wings, guardian, radiant. Fur, nuzzle, unicorn.* Very nice nonsense.

Now I set myself a dreamstream from the sea dial. I use it a lot. There's always loads of activity on it.

I carry my stream of sea dreams with me, and wander out to buy breakfast. My usual route's blocked by police incident tape. I keep trying to get around, taking the next available road, hitting tape again until I realise the pastry shop is the epicentre of the disruption.

I ask a policeman, hiding my nosiness behind a neighbourly air: just moved in, everything OK? He says there's been a fight but he's too professional to offer details.

"It was carnage," says a short unshaven man with no such scruples. He saw it: a proper brawl, a dozen guys, heads banged on pavements. There's been a lot of that recently, in Shoreditch. The free newspapers blame bad drugs and hot days. I walk away while the man's still talking.

I wonder if these fights are the first signs of the tide properly turning. There's not enough money around, and not enough optimism to fill the gaps. Overstretched hopes collapsing, leaving people wild and violent. I bet there were a lot of fights in failing gold-rush towns.

Then again: craft beer is strong. The fights don't need a deeper explanation.

I go back to the flat, back to bed. Barricade myself in pillows. Open up the dials again for some more soothing babble, but the words get murkier. *Inspector, scrutinise. Sword, Principality, coruscate. Nest, harrier, vermin.* I scrape away that top layer, go deeper into the chains. There's no comfort there. *Intrude, invade. Wrath, radiant, judgment. Tusk, tooth, carrion crow.*

•

One last Sandpit meeting with Oliver, one more night together in my flat. I haven't invited anyone else into my bed, in between. If I visualised the data of my love life there would be a years-long flat patch, then one big bar.

I've been dreaming about sex at night, daydreaming about it at work. Not Oliver, specifically. I just feel a pull; I lean towards something, all the time. I shouldn't have given in to it. I didn't miss it, before.

"Do you want to know what I do with your data?" says Oliver in bed.

My heart sinks because this means he's not coming back, doesn't it? The secret was part of our flirting. So he's saying he doesn't want to flirt with me anymore.

"Nah."

He's lying curled up close around my back. I thought he'd be very crisp and cool, like hotel sheets, but he isn't. He's very tender. Which is disconcerting, when you're not in love.

"Oh go on, let me tell you. There's no point in having secrets if nobody's interested."

Maybe he wants us to share the secret. Maybe he wants us to go into business together. That could be my passion. "Tell me."

"My clients are interested in catastrophic events."

"What events?"

"World-ending things. Or civilisation-ending. I use your dataset as a kind of barometer, so I can warn them."

"That's bonkers. Dreams aren't predictive. Have you read them? They're all about drowning and toilets and public speaking."

"They don't need to be prophetic. I do all the interpretation, the dreams are just... sensitive. You know how animals run away from earthquakes?"

But my dataset isn't a rabbit stampede. "People pay you for that?"

"It's a tiny risk. But with huge potential consequences. So they pay me a teeny-tiny proportion of their massive-massive wealth." He sounds so calm and sensible. His skin is warm all along my back.

"Was it all your idea?"

"Pretty much. The Tokyo earthquake set me off..."

Tokyo again. I'd thought it was my gorgeous interface that had attracted Oliver.

"Tokyo isn't true."

"Check your records." He kisses my shoulder.

"That's mad," I say. "That can't work."

"It works. I had to analyse dreams from around the time of a lot of unpleasant events. But it works. People notice more than they think. Then that affects their dreams in ways I can interpret."

"I don't believe you."

I feel him shrug. "My clients believe me."

"But how long are people going to keep paying you, when the world doesn't end?"

I squirm round in his arms so I can see his face. I should have done that sooner; he's not amused.

"Dil, you work in *Shoreditch*. My work makes more sense than a robot shoe you turn on with your bloody phone." He's so out of touch, even his sarcastic tech ideas are outdated.

Too late, I realise that he might love his data as much as I love mine.

He's not my boyfriend. I understand that. But I'd thought that he was clever, and that we were collaborating. Now I suspect he's a deluded con-man.

"This whole part of town's built on ridiculous fantasy," he says. "It couldn't survive without it."

"That's optimism. It's not the same thing."

"It's optimism combined with incredibly long odds. That's fantasy."

"Some people make it big!"

"Vanishingly few, Dil." Now he sounds withering, worldly-wise. As though I'm young and foolish and I'll grow out of working and start hunting unicorns like him. He's not just deluded, he's being a dick.

I don't like feeling angry and patronised and heart-sick and hope-dashed, so I go out to buy brunch. I want to call Monifa and cry on her shoulder. But she warned me he was dodgy.

As I walk, Oliver diminishes in my mind. His eccentricity makes him more fallible, less intimidating. I buy expensive pastries and go back to the flat and kiss him. I might not see him again, so I may as well do everything I've ever daydreamed about doing with him, while I have the chance.

•

Two days later, I haven't contacted Oliver. I don't believe that dreams are stirred by a wind that blows from future disasters. Whenever I think of his ideas I feel tired. That makes it harder to do my job.

Oliver hasn't contacted me, either.

I don't sleep well. I still listen to the dreams as I fall asleep, but they don't soothe me like they used to; when I upload my own, I have to tick the boxes for 'nightmare' and 'adult'.

Julian yells at Nate all the time. "We need some good publicity!" Morf the dream rapper has been found on Brighton beach. He might have jumped off the pier.

One night I run Oliver's dashboard backwards, back to the days before the Tokyo earthquake. To utterly disprove his stupid theory.

The dials are red: *shaking, falls.* It doesn't prove anything.

Monifa's verbal outputs say: *significant words today are crushed, dust, lost.* I hide that from all users.

From my email trash I salvage a message from a recruitment company which I'd deleted the previous week.

•

I've never called a recruiter before, and I don't know my lines. Is it like being a secret agent, or on a blind date? But she sweeps in and butters me up very briskly. "You must know we're really pleased to hear from you."

I'm phoning the recruiters from a shop doorway on Redchurch Street, because I have to be at work in ten minutes, and every time a car goes past I cup the phone. Pretending to the recruiter that I'm indoors, pretending I'm more of a master of my destiny than this.

"So, there are some jobs, maybe, and I could do them?" I ask. Nice one, Dil, super smooth.

"'Scuse me." A bearded man nudges me aside to open up his shop, which sells raw denim. I settle in the next doorway along the street, for a shop which sells raw chocolate.

"Definitely. We have a really interesting position with a company who are keen to meet you."

So far, I've been motivated by queasy panic. But of course, I'm also running *towards* somewhere. Could I quit Sandpit and hop into a better gig? A lowlier role, but in a bigger tech company. One of those converted warehouse offices with a ball-pit and free smoothies.

"It's good news. It's Natwest!"

I picture the little Natwest branch on Haxby High Street, back home. Dogs tied up outside, pens chained up inside. My friend Dave's mum behind the counter.

"A bank?"

"Uh-huh. One of the fastest-growing multinational banks."

"I'd thought, perhaps, it would be something else. A tech company. Or another start-up?"

"Right! Of course!" She's as surprised as I am. "A lot of people we work with, in your situation, they really want to get out of start-ups. They really want to move to banks."

Stupid not to have thought of it. I mean, you can even see bits of the City, the financial centre of London, from here. The Gherkin looms out from behind other buildings like a big swollen innuendo. I can't imagine what the Natwest office would look like. I just see myself hanging in the air over London, in a misty glass cube.

"My clients from start-ups often want some security. To buy a house, or have a kid. Or just have the weekend off!"

"Oh, totally! Weekends, yes." I sound like an alien infiltrator.

"So, shall I set up a meeting?"

"Why not." I'm so lacklustre. I say it again with gusto, to pretend it's my catchphrase: "Why not! Go for it." My Mam will be pleased, at least.

The recruiter offers me a preliminary interview the following day. "Lunchtime. So you can be a bit discreet. Your boss doesn't need to know."

She doesn't know I never take a lunchbreak for longer than it takes to buy a bagel.

•

At ten a.m. the following day, Nate scoots over on his chair and whispers: "Where's the interview?"

"What interview?"

"Brand new shirt, Dil. You've got an interview. Unless you pulled, last night. Look, I'm not prying..."

"You're prying. I'm allowed to look for other jobs, aren't I? And there isn't anything you can offer me—"

"We might get bought."

"Flippin' heck!"

Start-ups long to be bought. It's pretty much the best way to exit, another company snapping you up. But start-ups get bought because they offer something that another company wants, or because they're competition. Surely we're no threat to anyone, and why would anyone want to absorb us?

"Why would anyone buy us?" I whisper.

"*Acqui-hire*." Nate sounds like he's choking.

"What, acquire-to-hire? Who would they want to hire?"

"All of us. You're in demand as much as Julian and me."

"But they could just offer me a job. They don't need to buy Sandpit to get me."

"Dil! Where's your loyalty?"

"What loyalty?"

"OK, where's your *selfishness*? If someone buys Sandpit to hire us, you get a salary, *and* a honking big pay-off."

This could be it. The dream come true. I can actually feel my heart hammering.

"Would they keep the site up? Would they close it down?" I picture the front page of Sandpit plastered with one of those miserable, mockable notices: *Thank you for being part of our incredible journey. We'll always remember the creativity and community that made Sandpit so special! Now get your shite off the site by Tuesday before we nuke it.*

"I can't guarantee they'd keep it going."

That gives me a pang. Could I let the site go? Could I shut it down? The cloud capped tags, the gorgeous messages; the solemn algorithms, the great graph itself...

"It's not a bank, is it, who want to buy us?"

Nate squints at me with suspicion. "Why on earth would it be a bank, Dil? It's another tech company."

I imagine myself in a different warehouse office. I'm at one of those two thousand dollar sitting/standing hydraulic desks, sipping a smoothie, in the glow of some neon art. But who's that, lurking by the ball-pit? "Nate, I don't want to work with Julian indefinitely."

"OK."

"By 'indefinitely', I mean 'ever again.'"

"Why not, do tell."

"You know why! He just smarms around showing off while we do the work." And, I want to add, because the two of you argue all the time. I used to think it was because of the stress, but I reckon if we got bought by Google, Nate and Julian would lie in the same jacuzzi in Palo Alto and bicker.

Nate blinks, as though the idea of escaping from Julian conflicts with his programming. Then he gives a tiny nod, more like a twitch. "I'll bear that in mind during my negotiations."

"You won't tell Julian about my interview?"

"What interview? Look, he'll notice if you sneak out. But I can distract him. When do you need to leave?"

"Midday?"

At 11:40 a.m., Nate picks up a sheaf of papers and crosses to Julian's door.

By 11:45 a.m., they're shouting. My noise-cancelling earphones can't blot them out.

"Well, one of us didn't have any sodding *choice*!" Nate shouts, with a melodramatic flourish. Julian is more bass and rumbling so I can't make out the words. I assume he says something about how everyone has choices, because then there's Nathan again, pretty much shrieking. "Not after you screwed up the last two companies!"

There's some inaudible back and forth as to whose fault that was. I imagine each company took more than a year to complete its nosedive, so compressing the recriminations into five minutes is impressive. Nathan is putting in nice rhetorical touches: 'I *told* you but ooh no, *you* wanted to..." Sometimes he repeats things Julian has said back to him, in a stupid voice. Classic.

Then Nate turns up the volume, so I can hear his knock-out punch: "How was I ever going to get a job with *Dial-a-Dog* on my fucking CV?"

Dial-a-Dog is a blast from the past. In the early days of the internet, it was one of those companies that achieved fame through failure. I rack my brain. It was a bit like InterFlora. Inter*Fauna*? Could you send a basket of bunnies, a bouquet of white hamsters? I want to look it up now, but Julian might catch me at it.

I rock in my chair, uneasy, and feel the lovely smooth action of the chair. I wonder if the chair came from Dial-a-Dog.

"Some of us," bellowed Julian, reaching at last a level of anger that makes him audible, "Feel a *sense of responsibility*!"

"Some of us like to *play God!*"

It's no use, I can't resist. I whip out my phone and cradle it, hide it under the desk and look it up on that. Dial-a-Dog: it was initially imagined as a way to send animals to friends, but it pivoted when every humane society protested and the police intervened. It became a way, instead, for pet owners to lend their animals to someone else in the neighbourhood. Dachshunds as a service! Because who didn't, sometimes, want to hold a puppy?

I'd still been at school when Mr Rupert Smythe used Dial-a-Dog to request every long-haired cat in Kensington be sent to Mrs Alicia Smythe, for an hour on a Saturday afternoon. Twenty Burmese and Persians were delivered. It's our anniversary, he said, as he ushered them all in. It'll be a surprise.

And it was a surprise, because Mr and Mrs Smythe were divorcing, and Mrs Smythe went into anaphylactic shock. She lay on the hall floor and watched a big Maine Coon clawing chunks out of her sofa. KILLER KITTEN FIRM DELIVERS PURR-FECT CRIME, said the *Mail on Sunday*. Although one of the owners had popped back early and stabbed Mrs Smythe with an epi-pen, and she'd survived. CATTEMPTED MURDER, said the *Daily Star*.

I black out my phone screen three times from guilt, and return each time from horrified fascination. This was the car-wreck that had preceded Sandpit—or preceded the company which had preceded Sandpit?—which had welded Julian and Nate into unholy acrimony.

Nate is using the biggest key he owns to wind up the boss, all for my benefit.

At ten to noon, Julian strides through the office. His face is crimson; he doesn't even glance at me before he's out of the door.

Nate emerges, hair wilder than usual. "Right on schedule! He won't be back this afternoon, I shouldn't think." I can't stop staring. Nate rolls his eyes. "We never *actually* killed anyone."

"Was that the company slogan? Did you get Monifa to write it?"

"Look, I'm helping you out, here. I've got rid of Daddy. You can toddle off to your treasonous job interview."

"Why are you helping?"

"While you're out, I can go back to the buyer and negotiate about whether Daddy's part of the deal. I'll probably know by the end of the day what's possible. So don't do anything rash, OK? Dil?"

Ping! An email from Oliver. Saying: call me!

I really wish he hadn't. I need to run through my responses to typical interview questions, casually list the three times I've shown Leadership and Initiative.

I step outside to phone Oliver.

"Dil! What are you up to, today?"

He's a business associate. I can't tell him I'm thinking of jumping ship. See, Nate, I do have a sense of loyalty. "Not much."

"Come to Derbyshire."

"What?"

"Come to Coton in the Elms. Get a train from Euston to Tamworth, then a cab. I'll pay for it."

"Why?" He doesn't sound passionate, or romantic, or even polite.

"I've got a little cottage in the countryside. Wouldn't you like to see it?"

"I'm not really into cottaging."

"Dil, something's coming. But it's not one of the big ones. A little something."

"A catastrophic event? How can that be 'little'?"

"Well, it's not the end of the world. It's just the end of... some stuff. Look, I can help you. I know what to do."

"You're mad."

"Oh, that's nice. Here I am, asking you to move in with me..."

"Are you?"

"Dil, in two hours' time I'll be in a stone cottage at the furthest point inland in the country. A long way from the Thames estuary, in particular. Do you want to be with me?"

It's too big to consider, so I fixate on something smaller. "Are you supposed to be telling me this?"

"It's confidential. But my London clients are all jetting off to Xinjiang, and none of them offered to take me along, so fuck 'em."

Is he drunk? "I'll think."

"Think quickly."

I see myself in a trendy office, sinking into a ball-pit. I see myself in a glass cube at Natwest. I see myself in the garden of an English cottage. I shake all three visions out of my head and go back to the office.

I look up Coton in the Elms. The map shows miles and miles of fields, and The Honeypot Tea Rooms. I look up Xinjiang. It's the furthest point inland in the world. They're expecting a deluge, a flood so big it could end this age and dissolve the world.

I go back to Oliver's dashboard. Half of his dials are red. One is *sea,* one is *beasts.*

I open ten related dreams at random. Each one is a nightmare. Their similarities are more than coincidence, more than Monifa's discursive norms.

taste salt in the air but couldn't see the waves

hauling itself towards me. I couldn't move and

wet, and stumbling as though it had too many

some kind of gills and my legs wouldn't

I want to be further inland.

No, I refuse to give in to Oliver's panic. He's being too literal. I want to explain to him: sea metaphors are everywhere. The sea's the start-point of everything, whether you're talking about Manu's missus stepping out of the water or Darwin's waddling fish. And dreams are like the sea—a parallel world, half-known, always shifting—which is why the sea washes into so many dreams. You can't look at a couple of rough nights and assume that everyone's going to wake up underwater.

I drill down into the geographical data. There's a huge concentration of nightmares round London. But that could just be user distribution, and timing: London's big, awake, and uploading.

I'll be late for the interview if I don't leave now. I suddenly think: *what if I don't come back?* Of course I'll come back. But I scoop the tiny brass statue of Ganesha out of my desk drawer, tuck him into my pocket, to sit in the silk folds of the tie I'm hiding.

I take the train, changing from the funky, orange Overground line full of hipsters to the serious, silver Jubilee line, which the bankers use. I get out my tie, can hardly remember how to knot it. I speed out to a new building near Canary Wharf. The office isn't a misty glass box, although it isn't far off. It's a bit corporate, but there's nothing wrong with that. I send a selfie to Mam, making sure I get the tie and the skyscraper in the picture: *got a job interview here today, bit scared.* She texts back *clever lad, good luck!*

Nobody asks me daft psychology questions at this interview. They know their stuff. "Would you mind the change of sector?" the head of the panel asks. I can sense that the panel want me to renounce any attachment to Silicon Roundabout, to show that I'm serious.

"I'd be excited!" I lie. "I was able to take on a lot of responsibility at Sandpit because..." Because my bosses were chaotic arseholes? "Because of the relatively informal structure. But it's not like I'm in *love* with start-ups," I sneer.

Everyone chuckles. I make some extravagant claims about my abilities and realise they're true.

I should go back to the Sandpit office, and work through the afternoon. Julian could turn up again and raise hell if I'm missing. But when the train slows to a halt at my stop, I don't move. I watch the doors close, and ride on to Euston instead.

As I come up from the underground into the station, I notice I'm jogging along the concourse to catch the train to Tamworth.

My carriage is empty. I pull a technology magazine from my bag and flick through it. It's glossy and upbeat. *No need to look back,* it tells me. *Don't worry about past failures. Look forwards! Go faster!* I set my dreamstream to positive words: *conquer, surmount, overcome.* A motivating burble flows from my earbuds.

The outskirts of London give way to fields. The light's fading, hours too soon for dusk; the sun's still there, a dim disk in an overcast sky.

I check Oliver's dials. I pull up the data, and find the dials stopped being representative hours ago. If they'd been analogue devices, they'd have over-clocked, swept back through leaf-green and amber and up to red for a second time.

I press my forehead against the window. In the premature dusk, I can see cattle grazing. I'm out in the countryside, out of London, out of danger.

I should phone Monifa, give her a chance to leave town. But what can I say? *That guy you warned me about is some kind of occult con-man and he thinks London's going to drown.* It's not as if I have proof. Wouldn't my phone be making more noise, if anything serious was going down?

I look at my phone. It's been turned off since the interview.

I turn it back on with dread. Are horrors swarming from the Thames? Does today's news resemble last night's dreamstream? Will it ping like a ricocheting bullet?

No bad news from London.

I call Monifa anyway.

"Hey, Mon. Should I go and work for a bank?"

"Hi, Dil! I'm *fine*, how are *you*?"

"Oh. Sorry. It's just a bit of a shock. I might be getting a new job."

"Nice to have options."

"They didn't offer me options. Oh! You mean ordinary options, not start-up options. Yes."

"I did. So, what's the problem?"

"Will I be boring if I get another job?"

"Ha! I don't mind you talking about your job, but to be honest? It's not your best feature."

I'm disconcerted. "I thought being passionate made people interesting."

She laughs. "If that was true, Shoreditch would be the most interesting place in the world. Is it?"

Yes. Maybe? "No?"

"Julian really wants things. Is Julian the most interesting person in the world?"

"Nooo." He doesn't really want things, though, he just expects to get them. And Julian fears losing them. I'm the only one with a pure keen flame of passion. "What's that noise?" Monifa asks. "Are you on a train?"

"I'm going to Tamworth." For increasingly incoherent reasons.

"Look, I'm working now. Call me when you're back, we can catch up. Properly, two-way, not you using me as an agony aunt, alright?"

Despite the scolding, Monifa has calmed me down. She's right, it's good to have options. That sense of choice makes Sandpit seem bearable. I could stick it out a bit longer, and keep expanding my site, its functions, its marvels…

My interview adrenaline leeches away, and the false anxieties Oliver planted in me have turned to anger. I phone him.

"Nothing's happening in London, Olly! And now I've walked out of work because of you, and it's all bollocks."

"You're on a train *now*?"

"Yes. I'm about ten miles from you. Are you still there?"

"Yes, but hurry up."

"How?" A noise from further down the carriage: doors slamming, shuffling. "Hang on, the conductor's coming."

"Good. Tell him to make the driver go faster."

"Don't be ridiculous, Olly. It calls at all these small stations…"

"Fuck the small stations!"

While Oliver advises me how to commandeer the train, I fish in my pocket to find my ticket.

"Can you book me a taxi?" I cut through Oliver's hijack fantasies to ask.

"I'll fetch you."

"Wow. You're going to leave your secret underground lair, just to—"

A dragging, lopsided sound at the far end of the carriage.

Not the conductor.

It's rough cloth—or scaled, loose skin—hauled over wet stone. A familiar weakness spreads up my legs.

I hurl myself sideways to break the paralysis. I fall to the carriage floor, huddle against the wall. My shoulder's killing me, but the dragging sound has ceased and I can move again.

Oliver is silent. No, my earpieces are missing. I pat the floor around me, grip the earbuds and stuff them back in my ears. "Dil? *Dil!*"

"Oliver, it's here," I whisper. "It's on the train."

He doesn't ask what it is. He whispers back: "You'll be OK." A pathetic reassurance from a man whose business is the end of the world. "You're nowhere near the epicentre. It'll just be a strand, a fragment."

But there's no bad news from London.

"Olly, what if *we're* the epicentre?"

"Us? Why would we be?"

"Not you and me. *Us.* Sandpit."

Memories close in: the art show, the dragging in the corridor. The fights around the street where I live, where I work, that I blamed on long summer evenings of drinking. Disturbances circling me, closing in.

Huddled on the floor of the train, I know what the dragging thing is, approaching. It's a nightmare I've had a dozen times but I don't know how it ends because I always wake. It's a thing with sagging skin and thick fins crawling out of the sea towards me.

But the sea is not the sea, it's a symbol. For dreams, for waking, for *evolution.* Something struggling to haul itself from one state to another. A new kind of creature, heaved out of the dream-sea.

Over the dragging sound, I hear a high fine note that I recognise.

"Can you hear it, Olly?" I mean: is it real? Is it just me? Let it just be me.

"I can't hear anything. The train's too loud."

It doesn't matter. It doesn't matter if the creature has pulled itself into the waking world, or if I'm dreaming without sleeping. Either way, I don't know how to escape.

The tug intensifies and mashes me against the seating. The whine is deafening, and it joins with the sound of scraping metal, and a long hiss. It's the brakes of the train. The tugging sensation was the slowing of the train. A sans serif sign in the gloaming tells me, thank God, we're at Tamworth station.

I struggle to my feet. "Open up, open the fuck *up*." I punch the door button three times, spill out of the train and charge through the station ticket barriers. My knight in shining armour leaning on a car by the curb.

He reaches over to me and pulls the earpieces from my ears.

"Hello, Dil."

The countryside is very quiet.

"I think Sandpit might have caused Tokyo," I tell him.

•

Oliver's cottage is in the heart of a wood. The path to the cottage winds around all over the place, conceding to every tree. With each step through dappled light, my breath comes easier. My hand in my pocket finds the comforting brass lump of the statue and curls around it.

"Isn't it adorable?" Oliver asks.

There are actual white roses growing round the door of his cottage. The sky's so overcast they're luminescing in the gloom.

"If you like that sort of thing."

"Doesn't everyone? Don't you dream of escaping to the countryside?"

"I grew up on t'moors, I dreamed about escaping *from* the countryside." Mocking him calms me down. "Did you nick this place off three bears?"

As he ducks through the low doorframe, I notice that the stone walls are very thick. Defensive, robust. The dense trees, the winding path and the thick walls are the point of this place, not the roses or the wood-burning Aga. They don't reassure me, though. Not now I know what's happening. Oliver thinks that Sandpit can predict the future. That's rubbish. My database, my lovely database, doesn't foresee disasters.

I think it *causes* disasters.

It runs dreams through a hundred minds; users listening to dreams, then dreaming, then uploading those dreams to be heard again. Churning the dreams, intensifying them. The cycle creates a whirlpool.

The whirlpool sucks things through.

"What would you like?" asks Oliver, resolutely normal. "Coffee? Slice of sponge?"

"Have you got broadband?"

"I have a LAN. I'm not a peasant."

"I need a monitor. Or two, if you've got two."

I commandeer the kitchen table (stripped pine). I set up all the kit I can scrape together. When I sit, my hand sneaks out automatically and grasps my earpieces. As I slip them snugly into my ears, the wrongness floods back around me, thick and swirling.

I snatch my earpieces out, stuff them deep in my bag and zip it shut.

I need to prove something. I rack my brain for places around the world where there have been terrible disruptions in the last six months: tidal waves, wildfires, that one big volcano. I feel like a ghoul, but it's vital. I check the dates, and crank back the time-frame on my dashboard. The associations blaze up, from a week before each incident. I test it again and again, get a chain of deathly associations: *drench, drift; crisp, crackle; explode.*

Oliver stands behind me, reading over my shoulder. He's vibrating with the desire to say, *told you so.*

"But look." Before he can get a word in, I point at the screen. "There are other disasters in other places, and nothing bad on the dials at all."

"So what do you think's happening?"

I bring up a map of user activity. "The bad stuff only shows up on the dials when the place is a hotspot for our users."

Oliver pulls over a kitchen chair and sits next to me. "Dil, you realise you've leapfrogged over me in terms of ridiculous beliefs? I thought people might be able to sense an earthquake. Now you think you've invented an app that can make one happen?"

He's got a point, so I ignore him.

"And if it's about the number of users," Oliver asks, "why wouldn't it be affecting New York? Or Mexico City?"

"Perhaps we're not big enough there? We were big in Japan. No, hang on..." I pull up more information. "This is it, I've got it! The people at those hotspots, they're super-users. They don't just post more, they're not always banging on about themselves..."

"Don't insult the customers, Dil."

"The people at these locations are more *connected* users. They read more of other people's dreams, they search more, and they have their dreamstreams playing *all the friggin' time.*"

Creating a vortex. Dreams passing into dream passing into dreams. The truth had popped into my head on the train, and now I had proof of it.

Maybe dreams evolve this way naturally. You tell someone a dream, and then a fragment of it passes into their imagination, their dreams, and the current grows stronger and the boundary weakens. But in the world, it would happen so much more slowly—how often would you tell someone your dream? How often would you listen to theirs? Whereas we've been breeding them in captivity, factory farming them.

It was the wrong thing to do, and the wrong place to do it, in the thin air of a gold-rush town.

"The circulation, the concentration of dreams. That's what it likes. That's what brings it closer."

Oliver raises one eyebrow. "It?"

The tugging tide, the dragging crawler. The thing I can feel, even now, whenever my hand twitches for my earpieces. "The thing that's trying to come through."

Oliver keeps his face blank. Either he doesn't believe me, or he's been hiding some pretty dark stuff.

I prod him. "When you thought Sandpit could predict things, why did you think it worked? I mean, you said it was like animals running away. Is it about vibrations, or chemicals, or..."

He shakes his head slowly. "Not quite."

"Something else."

"It's best not to look directly at these things, you know, Dil."

Condescending bastard. "That's rich! You can afford not to look at them. They're not bloody following *you*."

"You're overwrought. When did you last eat?"

He stands up and paces around the kitchen, assembling objects—crumpets, honey, side-plates—like a ridiculous English barricade against the darkness. Good, he'll be occupied while I wrap things up. It's weird to be working without the dreams burbling in my ear. I'm uninsulated, so whenever Oliver closes a cupboard door or sets down a cup, it jars me. I log into Sandpit's VPN, start drafting an apology for the front page of the site. I wonder if I've got time to phone Monifa. She'd know how to phrase it. *Thank you for being part of our execrable journey.*

"What are you up to?" Oliver calls over. The crumpets smell lush but I don't stop typing.

"I need to close down the Sandpit site."

"Now, hang on! Hang on." Oliver puts a hand on my arm. He's too classy to grab me but this is an emphatic hint.

Bugger that. I keep typing. "Sorry about your business," I say, as I type a different 'sorry' to the users, apologising in stereo.

"I'm not worried about that. I'm thinking of you, you'll be sacked."

"I can get another job. There are loads of places I could work." Natwest Bank, for instance. A month from now I could have a photo of myself on a plastic card, hanging round my neck, in case I forget who I am.

"You can get another job *now*, as things stand," Oliver argues. "You're the CTO of a successful start-up. If you become a paranoid malcontent who sabotaged your own site, nobody will touch you."

"Shit. But what else can I do? It's still happening. The site helps it to happen!" I look across at the other monitor, the existing Sandpit front page, and my eye catches on some dreamtext that's show-cased there and the words wriggle into my mind. They're genuine, they have that sincere but lopsided dreamvoice, and the current tightens around me. The outside edge of the whirlpool brushes me. It wants me to read, to listen, to glut myself until I'm just a conduit. I wrench my head away.

Now Oliver actually holds my wrist, so I can't type. "What do you need to do?" he asks.

"Shut it down."

"All of it? Are there more and less dangerous parts? What is it you need to put an end to?"

I try to get out from the drag and the panic. I try to think. "The cycling, the re-cycling. The dream sharing. The most dangerous part is when people listen to each other's dreams."

"Dil, you built the site up bit by bit. Surely you can take some of those bits out."

But it's all interlocked and connected. It's a city. How do you dismantle a city? Why can't I summon up half the wit I used when I built this thing?

I breathe deep. "I suppose I could disconnect the dreamstream."

"Good!" he says.

I crack open the code and start deleting.

"Wait!" he says.

I backpedal frantically.

"Users will notice. Nathan and Julian will notice. They could sue you, even."

"There's no other way!" I'm wailing because the starting and stopping, pull and release, is making me seasick.

"Didn't you once tell me half the dreams were made up?"

"Jesus, I shouldn't have. Did I?"

"Pillow talk."

"Oh. I'd forgotten. You're right, half of it's codswallop." That used to annoy me, but maybe it was a blessing in disguise. Maybe it slowed the awful progress.

"If only you could just keep the made-up dreams."

I reach the same conclusion just as he says it. "Genius!"

Oliver smiles a modest smile, the smug git. "I mean, I suppose it's nearly impossible to tell the real dreams from the fake."

"It's not impossible. I can do it. Don't stare at me, go and do something useful."

I plough into the database. As Julian always insisted, we can't tell people what dreams are. But I can certainly tell you what they're not: things you stole, that someone else wrote, aren't your dreams. So I set up a system to pluck up any dream that matches any other online text. A plagiarism alarm.

You know what else aren't dreams? If something's actually sexy and narratively coherent, it's almost certainly not a dream. It's carefully crafted porn which someone has slipped into the Sandpit, to find a wider audience for their fantasy. I get the system to scoop up the most popular dreams with sexy keywords.

I dam up these two pools—one pool for theft, the other for filth—and I leave them connected to all the functions of the site.

Every other dream, I disconnect.

I've not destroyed them. I haven't deleted a word. You can still read any dream. You can still find them, if you look for them. But they won't feed into anyone's dreamstream, they won't be recommended to any readers, they won't be part of the dangerous churn.

I've walled off that great database, made a lagoon of fears and non-sequiturs and mangled memories. I've never been more proud of it than in the moment I isolate it. So big! Much bigger than *War and Peace*. So communal, so sociable, and yet so personal. It was a city, it was Atlantis. It was so fucking weird it probably bent dimensions. Will I ever make anything as marvellous again?

I slump in the unyielding kitchen chair. I ache, and I miss the back support of my suave leather office chair. But I feel lighter, now I've fixed things.

"Done it," I call. Oliver returns from the sitting room.

"Good. Your tea's gone cold."

"Can I have coffee?"

"Will anyone notice the difference? On the site?"

"Anyone coming in to work on the code would notice, but Nathan, or Julian? Never. And the users probably won't notice, they'll just… Over time, it'll be less interesting. Less quirky. There'll be more proper plots. Oh, and more rutting."

"You don't sound happy."

"I was giving them dreams. Now I'm just giving them some kind of shoddy repackaged bollocks, and *telling* them it's their dreams. Half of it's stolen. Most of it's tits."

"Welcome to capitalism." He sets a cup of coffee down next to my shaking fingers. "Are you better, now?"

We watch each other across the table. Each of us is convinced that the other is deluded. He thinks that dreams can predict the future, and I'm still reasonably sure that's bobbins. I think that dreams can endanger the future, and he's viewing me with amused indulgence.

He genuinely wants to know if I'm OK, though.

"I don't know." I try to unclench my shoulders. I think the sun's got brighter, outside, and it's so quiet. Shoreditch is never this quiet. There's only a soft buzzing, which in my flat would be an Overground train passing or the router, but here I think it might be coming from actual bloody bees.

But even when I'm totally at rest, and everything's silent, I can still feel that faint pull.

The things are still writhing, trying to get through. They're further off now, or deeper down. But they're restarting their incredible journey.

"It's not just the site. It really is me, I think."

"Narcissist."

"I'll delete my account."

"Oh no! The last resort!"

"Oliver..."

"Sorry!" He puts his fingers over his mouth.

I delete my Sandpit account. It takes sodding ages. Julian insisted people should have to press at least three buttons and reply to a confirmation email, and I resent that I didn't stand my ground and make it simpler. Even though I'm CTO it's like rooting out a tick. Finally, though, it's dead and gone.

I smell coffee, cut grass, roses. I gulp down Oliver's anaemic Americano. I don't want to be here, in the ruins of my city. I want so fiercely to be back at my desk, with a fancy macchiato with sprinkles, facing a day of hard coding.

At the thought of that an invisible swell twists round me, and threatens to carry me away.

"Olly. There's something snagged. Inside me. It's got a hook in me." Something to do with wanting: with dreams, desires, passion. "I need to resign."

"You can't resign! Look, I shouldn't tell you this, but Nathan told me: Sandpit is going to be bought. You could get a huge pay-off, and end up working for a totally different company. A much better company..."

As he speaks, the undertow grows and grows until I need to grip the table.

Oliver springs up, to peer out of the window. "Is it me, or is it getting darker?"

I follow him out into the garden. Beyond the fence, there's movement in the trees. The top branches dance, the thicker ones creak as a wind whips round and round the cottage.

Ping!

My phone's picked up a message, now it's outside those thick stone walls. I see the recruiter's name on the screen.

"Shit, it's the bank job..."

"What?"

"I went for an interview today, a corporate job."

"Are you going to take it?"

I think about it. I think I will.

As soon as I think it, the wind drops.

It's like flippin' telekinesis. I picture myself in that bland, glassy office, and the clouds draw back. I imagine trying on ties and spending a grand on a proper suit, and the undercurrent ebbs away and the sun peers out.

Ping! Text from Mam: *Still got fingers crossed for you but are you sure? I know you love Sandpit.*

I flick it away. *Ping!* It's an email from Nathan. I can read the first words, in the notification: *Dil, we've done it! We're going to be so*

The tide rises to grip me, the birds fall silent and the trees thrash about.

"I have to take the bank job! I have to take the bank job."

It makes perfect sense. Ever since I heard of Silicon Roundabout, I've wanted to work there. Like a kid turning up with a spade in the Yukon, I bought into the adventure. It was my dream. And it spiralled round with all my other dreams, and other people's dreams, and brought us to this place. I have to end it.

"Sandpit was my dream job. That's the problem."

"Dil, you always got so angry when people confused 'dreaming' and 'really wanting a thing'. Remember the headlines? Dream Boys, Dream Team..."

He puts his arm round me, which is nice, and helps with the shaking, but I think he's doing it to show he's reasonable while I'm coming unglued, so I shrug it off again.

"I think they might be mixed up, for me." In Shoreditch where the air is thin because everyone lives at such high altitudes of imagination. "It gets worse when I want things."

Oliver sighs. "So you have to give up everything you want?"

"I need to try."

"Then I'll get us a drink. To celebrate your new position."

I open the recruiter's email. The bank liked me, they're suggesting an astronomical starting salary. I tap out a hasty acceptance.

Oliver returns with glasses of fizz, and we sit in the garden in deck chairs. We watch the trees calmly sway, the unearthly louring clouds give way to fluffy cumulus, and the livid dimness turn to restful dusk. As long as I don't think about Silicon Roundabout, nothing tightens in my chest. Nothing creeps towards me through the undergrowth.

Looks like it doesn't matter how young I am, how little I've managed to grasp so far. I need to fast-forward to another stage of life: turn my back on desiring things and shove off into the forest, or further.

Oliver coughs, self-consciously. "Dil, if I was to follow this to its logical conclusion, is it partly my fault?"

"What, because you invested in Sandpit?"

"No, I mean *us*. Am *I* a thing you want?"

He's watching me with unaccustomed care.

I look at him in his linen trousers, in front of his country cottage. I think of the places he offered to take me: Glynbourne, the Hay on Wye book festival. Was he my dream boyfriend?

"No offence, but I don't think so." I meant to let him down gently, but he gives me such a quizzical look—*how can I not be, for goodness' sake, I'm marvellous*—that I keep talking. "I mean, if I thought I'd end up with anyone, it would be some indie kid. We'd watch Fourth Doctor box sets and play Pandemic Legacy together." A bit of a skimpy description, but I put all my creative thinking into my job, not my love-life.

"I don't know what those things are," Oliver admits. "Does that mean, then, that you *don't* have to give me up?"

Oh heck, am I supposed to choose celibacy? Another thing I have to let go of, before I've really got hold of it. But I'm bargaining, hoping there's a loophole: if Oliver was my dream man, I'd have to leave. But he's not. So can I stay? I reach over and hold his hand. "I reckon we're alright."

He sips his fizz. "Do you think it will go away? With time?"

I let myself feel the ebb and flow. My desire to return to my site knots up inside me and I smooth it out. Breathe in, breathe out. Renounce, renounce. No hate, no desire. Keep far from here the rippling wind, the troubled deeps.

"I don't know," I admit.

I feel a fleeting panic: how can I live like this, desperate not to desire too much? How can I let go of everything, let go of myself? Not wanting, not yearning, not raising the sea-drowned.

I untangle my hand from Oliver's to start a text message. To Monifa, and Mam, bombarding them with questions. I want them to help me to fix it, right now, I want, I *want...*

I press delete. I start again.

To Monifa: *Sorry I called when you were at work. Chips are on me, next time.*

To Mam: *Got the job, don't worry, really glad!*

I let my phone fall to the grass, squeeze Oliver's hand again, watch the woods. Nothing stirs.

"Shall we go inside?" Oliver asks.

I breathe in, breathe out, enjoy the garden at dusk. "No rush, is there?"

Publication History

"A Day Without Sunshine" copyright © 2015, first appeared in *Escape Pod*

"No Children" copyright © 2019, first appeared in *Corvid Queen*

"There is a Willow Grows Aslant a Brook" copyright © 2016, first appeared in *Reflections* (ed. Adele Wearing, Fox Spirit)

"Lucidity" copyright © 2017, first appeared in *Unsung Stories*

"My Rightwise Home" copyright © 2015, first appeared in *Expanded Horizons*

"Not Smart, Not Clever" copyright © 2014, first appeared in *Apex Magazine*

"Windows into Men's Hearts" copyright © 2015, first appeared in *Tales from the Vatican Vaults* (ed. David V. Barrett, Robinson)

"Sunslick" copyright © 2018, first appeared in *Mycelia* (ed. Simone Hutchinson, Hedera Felix)

"A Marvellous Neutrality" copyright © 2015, first appeared in *Aghast*

"Since You Ask Me for a Tale" copyright © 2022, original to this collection

"The Librarian's Dilemma" copyright © 2015, first appeared in *The Journal of Unlikely Academia*

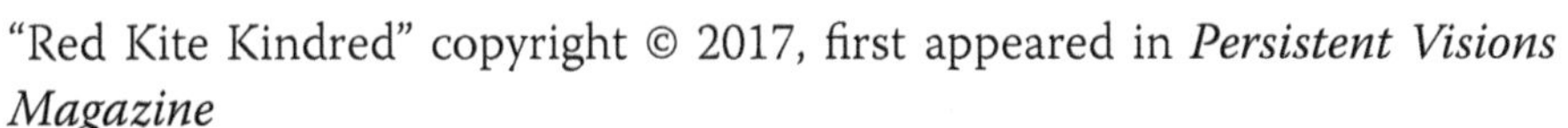

Acknowledgements

Enormous thanks are due, and no blame should accrue, to A.C.Wise, Alexandra Mitchell, Alice "Huskyteer" Dryden, Anne Perry, Daniel Nye Griffiths, Dan Lowe, Iona Datt Sharma, James Sinclair, Georgina Voss, Helen Gould, Jared Shurin, Juliet Kemp, Laura Mauro, Sarah Pinsker, Tom Armitage, Treadwell's Bookshop, and members and organisers of the T Party and Greenwich Writers. Everything is better for your input and support.

Thanks also to all editors and publications who originally published the stories reprinted here, and the illustrators who reimagined them. Thanks to John Darnielle and John Finnemore for inspiring titles. Massive gratitude to Steve Berman and Lethe Press for the opportunity to bring it all together.

About the Author

E.Saxey is a queer Londoner who works in Universities and volunteers in libraries. Their work has appeared in *Apex Magazine, Escape Pod* and *Best of British Fantasy 2019* among other places, and been described as "idiosyncratic" by *The Guardian*.

www.ingramcontent.com/pod-product-compliance
Ingram Content Group UK Ltd.
Pitfield, Milton Keynes, MK11 3LW, UK
UKHW041637190726
13854UKWH00006B/2536